An English Garden
MURDER

BOOKS BY KATIE GAYLE

An English Garden MURDER

KATIE GAYLE

bookouture

Published by Bookouture in 2022

An imprint of Storyfire Ltd.
Carmelite House
50 Victoria Embankment
London EC4Y oDZ

www.bookouture.com

ISBN: 978-1-80314-067-4
eBook ISBN: 978-1-80314-066-7

This book is dedicated to the Julia Birds of the world – the kind, capable, rather interfering women who make the world go round.

Julia stood at the front door, engulfed in a bower of scented purple wisteria, and waved goodbye as her husband – her ex-husband, *ex* – started his car and drove slowly away from her.

How familiar the shape of his head was, just the top half, above the car's headrest. A little egg-shaped – not that she'd ever mentioned it – and just a tad more pointed on the top than the second head, in the passenger seat, an inch lower than her *ex*-husband's.

She noted the way his head darted rather anxiously left-right-left to check for cars before turning. The way he edged nervously forward, and then accelerated the car into the road a little too suddenly. All completely, unconsciously familiar.

Their marriage was truly, permanently over and she really was absolutely fine with that. It was only habit, nothing more, that caused her to forget the 'ex' part, even in her own thoughts. Those two little letters which signalled the end of almost three decades of comfortable cohabitation. It was, after all, habit that had kept it going all those years.

Habits. They were going to be tossed aside and replaced with new adventures here in the Cotswolds where she would begin the next phase of her life, starting now. In this pretty cottage. If only she knew what to actually *do*.

Julia had never had spare time. Now she thought about it, her entire life had been geared towards ensuring the absence of spare time. She worked, that's what she did. Conscientiously, devotedly, time-consumingly, she worked. Well, no more. Her long career as a social worker, like her long marriage, was over. And, like her marriage, it had ended suddenly, under circumstances that she would rather forget – even though everyone had said, in respect of both the marriage and what had happened at work, that it wasn't her fault.

But those were worries that she was going to put behind her. Out with the old, thought Julia, turning back into the hallway and closing the door. It was satisfyingly heavy, and made a good solid thump.

She walked through to her sitting room, which was bathed in a buttery late-afternoon light, and hoped that a useful activity would present itself. She reached for a vase of meadow flowers and grasses, intending to fluff them up a bit, but withdrew her hand. They had been picked and artfully arranged by Christopher – he of the less egg-shaped head – to look perfectly wild and carelessly tossed into a jug. Julia was not much of a fluffer by nature and would doubtless spoil the effect. A bit mortifying that her husband's – ex-husband's – new lover was a better homemaker than she was.

She picked up a cushion and put it down where she found it. Straightened a small oil painting of a waterwheel, although Peter had hung it meticulously with the help of a measuring tape and a pencil this very morning, and it was perfectly straight. Ran her finger over the coffee table in search of dust, but it came up clean.

The house, which had been full of activity and warmth and conversation when Peter and Christopher were there, seemed very quiet now that they had returned to London. Three empty teacups sat on the table next to the sofa, the only evidence of her visitors ever having been there.

She wondered, briefly, if the move to a village in the country had been rash. When she and Peter had agreed to split up and sell the London house, and having resigned from her job, she had decided to move out of town for a proper change. In an uncharacteristically poorly researched decision, she had chosen the place based on a few enjoyable weekends staying with her friend, Tabitha, who had moved here fifteen years ago when her own marriage had dissolved. What if she'd made a mistake?

Julia's second-guessing was interrupted by the sound of the front door opening. She felt a prickle of fear. A break-in? Vandals? She should have locked it.

'Who's there?' she shouted firmly, to scare him off.

'Where are you?' called a woman's voice.

Not a robber, then, but Tabitha, her oldest friend. Was this how it was going to be, living in the country? People simply entered your home without knocking?

'Coming,' she called back, as she walked towards the little entrance hall. 'Glad it's you. I thought you were a robber.'

'Oh come on,' Tabitha said with a laugh, hanging up her coat on a hook set in a wooden plank next to the front door. She was tiny, and had to stand on tiptoes to reach it. 'Whoever heard such nonsense. *Robbers?* We don't have robbers in Berrywick. A lovesick teenager pinched our copy of *Love Story* from the library once, slipped it under her coat. That's about it for *robbers.*'

'What did you do about the teenager?'

'What? Oh, I just asked her to give it back. She did. And wrote me a very heartfelt if somewhat poorly spelled apology. She still comes to the library, and we've never mentioned it again.'

Julia thought of her own experiences of dealing with troubled young offenders and decided that village life might be a nice change after all.

'Well, that's good to hear. Sorry, I've seen far too much of the worst side of human nature in my career. I fear it has made me a cynic.'

'Lucky you moved here then – hopefully just in time to restore your faith in humanity. What lovely hyacinths,' Tabitha said, bending down to inhale the deep scent from a blue and white Chinese pot planted with three white bulbs on the little hall table. 'They smell like heaven.'

'Christopher,' said Julia, by way of explanation.

Her friend bustled past her into the sitting room, where she stood, hands on hips, and surveyed the scene, nodding in approval. When Tabitha nodded, she made a soft tinkling sound as her earrings jiggled and her bangles clacked together. Julia was more of a 'pair of pearl studs' kind of accessoriser and had always felt like a dowdy chicken next to a peacock when she was with Tabitha. When they were younger, Tabitha had worn her hair in complicated plaits and cornrows, but now that they were older, she allowed her greying curls free range. Julia had met Tabitha on her first day at high school – enchanted by her exuberant personality and the way fun things always seemed to happen when Tabitha was around. They'd stayed best friends through school, university, marriages, children and divorces. And now here they were, living in the same village again. Julia didn't know what she would have done without Tabitha to turn to.

'Goodness, you've made marvellous progress,' said Tabitha, looking around. 'I can hardly recognise the place. It's all so... so lovely. Cosy. Elegant. And the flowers!'

'Christopher,' said Julia again.

'Gosh, you are lucky to have him,' said Tabitha, and then blushed and stammered. 'I mean, not the divorce, obviously, or the, you know, the relationship... I mean Peter...'

'It's okay, I am lucky I suppose. If one's husband must fall in love with someone else, one couldn't do better than Christopher. He couldn't be nicer and he really is very clever with the garden and so on.'

'Yes, handy having a landscape gardener in the family,' said Tabitha. At this point she presumably remembered that Peter had in fact met and fallen in love with Christopher when Julia had engaged him to redo their little back garden. 'I mean, gosh, I really am putting my foot in it.'

'Don't worry, it's all a bit awkward, but you'll get used to it. I have. Anyway, he gave me lots of good ideas. Do you want to come and look?'

The next half hour was pleasantly spent on a slow tour of Julia's garden, with garden commentary taking turns with snippets of village gossip and information. It wasn't a huge garden, but big enough for deep borders filled with delphiniums and roses, lavender and dahlias. A few large trees were well-placed on the perimeter. Julia and Tabitha admired them individually. They discussed where to put a bird feeder. They agreed that the small lawn would be easy enough to maintain, and perfect for a couple of deckchairs and a jug of lemonade, or even Pimms, come summer. Julia felt pleasure at the thought of sitting in the sun with her old school friend, the birds availing themselves of the bird seed in the feeder.

Julia led Tabitha round the side of the house, along a walkway which separated the lush flower garden from the back garden. A paved path ran to the back door.

'This is going to be my kitchen garden. It's been very neglected. The old couple who lived here didn't have the energy for it the last few years. But Christopher is going to plan it properly and help me get it going.'

The two women surveyed the patchy grass, the two little fruit trees, the untended pots and the sagging wooden shed in the far corner.

'A project!' said Tabitha, enthusiastically. 'Just what you need to help you settle in. I can't wait to see what you do with it. I'm happy to help, you know. It'll be fun.'

'Yes, I'm looking forward to it,' Julia said, although in truth she found the whole thing rather daunting. 'We talked about a sundial, but I think a bird bath would be nice. Oh, and I'm getting chickens. I'm going to put in a chicken run. Maybe over there, where the old shed is now. Or possibly by the back wall, near the plum tree.'

Julia was genuinely and surprisingly delighted with the idea of chickens. Such sensible, productive creatures they were. Rather like Julia herself. She turned to her friend. 'That's something you might be able to help me with, actually. I need someone to build the coop. Do you know anyone in the village who could do that?'

'Oh, it's Johnny Blunt you want. He does odd jobs and building and such.'

'Excellent. Can you give me his number?'

'I don't have his *number*,' Tabitha said, as if this were an outlandish suggestion on Julia's part. 'I haven't ever phoned him. Why would I phone him? But you'll find him in the cafe tomorrow morning. Always there, nine o'clock sharp, for his breakfast.'

'The cafe?'

'The Buttered Scone. Don't tell me you've not been to the Buttered Scone? In fact you have for sure, I took you there last time you visited from London, remember? We had lunch.'

'Of course, yes, I remember now. Nice little place down the other end of the main street. I had the smoked trout salad. But surely I can't just arrive and find Johnny? And how will I know who he is?'

'Ask anybody. Or just look for him. He wears a blue knitted cap.'

'So I should just go to the cafe at nine tomorrow morning,

approach a stranger in a blue knitted cap, and ask him to build me a coop?'

'Exactly.'

Country life really was most peculiar. But Julia thought she might like it.

'All right then,' she said with a smile. 'Well, that's what I'll do.'

2

The thing Julia missed most about married life was coming down to breakfast – having enjoyed a tray of Earl Grey tea in bed with the morning papers – and finding a nice bowl of steel-cut oats, drizzled with honey and topped with sliced banana. Peter had been responsible for the tea and the tray, the oats and their toppings, even the newspaper subscription.

Out with the old... she thought, flipping on the kettle and reaching up for a mug. While the water boiled, she surveyed the fridge. She hadn't bought more than bread and milk and the most basic provisions in the week she'd been here. Too busy with the boxes. Peter had brought a lovely selection of picnicky foods for 'Help Julia Sort Her House Out Day', the remains of which sat sadly on the middle shelf – two cheeses, a free range organic pork sausage, half a tub of salmon pâté, some salady bits. There was, additionally, half a bottle of milk, a stick of butter, and two apples, slowly browning, which she'd bought on the drive down from London.

It was a disheartening sight. *Buck up, Julia,* she told herself firmly. *Nothing for it but breakfast at the Buttered Scone.* It was decided. She'd have her tea, get herself dressed and walk down to the cafe in time to meet the blue-hatted coop-builder. Then she'd shop for provisions and come home and fill the fridge and pantry with sensible meal options for the week. She would take care of two very necessary errands before lunch, and get to know the village a little better as she went about her business. She felt better already at the thought of these mild achievements, trying hard not to think of a time when her day had been filled with important tasks. That was the past; and having a plan *did* make her feel better.

You see, Julia? You always feel much better when you have a plan. Now enough of this drooping about, time to get started on the day. You've plenty to do. When giving herself a stern talking-to, Julia tended to employ her dead mother's voice, and her clipped and direct tone. No doubt a psychologist would have a field day with that, but the fact was that it worked. She felt herself buck up.

The day was lovely. Overnight rain had freshened the air, but the sky was clear and blue. Julia stepped out and locked the door behind her. Despite Tabitha's claim that there was no crime in Berrywick, Julia saw no point in tempting fate.

She strode purposefully down her little lane, past her two neighbours – both houses similar to her own, old stone cottages, previously the outbuildings of the Big House. If she so wished, she could have crossed the lane and walked down the small embankment to the walking path along the stream that ran parallel to her road, and which had given it the name Slip-stream Lane. If she chose the walking path, she could have turned right, away from the village, following the stream until it came to a small lake, that Tabitha had assured her was the gathering place of local swimmers, dog walkers, picnickers, and, as the sun set, young lovers. Julia noted that there was already a woman heading along the path in that direction, accompanied by five Yorkshire terriers, bouncing along, tails wagging. The woman had a scarf on her head and a sturdy walking stick, like she meant business with this morning ramble.

But Julia headed left, down the lane, turning right at the end, onto a road that took her across the stream and towards what she had found herself calling 'the big intersection'. At the intersection, one could turn right, and pass a patchwork of cottages, first so close to each other that they were like a party of drunken old men, propping each other up, and slowly becoming more and more widely dispersed, until the road was flanked by fields leading to the next village. If one followed this road far enough, one could reach Gloucester – 'the ancient Roman route' boasted the guidebooks.

This morning, Julia was intent on turning left at the big intersection, into the main road that led to the village. The pamphlet that the estate agent had given her, listing the wonders of Berrywick, had bragged that Berrywick, unlike many other Cotswolds villages, boasted a traditional town centre. In other words, you could find the butcher, the baker and the artisan scented candle shop all along the road. The shops and facilities like the post office and library were also found in this central area, with restaurants and pubs scattered through the village.

As Julia headed down the lane, over the bridge, and along the road to the intersection, she admired the pretty houses which lined the road, each with a profusely planted front garden. It was easy to see why this area attracted so many day trippers in the summer season. Everything was just ridiculously pretty.

Julia had crossed the bridge and was about to turn, when she was jolted out of her pleasant rambling by a shout.

'JAKE!' came a voice, in what sounded like a wail of despair and fury. 'You *bad* boy...'

Before Julia could determine who Jake was, or where, something large and brown and heavy barrelled into her, sending her sprawling on the verge.

Bear! was Julia's first, and wholly illogical thought. And now the bear was licking her!Only it wasn't a bear of course. When Julia managed to disentangle herself from her handbag – which had somehow pinned her arm to her side in the fall – and the licking bear, she discovered that the barrel of brown enthusiasm was, in fact, a half-grown chocolate Labrador, trailing a lead behind him.

Running down the road after him was a dishevelled looking woman, dragging three more Labrador puppies behind her.

'I'm sorry, I'm so sorry,' the woman was yelling as she ran. She came to a stop, and pulled the bear – Labrador – off Julia.

'You are such a *bad* boy, Jake,' she said, in the tones of one who had said this many times before. She reminded Julia of a client she'd worked with who'd had too many children and was constantly telling them how awful they were. No longer Julia's problem, thankfully. Julia hauled herself to her feet and brushed grass from the trousers. No harm done.

'I'm sure he's not a bad boy all the time,' she said to the frazzled apparition before her. 'And he is rather pretty.' Jake lifted his leg against a tree, splashing Julia's brand-new country shoes. Julia and Jake's owner looked at this clear proof that Jake was still a bad boy. 'Bad boy, Jake,' muttered the owner. 'I'll reimburse you,' she said, nodding towards the shoes.

'No need,' said Julia. 'I'm sure they'll be good as new after a wash.'

'I'm Pippa Baker,' said Bad Boy Jake's mum. She tried to offer Julia a hand to shake, but found both her hands were occupied with dog leads. 'And these are the latest recruits for the local seeing-eye dog training programme. Sit!'

The two gold puppies and the black one deposited their bums on the ground and looked up at her proudly. Jake was investigating the bushes.

'Aren't they lovely?' said Julia, giving each a pat, making their tails wag happily. 'I'm Julia Bird. New to the village. I'm delighted to meet you and the puppies. What noble futures they have ahead of them.'

'Yes, they'll be going soon,' said Pippa, nodding vigorously, her blonde ponytail bouncing. 'Except, of course, for Jake. He hasn't made the first cut. I don't suppose you know anyone who might like a ten-month-old puppy? He's very dear really...'

They both gazed down at Jake, who had found a lipstick that must have rolled out of Julia's bag in the fall and was chewing it enthusiastically. His brown velvet muzzle was smeared in a fetching pink colour.

Pippa Baker sighed. 'I'll reimburse you for that too,' she said, picking up his lead.

'No need,' said Julia, again. 'It looks better on him than me.' Jake obviously knew that they were talking about him, because his tail started wagging madly, smacking against Pippa's leg. His litter mates were waiting, polite and patient. As charming as Jake seemed, Julia could see why he wasn't guide dog material.

'Well, Jake,' she said, 'and Pippa. It's been a pleasure to meet you both.'

'Oh, I doubt that,' said Pippa. 'Knocked over, pee on your shoe and a lipstick gone. I bet it's the worst day you've had all year.'

'Oh, Pippa,' said Julia, 'I'm afraid it doesn't even make the top ten.' She laughed, even though it was true. There was nothing to be gained from feeling sorry for herself.

'Sit,' she said to Jake, in the calm and authoritative voice she used with her clients – it had worked on the woman and her too-many children. He plonked himself down obediently.

She bent down and gave Jake's head a scratch. He wiggled and squirmed in delight, looking up at her with soft adoring eyes, but still sitting down as instructed.

'You're a superb boy,' she told the Labrador. 'Whoever gets you will be very lucky.'

Saying goodbye to Pippa, who was looking at her and Jake in astonishment, Julia continued towards the Buttered Scone, feeling strangely invigorated from the encounter.

Johnny Blunt was easy to find. He was indeed seated in the Buttered Scone, wearing a blue knitted cap, and glaring at the headlines of *The Sun*.

'Are you Johnny?' Julia said, tentatively approaching him. 'Johnny Blunt?'

'That's what they call me.' Johnny Blunt said so loudly that two tourists, poring over a walking map at the table next to him, glanced up nervously.

'I'm Julia Bird, a friend of Tabitha's. She said that you could help me build a coop,' said Julia, quickly.

'A hoop? What do you want with a hoop?' He sounded quite affronted by the suggestion.

'A coop,' she enunciated clearly. 'For chickens.'

'Why didn't you say so?' yelled Johnny. Julia didn't think this was quite fair, seeing as she had just said so. Julia prided herself on coming to the point. However, it seemed the question was rhetorical.

'I love building things,' said Johnny, voice still booming. 'Don't I, Flo?' he shouted at a passing waitress.

'You *do*, Johnny,' said Flo. 'You really do. Why don't you let your lady sit down and she can tell you all about her coop.'

Julia wasn't thrilled to be referred to as 'your lady', but she admired the easy way that Flo managed Johnny – she'd clearly had some practise.

'Sit down,' boomed Johnny, 'and tell me about your coop.' He said it as if it was all his idea.

Sitting down, Julia had a chance to observe Johnny better. His blue knitted cap was pulled down so low that it appeared to rest on his bushy grey eyebrows. Hooded blue eyes looked at

Julia over a beaked nose. Despite his intimidating demeanour, there was kindness in those eyes.

'Well,' she said. 'I want to get chickens, and they'll need a coop. I've got some ideas off the internet. I'm still deciding where it should go, though.'

'Excellent,' bellowed Johnny, and the woman two tables away jumped slightly in fright. 'Chickens are fine animals. God knew what he was doing the day he made chickens, that's a fact.' Johnny picked up his mug of tea and gave it a good slurp. 'Feed them rose petals,' he said, after having savoured the sip. 'Just the ticket for chickens.'

'Rose petals?'

'Definitely. Isn't that right, Flo? Rose petals for chickens?' He yelled this at Flo, who was standing on the other side of the small restaurant, tapping on the antiquated cash register.

'Right you are, Johnny,' Flo shouted back. 'Just the ticket.'

'Okay. Right. Got it,' said Julia. 'Rose petals. So, about my coop. There's a good spot by the plum tree. I'm thinking of putting it there. Could you come and have a look, and maybe get started?'

'Right. I'll come tomorrow after breakfast,' said Johnny. 'Chicken coops vary in cost, depending what design you choose in the end, but it won't be more than a hundred quid. That okay?'

'That's excellent,' Julia beamed. She'd expected to pay rather more for this project, and now would be able to get a few more chickens than originally planned. 'I accept.'

It turned out that accosting strangers in the local tearoom was a surprisingly efficient system.

'Haven't you forgotten something, lass?' bellowed Johnny.

Julia, somewhat thrown at being called a lass on the wrong side of her sixtieth birthday, couldn't think what.

'Your address.'

She laughed. 'Oh yes, of course. I'm at Rose Cottage. Do you know the Steadmans' old place?'

Johnny paused. He looked uncertain, 'Ah well, I'm not sure if I...'

'It's on Slipstream Lane,' she said.

'You know Slipstream Lane, Johnny,' Flo butted in loudly, as she leant over to take his empty mug. 'There by the Big House.'

'Bit deaf,' she muttered to Julia under her breath.

'Oh yes, well, I suppose I do. Under the plum tree, you say?'

'That's what I'm thinking.'

'All right then,' said Johnny. 'Chickens do like plums.'

'Wonderful, see you tomorrow then. Let's say ten,' said Julia, getting up from the table. 'Lovely to meet you, Mr Blunt.'

3

Julia stirred the oats, peering through the steam to assess their creaminess. She looked at her watch. Yes, ten minutes, and they seemed perfect. She turned off the stove and scooped them into a bowl.

No more bemoaning the loss of Peter's perfect oats. She had mastered them herself. If anything, hers were now *better* than Peter's, thanks to the experimental addition of cinnamon and a small blob of butter, which was melting oozily into the honey. Julia sliced a pear on top – she'd moved on from banana – and sat down at the kitchen table feeling pleased with herself. Not just because of the oats, but because of her general resourcefulness and organisation. She ran through her achievements in her head while spooning buttery porridge into her mouth.

First, she had stocked the fridge and pantry and made a few decent meals, halving each one so she had one for her supper and one for the freezer. This simple act made her feel like some pioneer homesteader in the American Midwest, bottling plums or threshing corn or whatever it was they did.

Secondly, the shouty man was coming to get started on the coop this morning. She had decided that it would go where the shed was, rather than under the plum tree. She had realised that the plums would fall onto the coop, which could be messy. Besides, the old shed was an eyesore. A coop would be much better in that corner. So the shed would need pulling down first. She hoped he'd be up for that too.

Thirdly, she was making friends. Not friends, exactly, but she was getting to know the inhabitants of the village. She'd already met Pippa the dog wrangler, shouty Johnny, and Flo in the cafe. This evening, at Tabitha's insistence, she would be attending the Berrywick Book Club. When Tabitha had first come to the village with her second husband, she'd worked in the local bookshop. But when Margie MacGregor had died, Tabitha had taken over as the local librarian. And when her second husband had left her, and the village, she had stayed. Julia felt that being a librarian was at least a slightly better use of Tabitha's doctorate in English Literature. As the librarian, Tabitha had also started a local book club, which she described to Julia as 'small, but fierce'. It was to this that she had invited Julia. Julia felt a flutter of social anxiety at the thought. Peter had been the social motivator in their marriage, but she had resolved to *buck up and get out there.* Starting tonight.

She was racking her brain to come up with 'Fourthly...' when she heard a sharp rap on the front door.

At the door, she found a nice-looking young man, who was already blushing before he'd even started speaking. 'I'm Brendan,' he said. 'Johnny's grandson.'

'Come in, come in,' said Julia, stepping back and indicating that Brendan should enter. He wiped his feet carefully on the mat, before stepping into the house like he might break something. 'Where's Johnny?'

'Grandad went to collect his tools. Left them at the Wesleys, he did, daft old bugger.' He said this fondly. 'Anyway, he said for me to come and start by preparing the ground.'

Julia led the young man out to the back, sensing that he felt more at home in the outdoors. She showed him the two sites she'd considered, and where she planned to put in the vegetables. 'So I've decided that I'd like the coop where the shed is now,' she said, at the end of her tour.

'That's a good idea,' said Brendan. 'Good sun, but not too much, if you know what I mean. Near the veggies, but not too far, if you know what I mean.' He looked worried, like he wasn't exactly sure what he meant himself.

'Indeed,' said Julia, in what she hoped was a reassuring voice. 'D'you think you and Johnny will be able to pull the shed down for me?'

Brendan puffed up slightly.

'I reckon I can do it myself, and have it all ready to show Grandad when he arrives,' he said. 'Reckon that would be a good surprise for him, if you know what I mean.'

Julia recognised the signs of a young man eager to take the initiative and prove himself. She was pleased that she had created an opportunity for him to do so.

'Wonderful,' she said. 'I'll leave you to it, then.'

It was some twenty minutes later when there was another knock at the door, accompanied by the now-familiar bellow of Johnny Blunt.

Julia opened the door to find Johnny in the same blue hat as yesterday, his van parked outside the house.

'Your grandson has got started outside,' said Julia, as she showed Johnny into the house. She decided not to mention that he was pulling down a shed by himself – let the boy show off his work to his grandfather. 'He's a good boy, that one.'

'That he is,' agreed Johnny, beaming as he bellowed. 'The apple of me eye. His father gave me a grey hair or two, growing up. But Brendan hasn't given us one moment's worry. Stellar lad.'

'Oh, I forgot to ask when we spoke – how long do you think you'll take to build the coop? It would be nice to get the chickens really soon.'

'Steady on. It's not London, you know,' Johnny bellowed so loudly that Julia winced. 'It'll take as long as it takes, now, City Miss.'

Brendan peeped his head around the back door. 'Thought I heard you, Gramps,' he said, with a cheeky wink at Julia. 'Me and most of Berrywick. Gramps, shouldn't you have your hearing aids in?'

Well, *that* explained the shouting.

'What's that you say?' Johnny enquired at a hundred decibels.

'Your HEARING aids?'

'Not wearing them. I don't want to hear all the banging and crashing when we build now, do I? Nor all that chattering and yammering that everyone's doing nowadays.'

'But, Gramps, the doctor said you need to get used to them.'

'I'll wear them when someone's got something sensible to say. Not that I expect that to happen any time soon,' Johnny bellowed, looking pointedly at Julia, and then at Brendan. 'Now, come on, lad.'

'Gramps, why don't you let Mrs Bird show you her ideas for the coop while I finish out here, get it all ready for you to start building.' Brendan gave Julia a meaningful look, which she took to mean that he hadn't quite gotten as far as he had wanted to with the shed and wanted her to stall Johnny.

'Indeed,' said Julia. 'And I can offer you tea while we look.'

'And biscuits if you have any,' bellowed Johnny, eliciting another apologetic smile from Brendan.

Brendan smiled. 'I'll be getting back to work while you chat.'

What a nice polite boy he was, Julia thought, putting a cup of tea and some biscuits down in front of Johnny.

'I've got some ideas for the chicken coop,' she said. 'I'll show you some plans and pictures, see what you think.'

'Plans and pictures for a coop, well I never... Let's have a look then,' he barked, grabbing the papers rather rudely, and looking at them while he sipped his tea. He shuffled the papers, nodding, looking between them and the site, turning this way and that. For once, he wasn't bellowing, but talking quietly to himself as he nodded and traced his fingers over the drawing. 'Could work. Fix it onto the back fence there... What's that, four foot? Could make it five... A step there... Hmmm.'

She listened to him, imagining the friendly wooden structure with its ladder up to a row of nesting boxes and its nice bit of lawn safely enclosed in wire to keep foxes out. She'd already sourced some fine red hens from a chicken farmer down the road. As soon as the shed was out and the coop was up, she'd fetch them and get them settled in. She pictured the nesting boxes full of warm fresh eggs. Happy hens, clucking in the grass.

She realised with a small jolt that she was enjoying herself, the sense of achievement and improvement. She even felt warmly towards shouty Johnny Blunt and his nice grandson. This village life was rather fun, and sort of wholesome.

'Grandpa...'

The boy's voice was high, and loud enough to reach them in the kitchen. Almost immediately, Brendan's head appeared around the door again. 'Gramps,' he said.

Julia's instincts and training made her turn sharply towards him – there was panic and anxiety in his voice. His eyes were wide with shock as they met hers.

'Gramps, I was pulling down the shed for Mrs Bird,' explained Brendan, in a rush of words. 'She wants the coop there. So I wanted to get it all done for you. But, Gramps, there's something there... In the ground... It might be...'

He was as white as a sheet. He swallowed and tried again.

'There's something buried there, Grandad. Bones. I think it's a body. A person. I think I can see an arm.'

4

'A *body*?' Tabitha asked, her eyes wide. 'A *human* body? In your garden?'

'Under the shed,' Julia whispered. She realised that they were both whispering, despite being the only people in the library, and wondered whether it was out of obedience to library rules, or due to the presence of death.

'Well, who is it?' Tabitha asked, with a shiver that made her long silver earrings sway and jiggle.

'No one knows. They... he... she... *the person* died a long time ago. It's an old body, been there a long time, the policeman said.'

'Well, that's good, I suppose. I mean, if there *has* to be a body at all...'

The door opened and they sprung guiltily apart, as if they'd been caught gossiping.

'Hello, hello, come in,' Tabitha said warmly to the new arrival. To Julia, she muttered under her breath: 'Don't mention the body. Village gossip travels fast. We'll talk about it later.'

The reading area was at the front of the library, next to a large window that showed the comings and goings of the village.

The space was set up with comfortable chairs and a table with a hot urn, cups and saucers, teabags, milk and sugar. The new arrival plonked down a big plate of delicious-smelling sausage rolls, glistening and golden.

'Home-made,' he said, looking justifiably pleased with himself. He turned to her, 'We've a new member, I see. Sean O'Connor, pleased to meet you.'

Julia was momentarily confused – she'd heard 'Sean Connery', and in fact the man looked rather like the old James Bond (her personal favourite amongst 007s, it must be said). He even sounded like him, with his rough Scottish burr.

'Julia Bird, hello. I'm a friend of Tabitha's. I've just moved to the village. This is my first time at book club.'

'Well I hope you know your Dostoevsky; we are working through the canon,' he said sternly.

Oh heck, thought Julia. She was here for some light fic and good company, not for the bloody Russians.

James Bond burst out laughing. 'Got you! Don't you worry, it's mostly thrillers, spies and adventurous women finding love in Kenya.'

'Well, that's a disappointment. I did my PhD on Dostoevsky,' Julia said, sadly.

'Really? Goodness, well...'

'Got you,' she snapped back, and they both laughed.

'Oh, it's you! The puppy whisperer!' came a friendly voice. Pippa, the exasperated dog wrangler, had come in, mercifully free of her charges. Pippa had smartened up a bit, and her hair hung loose around her face. She was accompanied by a very tall woman, in her thirties like Pippa, with very long red hair and a very long green coat. She looked rather Christmassy, Julia thought, if not terribly jolly. Pippa introduced her: 'Diane, my cousin. Di, this is who I was telling you about. Jake, you know... Julia.'

The new arrival said her hellos.

Just when Julia thought it was going to be all ladies, with Sean as the sole bloke and local wit, in sloped a pale young man dressed in an open checked shirt over a shapeless sweatshirt, big boots and a knitted cap – a look she knew well from her youth work and thought of as 'homeless Canadian logger'.

'Hello, Dylan,' Tabitha called brightly.

'Hey,' he mumbled, and poured himself into a chair.

'I think we should get started. Not sure where Jane is; she's always so punctual.'

For a horrible moment Julia imagined that Jane was lifeless under the shed, but that was absurd, of course. Whoever was under the shed had died years ago. And was no longer under the shed, but presumably in the coroner's examination room, spread out on a table somewhere. She gave a little shudder at the thought.

They took their chairs, Julia lingering in case there were established places, and then taking an empty seat next to Diane.

An elderly tortoiseshell cat sauntered into the circle and made a beeline for Julia, rubbing itself against her leg and giving a throaty purr. 'Hello, pretty boy. What's your name?'

'Girl. She's the library cat and believe it or not, her name's Tabitha,' said Diane with a laugh.

'Really?'

'She pre-dated me,' said Tabitha the Human, looking mildly embarrassed. 'To avoid confusion, we call her Tabitha Too, or Too for short. Strictly speaking, I should be Too, as she got here first, but seeing as she doesn't respond to any sound but the opening of the fridge, I kept our name. Now, let's start, shall we?'

Tabitha introduced Julia as their newest member, and briefly explained the format – everyone presented a book they'd read, five minutes each, then a bit of discussion, then tea. Sometimes they had a theme, but not always. Any genre was acceptable. If you didn't have something to share every time you weren't to worry, you were still welcome. It all sounded rather casual, except for a very strict roster related to snacks – the sweet vs savoury debate, the group position on allergies, and so on. And there was a WhatsApp group: 'To be used *solely* for book recommendations, and book club arrangements,' Tabitha added threateningly. Diane looked guiltily at the floor, which Julia took to mean she had been sending memes and jokes.'Who wants to start?'

There was a bit of shifting about, but before a volunteer surfaced, the door rattled open, shouldered by a flustered-looking woman with short grey hair, a big sling bag full of books over one arm, and what looked like a lemon drizzle cake in her hands. Jane, Julia assumed.

'Sorry I'm late. But you'll never guess what? There's been a murder!'

'In real life?' asked Diane. It was, after all, a book club.

'Yes, in real life. My Graham told me, he saw the police van out in the road over at the Steadmans' old place, asked the coppers,' said Jane, depositing the cake on the table.

Pippa turned to Julia.

'But isn't that where you...?' said Pippa, drawing away from Julia.

'Yes. That's where I live.'

All eyes were on Julia now, and they all spoke at once:

'Good Lord.'

'Someone was murdered at your house?'

'How...?'

'Who...?'

'What did...?'

Even Dylan was roused to enquire, 'Did you see the killer?'

Tabitha put up her hand. 'Please, let's not badger Julia with questions.'

'It's okay, I'll tell you what I know,' said Julia. 'It is an old body, actually more of a skeleton. Years, maybe decades old. It was found in the garden when I was doing some landscaping. The police have taken it away for tests.' Julia paused. She wasn't going to tell them how poor young Brendan had been completely beside himself, and had needed to sit down with a sweet cup of tea before he could stop shaking. Or how old Johnny had gone so pale when he saw the bones sticking out of the soil that Julia had thought he might have a heart attack then and there. The discovery of a body in the garden had been very upsetting.

Another torrent of questions and comments.

'A suggestion, if I may,' said Sean. 'Should we start on the tea while we talk? I know it's unconventional, but under the circumstances... And the sausage rolls are still nice and warm.'

There was resounding approval of this course of action, and a veritable stampede towards the tea and eats.

Jane plonked herself next to Julia, giving Julia a chance to examine her properly. The short, plump woman had warm brown eyes, which currently sparkled with interest. A spray of laugh lines around her eyes and deep creases around her mouth gave Julia the idea that Jane laughed often and easily. She wore a pretty white blouse that billowed over bright red, loose trousers. A necklace of large red beads brought the outfit together. She seemed like the sort of person that Julia could make friends with.

Jane's bright eyes were focused on Julia. 'Poor you,' she said. 'It must have been such a shock. You've only just moved to the village, and already a murder, right in your backyard.' She gave a little shiver of fear, or more likely, excitement. Julia had seen it before in her work – that tickle of a thrill that came with proximity to drama, especially death, and from a safe distance.

Jane continued, 'Good that you managed to come to book

club despite, you know... the murder.' It wasn't clear if this was more sympathy, or a criticism. Perhaps it wasn't village etiquette to go out socialising right after finding a body.

Julia wished Jane would stop using the word 'murder'. 'Tabitha is my friend, I wanted company. And there was nothing I could do at home,' she said a bit defensively. 'And we don't know that it was a murder. The body could have just been buried there.'

'Of course, of course,' said Jane, clearly not buying any of it. 'So you bought from the Steadmans when they went off to the retirement home. How long were they in the house, d'you know?'

'Oh, ages,' Pippa chipped in. 'They were there when I moved here ten years ago.'

'They'd been there at least fifteen years, maybe twenty. Bert Steadman always had a funny look,' said Diane. 'Sort of shifty, never quite looked you in the eye.'

'He had a squint,' said Tabitha, sternly. 'From an injury. That's quite a different thing.'

'Of course, yes,' Diane said quickly. 'I didn't mean... Lovely man. And Annie was lovely, of course. So helpful and kind; we'll miss having her at the chemist. She was such a help when my kids were babies. Definitely not the sort to bury a body.' Pippa gave a bark of laughter – Julia presumed at the thought of Annie Steadman being a murderer.

'Old man Bailey was there before the Steadmans, wasn't he?' asked Sean. 'He certainly didn't strike me as a killer. Unless the person died of boredom. That man could talk for Britain.'

The village gossip settled down for a minute while they drank their tea and contemplated the relative likelihood of any of the previous owners being a killer.

'Oh, come on now,' said Pippa. 'The Steadmans wouldn't murder anyone, and neither would Dermot Bailey. We all know that. If you want my opinion, it will all turn out to be some sort of muddle or misunderstanding. A Viking, or a cow, or... I don't know. But no one murdered anyone in Berrywick. This is not that kind of village.'

The evening went on, but the books were never even mentioned.

5

The light was falling as Julia made her way home. Her house, so pretty and welcoming this morning, seemed gloomy and brooding in the evening light. Maybe it was the awful situation with the ancient skeleton which had unsettled her and dampened her spirits. Or maybe it was just coming home to an empty house. Not that Peter had always been home before her; there had been plenty of times when he'd worked late or gone to some work-related function. But for nearly thirty years she had known that he'd be back, there was another place at the table, a warm body in the bed, someone to tell about her day.

Maybe she should get a cat. Like Too, the one in the library. Wasn't that what ageing single ladies did? She could tell the cat about her day – not that it would care – and it would be a warm body on the bed. Maybe she'd be able to confide in the chickens, when she got them. Fine animals, chickens, as Johnny had shouted. Although she didn't think she could share a bed with one.

Julia turned on the kitchen light, which helped brighten things up, and put away the single plate and single cup that rested sadly in the drying rack. She wasn't hungry – 007's sausage rolls had taken care of supper, with lemon drizzle for afters – but she poured herself a small glass of wine. The clock on the oven said it was nearly 7 p.m. but the light was soft and warm outside.

She took her wine glass and walked around her front garden, following the little paths and admiring the beds of lush summer flowers. The air was fragrant with lavender and early roses and she breathed deeply, feeling herself relax.

She hadn't intended to go to the back garden, the scene of the crime, so to speak, but she found herself walking round the side of the house. The shed was no more, its constituent parts stacked in a pile, ready for removal. In its place, a square had been demarcated in yellow crime tape, strung between metal poles. The bones had been removed, along with the rubble, leaving a shallow indented rectangle of rich brown earth. She walked closer, although there was nothing to see, and it was nearly dark now anyway.

There was a rustle in the bushes and Julia felt a flush of fear. She knew it was perfectly irrational, there was no murderer waiting in the bushes, but she pulled her phone out of her pocket anyway and used the little torch to scan the area. The beam probed weakly into the undergrowth. There was no one there, of course. It had probably been a bird or a rat. She drew the beam broadly across the tape and the soil, thinking how strange it was that someone had been buried there for years, until this morning. She wondered who it was. She wondered if someone was still out there, wondering what happened to the person who had died. She hoped not.

The soil was churned up where the police had dug up the bones, the ground around that area flat and dry, with the occasional weed that had managed to flourish despite being under a shed. Probably nourished by the body, thought Julia bleakly. The weeds annoyed her. Christopher had read her the riot act about weeds when he'd walked around the garden advising her.

'The moment you see them, you rip them up,' he had said, ripping up things that looked like perfectly healthy plants as he spoke. 'If you leave them, they will take over. Take. Over.' He'd made it sound terribly dangerous.

Before Julia could think about it, she found that she had put her phone back in her pocket and stepped over the police tape to start pulling up the weeds. This hardly counted as interfering with a crime scene, she told herself, as she pulled up the first one. This was gardening. The second weed was stubborn. She had to put her wine glass down to use both hands, tugging at it. Eventually, it gave up its tight hold on the ground, coming loose suddenly and spraying Julia with a shower of soil.

'Dammit,' she muttered, stepping backwards and almost falling. Maybe night-time gardening wasn't the best idea. Carefully taking the weeds with her – 'Don't just throw them into the garden,' Christopher had warned – she climbed back over the police tape. 'Dammit,' she muttered again, realising that she had left her wine glass behind. She took her phone out again, and using the torch, made her way to where the glass was standing, tipped perilously and with lumps of soil floating in the wine.

She picked up the glass and looked at the flotsam. What a waste of good wine. There was something else in there though, with the soil. An insect body? She fished it out. It was a strange hard oval shaped disc, covered in earth. Not an insect, that was for sure. She put the object in her pocket, and moved her torch back and forth over the area where she'd pulled out the plants. Something glimmered. She took a step to the left and bent her knees to get a different angle, then tried again, sweeping the beam over the soil. There it was, a glint in the soil where the weed had come up. She held the torch steady, knelt down and took the glittering object out of the soil. As she did so, she noticed a third one nearby and, running her hand over the soil under the beam of her phone, a fourth. She picked them up too, dropped them into the palm of her hand and walked through the gloaming to the back door.

In the kitchen, at the table under the light, she opened her hand to see four discs, small and hard, caked in soil, gold showing through. She rubbed the dirt away from one of them to reveal a thin plastic oval, a golden colour with a sheen that glimmered in the light. She had absolutely no idea what they were, or if they had any significance at all. But she knew she had just tampered with a crime scene.

Her hands shook as she filled the kettle – having briefly considered, then rejected, a second glass of wine – and took out a mug, a teabag and some milk. Whatever the little gold discs were, they likely had nothing to do with the skeleton, she decided, pouring the water into the mug. *No matter,* she told herself sternly, *you'll go and hand them over to the police tomorrow, and that will be that. Then, chickens.* She deposited the four little ovals in a small china bowl on the sideboard for safe-keeping, and went to bed.

Julia didn't have to call on the police. The next morning, they called on her, in the person of a younger woman and her colleague.

'Mrs Bird? DI Hayley Gibson,' she said, when Julia opened the door. 'And this is DC Walter Farmer.'

The uniformed young man behind her nodded. 'Morning, ma'am.'

DI Gibson was shorter than Julia, with bright blue eyes and short dark hair, peppered grey at the temples. Julia estimated that she must be in her early forties. She was dressed in plain clothes, and wore plain black trousers, a blue collared denim shirt and sensible black shoes. Ideal for chasing down a criminal, thought Julia. She looked the type of woman who took no nonsense, but might be kind in a crisis. Her handshake was firm, and warm.

The DI got right down to business. 'Do you have a moment? Just a few routine questions about the, er, the body.'

'Yes of course,' said Julia, stepping back to let them in. 'I was going to phone you and see if you had any news.'

'The, um, remains are with the coroner's office, and we don't have results just yet, but we would like to get some background information from you if we can,' said DI Gibson. DI Gibson didn't seem at home with the terminology of death. Julia supposed that as a DI in this area, she seldom dealt with this type of crime.

'Happy to help,' said Julia. 'Although as I told the policeman who was here yesterday, I've only lived here just over a week, so I'm not sure how much help I'm actually going to be.'

'You never know what will turn out to be useful,' said Gibson, without much confidence. 'Although it's clear that the body is quite old.'

'Oh really? Like decades?' asked Julia.

'I'm not at liberty to share details of the investigation, ma'am, and besides, we don't have the results of the post-mortem. But she has been here a good while. Now, what can you tell me about the people you bought the house from?'

So it was a 'she' then, Julia noted, before answering: 'The Steadmans. Bert and Annie. Seemed like a nice couple, they were moving to a smaller place. They had been here fifteen or twenty years, I think, maybe more.'

'Well, the body's definitely been here a long time – might have been here that long, or even longer,' said Gibson, thoughtfully. Julia was relieved to hear it was at least that old, although it seemed unlikely it would be a Viking, as Pippa had suggested. That said, a Viking *would* have been better. Fifteen or twenty years, when you thought about it, wasn't that long at all. Hadn't

Tabitha moved to the village fifteen years ago? And she said that some of the villagers still called her a newcomer.

'We'll have to speak to the Steadmans,' DI Gibson was saying. 'Do you know where they are living?'

'A retirement village, somewhere local I think, but I don't know exactly where. I have a phone number for them, if that helps?'

'Yes, thank you.'

Julia read the number off her phone and Gibson took it down on a little notepad.

'What do you know about them?'

'Really not much, I only met them once. He was an accountant, I think. He had a squint. Not that that...'

'No, of course not. Well thank you, you've been...' The sentence tailed off. Julia knew she had been going to say helpful, but in fact Julia had been rather useless in terms of information. She'd learnt more from DI Gibson – that the victim was female and had been there at least fifteen years – than the DI had learnt from her. The DI patted Julia's arm, as if to say there were no hard feelings that Julia was such a dead end of a witness.

'Not to be impatient,' said Julia, 'but how long before the tape will be down and I can use the area? I want to get working on the garden, you see.'

'Oh, I don't know about that. We'll have a word with crime scene. They took the surrounding soil, and the fragments of clothing and so on of course. I think they're finished, but you can't do anything until they take down the tape. That would be tampering with a crime scene. A serious criminal offence. There wouldn't be much in the way of clues after all this time, I don't think. It's not what you'd call a priority, such a cold case. Not as if there's a serial killer on the loose now, is there?'

Walter Farmer, who had hitherto been entirely silent, gave a snort at this witticism, and said drolly: 'Hardly.'

Julia remembered the little oval discs. They were probably just rubbish. The crime-scene people would have taken them if they'd been important. There was no point in handing them over, and it would mean admitting she'd tampered with the crime scene – 'a serious criminal offence'. Julia knew that just a year ago, she wouldn't have hesitated to hand them over. But the events of her last months of work, with all the accusations and finger pointing, had made her wary of any sort of trouble. That trouble had been smoothed over, of course, but the scars were still fresh. Julia did not fancy being accused of anything sinister; she'd keep the little gold ovals to herself.

'So you'll check and let me know?' she asked.

'Sure,' said DI Gibson. 'Walter, give them a ring when we get back to the office and let Mrs Bird know. Right, we'll be off. Got someone down the next village with a stolen bicycle. Criminals never sleep, Mrs Bird.'

'I hear you, DI Gibson. I used to be a social worker in London, and my ex-husband is a solicitor, so I've had a brush or two with the criminal justice system.'

DI Gibson looked at Julia with interest. 'Social workers have useful skills, Mrs Bird,' she said. 'One of these days you'll have to tell me more about it.'

Once the officers left, Julia felt her sense of unease from the night before returning. She'd tampered with a crime scene in her very own back garden. The place that was supposed to be her refuge and her new start. Now thanks to this skeleton, she was feeling alone and unbalanced, which was exactly the feeling she had wished to avoid. It was a feeling that had grown too familiar in those last months in London, between work and Peter leaving her. It was the reason that she had come here. She fetched herself a glass of orange juice and went to sit on the small bench by her front door. Christopher had placed it in exactly the right spot and the right angle to afford her a view of the stream, and the passing dog walkers.

What she needed to do, Julia thought, was figure out how to get her garden back to being a garden, instead of a crime scene, as fast as possible. The quickest way to do that, she realised, would be to get hold of the Steadmans herself. The case was cold and not at all urgent – the police had said as much. They were right now heading to the village up the way, looking for a bicycle. And who knew what other village crimes they might have to investigate before they got round to the Steadmans – a stranded cat? A pilfered peony? And tomorrow was the weekend. It could be a week before that crime-scene tape was removed and the chicken coop installed.

But there was nothing stopping Julia from making a call or two herself to get things moving a bit more quickly. Julia was good at talking things through and sorting things out. That's what she had done for a living for nearly forty years. That's what she would do now, and she could get her chickens, and perhaps a cat, and return to her plan of a peaceful village idyll.

'Jake, no!'

A familiar voice interrupted Julia's musings, and a familiar brown shape came bounding down the lane in hot pursuit of a swan. 'Jake, stop!' yelled Pippa. 'Killing swans is treason, you idiot dog! They belong to the Queen.'

Julia stood up, unsure how she would be able to help exactly, but she couldn't just sit there doing nothing.

'Jake,' she called tentatively to the fast-approaching hound. And then a bit louder, and with authority, 'Jake! Come here.'

To her surprise, and to Pippa's amazement, Jake did, in fact, stop. He came to a skidding halt in front of Julia's cottage. The swan took the opportunity to leap aside in a flutter of great wings, and came down on the water.

Jake turned to look at Julia, his large brown head tilted to the side, his chocolate-hazel eyes taking her in.

'Okay,' he seemed to be saying. 'I stopped. Now make it worth my while.'

And suddenly, Julia had quite the most magnificent idea she had had in a while.

She waited for Pippa, and Jake's siblings, to catch up to him, and went out of her gate to meet them in the lane. Jake was still waiting, his eyes on Julia. He didn't even flinch when Julia took his lead.

'Pippa,' said Julia, before she could change her mind, 'if Jake is still available, I would very much like to give him a home.'

'Oh, I couldn't possibly ask you to do *that*,' said Pippa, which was not quite the outpouring of gratitude that Julia expected. 'This dog is a horror. Untrainable. He'll destroy your home and your peace of mind.'

Julia looked down at Jake and thought of all the times that she had heard words like this in the foster care system. Those children that nobody believed in, who just needed one grown up to take their side. Julia knew the power of love and recognition better than most. Jake's eyes met hers, and she could swear he knew what was going on.

'I'm quite sure, Pippa,' she said. 'I would like Jake to be mine.'

6

Julia's phone rang on the dot of 8 a.m.

'Mrs Bird? It's DI Gibson,' came the voice. Julia wondered if there was some police rule that you only phone after eight, unless of course it was an emergency.

'Oh, hello. Any news about the case?'

'I'm just checking on Bert Steadman's phone number. I think I might have taken it down wrong, because I haven't been able to reach him.'

'Hang on a mo,' said Julia, putting her phone on speaker and fiddling around to get to her contacts list. She managed to find the number without cutting off the copper, which was quite an achievement in itself. She read it out.

'That's what I've got. Strange. Okay, thanks.'

'My pleasure. Any news on the crime scene? I don't mean to...'

'Yes, I quite understand. I'll follow-up with Walter, see if he's got hold of them. Was up to my ears in the bicycle theft yesterday. Turned out it wasn't stolen, just misplaced. But still, what a run around.'

'I can imagine,' said Julia sympathetically, although she

really couldn't. In Julia's experience, if you asked the right people the right questions, things tended to get sorted out quite quickly.

'I'll try and get hold of the crime-scene chaps this morning. The forensics weren't backed up for once, so the examination of the bones is complete, and the fabrics are with a specialist department, so I shouldn't think there's much more to be done. But I'd better check.'

'Thank you. Of course, anything I can do to help...' said Julia vaguely, feeling rather bad about hurrying the crime scene along just so she could get free range organic eggs. 'Clarify anything?'

'Yes, thanks, but unlikely. As we suspected, the body's been there a good while, long before your time.'

Bert Steadman's contact was still up on Julia's phone screen when the call with DI Gibson ended. On a whim, Julia hit the little green button. No answer from Bert Steadman's phone. Just a rather strange series of beeps and then nothing – not even 'please leave a message'. Odd. She had used the number just weeks before, discussing the logistics around the move. Perhaps the phone was broken, or he had a new phone. Still. Odd.

How long is 'a good while'? she wondered to herself, thinking about what the police lady had said. It seemed that the body must have been dumped at the same time as the shed was built. So the question was, who had built the shed, and when? If Bert and Annie Steadman had built that shed, they were the ones most likely to know how that body got there. Or, even – she thought with a shiver – killed that person.

Nonsense, Julia, said her stern inner voice. *You're in the Cotswolds, for heaven's sake. The other big crime on the go is the theft of a bicycle – and even that turned out to be a misunderstanding. There's no way Bert and Annie – an accountant and a village pharmacist – have anything to do with this.*

She looked at the contact, noting the email address, thesteadmans@janmail.com. She had a thought.

Now, Julia knew that she had a tendency to be curious – it came with the job of being a social worker. And even though she knew how wrong things could go, a lifetime of solving problems and getting things done was a hard habit to break.

She opened her email app and started typing.

Hello Bert and Annie,

I hope you are both very well. Just checking in to let you know that I've settled in and all is well here at Rose Cottage.

Spring has sprung, and I've been busy in the garden. My next project is to build a henhouse and buy some chickens. I think I'm going to get rid of the old shed, and put them in that corner. What do you think?

Everyone has been very welcoming in the village.

I hope you've settled into your new place. It must be quite an adjustment after – how many years here?

All the best to you

Julia B

She pushed 'send' before she changed her mind. Another thing her work had taught her – in addition to taking matters into her own hands at times – was not to show your cards too early. *Let's just see what Bert and Annie say about the shed,* she thought. But in the meantime, tea.

She'd no sooner put the kettle on than there was a knock on the door.

As she reached it, she heard scratching and thumping from the other side, and then the familiar refrain, 'Oh, Jake.'

'Hello, Pippa,' she said, opening the door.

'Surprise!' said Pippa, gesturing to Jake who was at her feet, a beautiful red silk bow tied around his neck. She gabbled on: 'I thought I'd bring him round straight away, save you the trip. And here's all his stuff. His bed, he loves his bed. And I got you the extra large puppy food, he loves his puppy food...'

'Oh, gosh, I wasn't expecting... I mean, thank you for bringing him and the bed and the food.'

'And here's his chewy toy,' Pippa continued, handing over a big red rubber bone which squeaked horribly when Julia took it.

'Does he love his chewy toy?'

'No. He prefers my shoes,' said Pippa, and then added quickly, 'Just teething! He'll grow out of it.' And then, under her breath, 'I'm almost sure he will.'

Julia squatted down next to the dog and stroked his silky brown ears. 'Look at you, you lovely boy.' He sat still and gazed at her adoringly, his tail slapping the front step noisily.

'You really do have a knack with him,' said Pippa, shaking her head in wonder. 'He's so... calm.'

'Isn't he a love? Come in and have some tea,' Julia said, remembering her resolve to reach out to the locals. 'I was just about to have some.'

'Thank you, but I must dash,' said Pippa, who seemed very eager to leave. Or perhaps eager to leave Jake. 'Goodbye. And good luck!'

She set off down the garden path at an efficient clip, leaving Julia and Jake on the step. Julia was reminded of the day she and Peter had brought Jess home from hospital. The delight and amazement, mixed with that daunting feeling of, 'What are we going to do with this being? What the heck were we thinking?'

Julia hadn't had a dog for years. Their spaniel, unimaginatively named Charles, had died the year that Jess had gone off to uni, and he had never been replaced. It hadn't seemed fair, with the hours Julia and Peter kept. Well, that had changed. She now had more hours than she knew what to do with. One of many changes.

She put Jake's bed down in a corner of the kitchen where it would catch the morning sun. Jake immediately went over and lay down with a contented sigh. This dog ownership business was easier than Julia had imagined. While he lay there calmly and wagging his tail slowly, she sat down at the kitchen table and checked her phone. There was already an email from the Steadmans.

Dear Julia,

Hello from Sardinia! We are on the most lovely cruise.

So glad you've settled in, it's a lovely friendly village. We were there twenty-two years – high time for a change. Chickens sound lovely!

Annie

Well, there you go. Much loveliness, but no mention of the shed. Annie was obviously not the least bit concerned about it being pulled down. Which meant the Steadmans had nothing to hide. Not that she'd really expected them to.

She was about to close her email, satisfied with her morning's work, when another popped up.

That's a perfectly serviceable shed. Old Doug Harrison built it to last – it's got many good years yet. Where will you put your garden tools if you pull it down? I think you should reconsider. The chickens would be better over by the plum tree.

Bert

Interesting. Very interesting.

No time to dwell on what his reluctance might mean, because Jake had emerged from his thirty-second lie-down refreshed and invigorated. He was investigating the table legs, to chew or pee on, she wasn't sure. But trouble was bound to emerge from one end or the other.

'Come on, Jake,' she said. 'Would you like a tour of the garden? I can show you where Bert Steadman buried a body.'

She hoped she was joking. It was one thing buying a house with a dead body in the garden, but quite another buying the house of a murderer.

7

Julia took a table on the pavement, because of Jake. The unusually warm weather meant that all the doors were open, and tables spilt out onto the pavement, so even from there she could hear that the Buttered Scone was abuzz with the news: the body in the garden had been dated.

'The coroner has determined that the remains are those of a young woman, who died approximately twenty years ago. The cause of death has not been announced. The police have asked any Berrywick residents with information that might be relevant to the investigation to please come forward,' read Sean O'Connor in his unmistakable burr, before tossing the newspaper onto the white veneer table in front of him. 'Well. It's a sad day, I must say. A murder in Berrywick.'

'If it is a murder,' said Diane, who was wearing the same long green coat that she had worn to book club, her long red hair wound around her head in a complicated nest of plaits. She added hopefully, 'It might have been a mistake.'

'But why was nobody reported missing, then?' asked a mousy woman in a floral dress. 'If it was someone local...'

'Well, I was here twenty years ago, can't say I remember

anyone missing. What about you, Diane?' said Sean. 'You would have been here then.'

'Yes, I was just finishing up school. Lots of people coming and going, of course. Off to uni, or the city. But no one missing, no.'

'Could have been someone from out of town,' ventured another amateur police inspector, this one a young mum with a chubby baby asleep in a pushchair.

'Could be,' said Flo, who had hitherto busied herself with clearing the tables. She warmed to the idea. 'That makes more sense. Murdered in London or Manchester or somewhere and then dumped here, where no one would ever think to look. Nothing to do with anyone in Berrywick.' Flo said this with such certainty, you'd have thought she'd that morning got an email from the police.

There was a grim silence as they all pondered the dangers of the city, where people were doubtless being knocked off every minute, and then a lightening of mood, as they all came round to the idea that this abomination was likely nothing to do with them at all. Just a horrible coincidence.

Once they'd determined that, they sat back in their chairs and sipped their morning beverages, noting, almost in time with each other, that the harbourer of the dead woman was sitting there, on the pavement, with the world's worst dog.

'Hello, Julia,' said Diane. 'So you took him! Pippa said you would. Well done, you, I'm sure he will be perfectly...' Her voice faltered and she ended with a mumbled, 'I'm sure he won't be too bad.'

'He's an angel,' announced Julia. 'Just really misunderstood.' And indeed, Jake was lying next to the table, his chin resting on crossed paws, placidly observing the scene. You couldn't ask for more from a dog, really.

'Did you know about the body then?' asked Flo, arriving at Julia's table rather suddenly. 'Any inside track?'

'From the sounds of things, I know less than you do,' said Julia. She felt slightly put out about this. Surely, as the owner of the garden in which the body had been discovered, she should have been told the news directly?

Sean picked up his newspaper. 'It's all here,' he said. 'Here, have a read for yourself.' He stood up and brought the paper over to her. 'It's the local rag,' he said. '*Berrywick and Surrounds Gazette*. Not an inspiring name, but an unexpected source of excellent journalism.'

'Pah,' grunted Johnny Blunt, who had been so quiet that Julia hadn't even noticed him sitting at the table behind her. 'Journalists, what do they know?' Johnny was not reading the paper, nor was he eating his breakfast, which sat untouched on the table in front of him. Probably still the shock of finding a body in her garden, Julia thought, feeling guilty. Her own appetite hadn't been quite the same since. She shot Johnny what she hoped was a look of support and sympathy before turning to the newspaper that Sean had given her.

Julia carefully read the article in front of her. Just as Sean had read, it reported that the body was that of a young woman, and had been dead for about twenty years.

'A young woman,' said Julia, so softly that probably only Jake heard her. 'That's awful.' Julia tried not to be the sort of mother who fussed and worried, but with Jess so very far away, and in such an exotic part of the world, sometimes it was hard for her. To think that the body of a young woman – probably around Jess's age – had been found in her garden made her feel quite sick. And it also made it much more likely that it was definitely murder. Young women didn't just drop down dead in people's gardens and mistakenly get buried under sheds. No more hoping that it might turn out to be a Viking, that was for sure.

Talk in the cafe had meanwhile moved on from the body.

'I couldn't believe it, could you?' Diane was saying to her

companion, a middle-aged woman that Julia had yet to meet. 'The cheek of her, selling something that I gave her, and in front of the whole nation, too.'

'She always was a dark horse,' said Diane's companion, nodding violently, dislodging one of the many decorative combs keeping her hair in place.

'In fairness now, Marilyn,' said Sean, from his table, 'she's not a dark horse at all. Just lonely. Happens to a lot of us when the young folk move on. And Diane, you did give her the jug. It was hers to sell.'

Julia sipped the coffee that Flo placed in front of her, trying to get a grip on the conversation. She didn't think she'd ever get used to the way everybody just yelled at each other, with no regard for whether they were invited to the conversation or not. Julia considered herself a reserved person. A nice quiet morning coffee was what she was looking for, not this shouting across tables.

'I'd never have given it to her, would I, if I'd known it was a Cody jug?' said Diane, her voice loud with indignation. 'Ugly bloody thing with that great big face on it. Didn't know it was worth more than a fiver.'

'A Toby jug, not a Cody jug, silly girl,' shouted Johnny, now poking at his breakfast. 'And a bloody valuable one, it turns out.'

'A collector's item, according to that telly programme, *Antiques in the Country*,' confided Flo, who was back at Julia's table, wiping a small spill that Julia hadn't noticed. 'I don't suppose you watch something like that, up in London.'

'Actually, my husband... my ex-husband... loves it,' said Julia. Peter could watch antiques shows for hours. He and Julia used to watch them together, trying to guess the value of things, and speculating what their own antiques and curiosities might fetch. It was probably something that he and Christopher did together now.

'Oh yes? Well, who should be on it but Maeve from up the

village,' said Flo, gesturing into the street as if that would shed light on where Maeve lived. Her voice dropped, and she filled Julia in. 'Sold a Toby jug. But the thing is, she got it from Second Chances, the charity shop where Diane works. A big box of things had just come in, and Maeve popped in and bought a few odds and ends. Diane went and said that she'd "throw in" the jug as a freebie. You should see the thing. Looks like old Johnny Blunt after a big night at the Pig & Whistle. Anyway, the manager, Wilma, hadn't evaluated the new stock, and Diane doesn't know a Chesterfield from a chestnut, stupid tart.' Flo said the last bit fondly, and smiled in Diane's direction. Diane was luckily too deep in conversation with wild-haired Marilyn to notice.

'Well, now Maeve has gone and sold it on *Antiques in the Country* for a record price for a Toby, and Diane is spitting.' Flo paused for a moment. 'I tell you this, if I were Maeve, I'd keep out of our Diane's way for a bit, I would.'

8

With that dire observation, Flo left to attend to the lady with the baby, who was now wide awake and bawling.

Julia went back to sipping her coffee, wondering whether Jake would allow her enough time to order something to eat. She glanced down at him. He was happily chewing on Sean O'Connor's newspaper, the words 'Contact the police... aware... missing women...' hanging out of his mouth. It was hard to read, with all the Labrador spittle splattered over it.

'Oh, Jake,' said Julia. 'No! Bad boy! Give me the paper back!' Jake continued chewing, his tail wagging at the sound of her voice.

'Sorry, Sean,' she called to the next table. 'The bloody dog has eaten your newspaper. I'll buy you another one.'

Sean glanced down at the dog. 'My advice to you is not to offer to replace everything that dog chews, or you'll be replacing things the length and breadth of Berrywick. Apparently Pippa doesn't have a pair of shoes to her name.'

'You're a fiend, Jake,' said Julia to the dog. Jake looked at her with melting brown eyes, and rested his chin on her foot. The word 'body' had somehow stuck itself to his nose. He looked proud of himself, and perhaps ready for a nap.

When she looked up, Johnny Blunt had sat himself down at her table, and was observing her with a glint in his blue eyes.

'Taken on quite a hound there, haven't you?' he observed. 'Dogs, though. God knew what he was doing the day he made dogs, that's a fact.' Julia remembered he'd felt much the same about chickens.

'I'm afraid that our chicken project will have to be on hold for a bit,' she said. 'What with the body.'

'What a thing to have happened,' said Johnny, shaking his head. It looked to Julia like the whole experience had aged him slightly, and she felt another stab of guilt. She had to remind herself that she had no part in putting the body under her shed and upsetting poor Johnny Blunt. 'What a thing,' he repeated, with a sigh.

Julia noticed that he was talking at a perfectly normal volume. A surreptitious glance at his left ear showed a glint of silver below the blue hat – Johnny was wearing his hearing aids. All the better to hear village gossip, perhaps. And, perhaps, all the better to share it.

'Johnny,' she said, trying to inject a sort of idle curiosity into her tone. 'What sort of chap was Bert Steadman?'

'Bert? Never liked the fellow, to be honest.'

Julia waited.

'Typical accountant. Always counting the pennies. Did a job for him once, and he asked to see the invoices for the paint. Invoices! I ask you. Can you not trust an honest man to do an honest job?'

Julia nodded solemnly as if this were indeed a madly unreasonable request. 'But apart from that...' she said.

'Oh, he was all right.'

'Not, you know... difficult?'

'You could call him difficult. A bit of a know-all. You know the type. Has his opinions.'

'I mean, did he have a temper?'

'Bert? Good heavens, no. Why would you be worrying about Bert Steadman's temper?'

'I don't know... I was just wondering.'

Jake broke the awkward silence by chewing Johnny's shoe, allowing them both to fuss and admonish and pat the dog.

'Do you by any chance know Doug Harrison, Johnny?' Julia asked. 'A builder, I think he is?'

'An all right fellow. Knew his way around a hammer,' Johnny said brusquely.

'Do you know where I could find him?'

'Of course I do,' said Johnny. 'In the far left corner of the cemetery at St Francis.'

Julia said goodbye to Johnny, left a tip for Flo, and got to her feet. She had a bit of shopping to do, and it was past nine. As evidenced by the small rush to the door a few minutes ago. Jake followed her obediently, staying close, trotting along without pulling. What a good boy he was.Goodness, who would have guessed that village life would be so busy and interesting and filled with drama? First the body in her very own garden, and then all that nasty business with the Toby jug. A quiet morning coffee at the local coffee shop had been positively brimming with intrigue.

Julia admitted to herself that she had entered into the spirit of things, fishing for info on Bert and the late Doug Harrison. It was her nature, she knew, to be a little... she would say *quizzy*, Peter said *nosy*. She maintained that she was simply interested in human nature. She was a social worker, after all. Well, Peter wasn't here to criticise her now. She could be as nosy as she wished.

She enjoyed the walk to the shop. She had hardly had a chance to explore the shopping street, so busy had she been with the house and then all the shed drama. She noted, as she had on her previous visits, what a very pretty street it was and what a pleasant mix of shops. Everything you could want – a hardware store, a stationer's, a florist, a sweet shop, a toy shop, a hairdresser – all gathered in the same place. A couple of pubs, a few restaurants. She had tried one or two on her visits to Tabitha.

She was about to enter the little supermarket when she remembered Jake. What would she do with him? What did people do with dogs? An ancient furry border collie was lying obediently at the edge of the door, waiting for her owner. Jake would not lie obediently at the edge of the door, waiting for his owner, that was for sure.

There was a SERVICE ANIMALS ONLY sign and Julia briefly considered making a case for Jake's guide dog status. But it seemed dishonest, given the expulsion.

Julia was rooted to the spot in indecision, when she saw Diane bustling past on the other side of the road.

Should she ask Diane to watch Jake for a moment? Julia was not the sort to impose, but Diane was sort of an acquaintance – a fellow book club member and a regular at the cafe. Besides, village life was different. She hesitated, and then gave Jake's lead a little tug. 'Come on, Jake. Let's see if we can find you a babysitter for five minutes.'

Before she could call out to her, Diane walked into a shop. SECOND CHANCES, read the sign, with the words CHARITY SHOP underneath in smaller writing. The scene of the great Toby jug heist. Diane was off to work.

Julia crossed the road, dragging the reluctant Jake away from a chip packet in the gutter, and paused outside the shop, where an argument was in full swing. She flattened herself against the door frame, out of sight. She couldn't see the arguers, but she recognised Diane's indignant voice.

'I'm sorry, but how was I to know? It's not as if I claimed to be an expert in hideous bloody jugs.'

Ah, so this was about the TV programme.

'You shouldn't have taken anything out of the box before I'd checked it.'

'To be honest, Wilma, it's not as if I was expecting to find the crown jewels. I mean, let's face it, people send us a whole lot of tat.'

'Tat?' said Wilma, enraged. Jake cowered slightly, and rolled his anxious eyes at Julia. 'Tat? Well if that's what you think of it...'

'I do.'

'Well thanks to you, we missed out on thousands of pounds that could have gone to the dogs and cats. Not to mention those poor dear donkeys.'

Wilma's voice wavered at the mention of donkeys.

'I'm sorry about the dogs and cats,' said Diane, tearily. 'And the donkeys of course. The poor, poor donkeys.'

What on earth was wrong with the donkeys? Julia wondered. She tried not to dwell.

Diane continued, 'I feel bad about it, honestly I do.'

Wilma made a conciliatory huffing noise. 'It wasn't your fault. That Maeve pulled one over on us.'

'You think she knew?'

'Damn right she knew.'

'She tricked us?'

'I think she did.'

'That means she effectively *stole* that money from us. From the donkeys! What kind of person...'

'A cold-hearted, swindling animal hater, that's who.'

'She seems so... mild.'

'They always do. But honestly? I always thought there was something funny about her. Cold.'

'She's strange, you're right,' said Diane, warming to the subject now that they were partners in outrage and she seemed to be off the hook. 'Known her since my school days. She was one of the mums. Samantha's mum. Never liked her, and she just got weirder.'

'And now she's stealing from the animals!'

Now that things had calmed down a bit, Julia announced herself with a sing-song, 'Good morning!' as if she'd just arrived at the door.

'Oh hello, Julia. Come in. This is Wilma.'

The manager gave her a tight smile. She was older than Diane, but a bit younger than Julia, with her blonde hair in a shoulder-length bob, and slightly streaked with grey. She was slim and fit-looking and wore the sort of clothes that suggested that she might take off for a run at any minute, or perhaps a quick session at the gym. Julia supposed that this was practical for the sorting and lifting that might happen at a charity shop.

Julia explained about the shop and the dog. 'Just for five minutes,' she said. 'Would you mind?'

'Of course not!' said Diane. 'We'd love to have him.'

She knelt down and fell upon Jake with squeals and clucks, rubbing his velveteen tummy, stroking his silky ears. Even the rather grumpy Wilma gave him a pat. He lolled about like a small furry princeling being adored by his lackeys.

'I'll be back before you know it,' Julia said, dropping the lead and scurrying out the door.

9

'He's very lively, isn't he?' said Wilma, when Julia returned from her shop. Wilma was surveying a shortbread biscuit which Jake had found and was busy extracting from its foil wrapper with his sharp little teeth and pink tongue. There was a small yellow puddle on the tile floor.

'Oh, I am sorry,' said Julia. 'I'll clean that up.'

'No worries. I've got it,' said Diane, placing a newspaper over the wet spot and giving Jake a scratch. 'He's just a pup really.'

'Well, thank you both for looking after him, I appreciate the favour. I'm going to come back without him though and have a look around. I've just moved in so I need a few things. I do love a charity shop.'

'You do?' said Wilma.

'Oh yes, I used to go and trawl the stands at Portobello Market with my ex-husband. He'd love this place, you've got some lovely pieces.'

'I don't suppose...' Wilma hesitated and then came out with it. 'I don't suppose you'd consider doing a shift or two? We are a bit short staffed and it would be such a help to have an extra pair of hands. Especially in the summer – it gets quite busy, what with the tourists.'

'Oh really, well that's nice of you to ask, but...' Julia's first instinct was to wriggle out of it, but it was rather awkward since the ladies had so recently done her a favour. And she had promised herself that she would be more accommodating, more approachable, and try to make friends. 'Okay, sure. That might be fun. I'd need to be quite flexible though,' she added, giving herself an out, and hoping that nobody asked why exactly it was that a woman with no job and no family needed to be flexible.

'Perfect. What's today, Monday? Well, how about you come in at nine on Wednesday, do a shift with me and Diane, and learn the ropes?' said Wilma, whose policy was clearly to strike while the iron was hot, or even lukewarm.

'Perfect,' said Julia brightly, hefting her shopping bag up onto her shoulder. She was just turning to leave when she noticed that Wilma and Diane were staring at the door where a new customer was standing. The thin woman with greying black hair, dressed in a neat skirt and blouse, hardly seemed to warrant the look of horror on Wilma's face.

'Well, you've got a cheek,' said Wilma.

'A right cheek,' echoed Diane, putting her hands on her hips.

'I just thought we should talk this through,' said the woman. She smiled hopefully at Wilma and Diane. 'Make our peace?'

Could this be who Julia thought it was? In which case, she was very brave coming into the shop like this.

'Maeve Harold, you should be ashamed of yourself,' said Wilma, two red splotches appearing on her cheeks. 'Tricking Diane and robbing the donkeys.'

'Wilma,' said Maeve. 'You know that this is how it works. I've sold things at a profit before. You know how I struggle to make ends meet. You've always been very supportive of me.

And Diane just gave me the jug. I even asked her if she was sure. I had no idea it was so valuable.'

Julia had to admit, this woman didn't seem like the evil schemer of the village gossip.

'Be that as it may,' said Wilma, 'you've pushed me too far.'

'I've always thought we were friends,' said Maeve, her voice breaking slightly.

'We *were* friends, Maeve. But we're not any more. I'd like you to leave.' Wilma pulled herself up to her full height.

There was a moment of silence as the two women stared at each other. Julia worried that there might be pushing and shoving, and Julia would have to step in. It wouldn't be the first time she'd separated fighting people, but it would be more complicated with an armful of shopping and a chocolate Labrador.

But after a minute, Maeve turned to leave. Her back was bent, and Julia felt quite sorry for her.

'Good riddance,' muttered Diane.

'Don't come back,' called Wilma, after the departing woman. 'Or I won't be responsible for what happens.'

The air in the shop was electric, and Julia thought it wasn't really her place to stay.

'Come on, Jake,' she said, injecting some cheer into her voice, 'say goodbye to your new friends.'

Jake obeyed her instructions enthusiastically, smearing spitty crumbs onto Wilma's white gym leggings and then getting a lock of Diane's long red hair, straying from her plaits, caught in his collar. After a brief flurry of wiping and wrangling, Julia waved them both goodbye.

It seemed you couldn't go anywhere in this village without a drama, thought Julia. Village life really was not at all what she had expected. But still, she enjoyed walking briskly down the shopping street with Jake trotting along happily at her side. Funny how Pippa had so much trouble with Jake, she thought. He was such a dear little thing, and apart from a bit of chewing, hardly caused any bother at all. Perhaps Pippa just wasn't good with dogs, Julia thought, inwardly complimenting herself on her own firm-yet-kind manner. That was what dogs needed. Just like the young people Julia had worked with in Youth Services. Firm-yet-kind, that was the ticket.

She was, quite literally, jerked out of her self-congratulatory reverie by Jake. He shot into the road, his lead slipping from her hand. A car squealed to a halt. An elderly man on a bicycle weaved and wobbled precariously to avoid the bounding beast who was in hot pursuit of a pigeon. The old man managed to stay upright, but shouted: 'Watch that dog of yours, it's a menace!'

'Sorry, ever so sorry,' Julia said over her shoulder, following Jake across the road.

A woman in gym clothes lunged athletically for him, but he slipped from her grasp, causing her to slide on the cobblestones, landing heavily on her bum.

Jake appeared oblivious to the chaos, engrossed, as he was, in trying to get the bird. It had evaded him (having the not inconsiderable advantage of flight), and was now looking down its beak at him from a lamp post.

Jake jumped at the pigeon a few times, and then decided to cut his losses and move on to easier prey. He turned to the little boy who was standing transfixed by the chase, and took a big slobbery bite out of his ice cream cone. The child dropped the cone, and Jake set about finishing it. It was astonishing that he could eat with all the wailing coming from the kid.

'The naughty dog ate my ice cream,' the boy bellowed, liquid seeping from his eyes, nose and mouth. 'Smack the dog, Mummy! Smack the naughty dog.'

His mother, thankfully, didn't smack the dog. She gave Julia an apologetic smile, her slightly buck teeth showing, a dimple in her cheek. She seemed to be in her early thirties, with that perpetually stressed look that Julia remembered well from the toddler years.

She reached down and gave her son a big hug, and calmed him. 'Ah, there, there, love.'

'Sorry, so sorry,' said Julia. 'Please let me buy you another ice cream.'

'Not to worry,' the mum said with a wave of her hand. 'It's nearly Sebastian's lunchtime anyway. I shouldn't have given in to the begging, but, you know how it is. Anyway, not your fault.' She had dark brown eyes and blonde hair – a combination that Julia always found appealing.

'That's very understanding of you. And again, apologies. He's only a puppy. I just got him.'

'Oh, I thought I recognised him. Pippa's dog, right? The guide dog school dropout?' She gave a merry laugh. 'Ah, so *you're* the one that took him. Good on you!'

'Yes, I'm Julia. And thanks. I think!' Remembering her vow to herself that she would be more friendly, Julia asked, 'So you know Pippa?'

'Oh, Pippa and I go way back,' the woman answered, absent-mindedly fishing a chocolate bar out of her bag and giving it to her son, thoughts of lunch obviously abandoned. 'Her mother and my grandmother used to go fishing together, so of course my aunt had to invite Pippa to her wedding so don't you know it, Pippa met her husband at that wedding, and the rest as they say it, is history. She's my godmother, as a result.'

Julia couldn't for the life of her figure out how this story all hung together, and was trying to drag up some sort of coherent response when a wizened old lady came tottering out of a nearby door, marched straight up to Jake and started talking to him as if they were old friends, of the same species.

'The fish are rising,' she confided in him. 'The hens are coming home to roost.'

'Hello, Auntie Edna,' said the younger woman, in a loud

voice. She took the other woman by her arm, speaking slowly and clearly. 'Auntie Edna. It's me. Nicky. Lizzie Watson's Nicky. How are you?'

'Lizzie Watson's a slut,' said Auntie Edna pleasantly, before tottering off.

'You have a lovely day yourself, now, Edna,' said Nicky in a friendly tone, unfazed by the maligning of her mother. She turned to Julia. 'Such a shame. Used to be the Chair of the Women's Institute and now she's completely barking. Dementia, Dr O'Connor says. Nothing to be done and she can't help it. We just try to be nice to her, you know? Even if she's not very nice back. She was a lovely lady before.'

'Gosh, you seem to know everybody,' said Julia.

'Well, I was born and raised here,' said Nicky. 'Lots of my friends left but, you know, I'd met my Kev, and we like it here, so we stayed.'

'How lovely,' said Julia. 'You must know everything about Berrywick.'

'Hard not to, around here, isn't it? For a start, I know that *you've* got a body in your garden. And the naughtiest puppy in Berrywick,' she said, with a laugh. They both looked down, but the naughtiest puppy in Berrywick had fallen asleep on the pavement, with little Sebastian leaning against his sleeping body, stroking his ears.

'Those idiot police, asking up and down the roads if anyone went missing twenty years ago,' Nicky continued. 'They should just come to ask people like me and Kev and our parents, and we could set them right. Missing! In Berrywick! As if. Can't get yourself knocked up without the news being around the village before you've even peed on a stick.'

'Right,' said Julia, wondering if this was a story from Nicky's own history, or more of an imaginary example.

'Yes, not much gets past me, I tell you.'

'What do you make of this Toby jug story?' Julia asked, out of pure nosiness. 'What a thing, eh?'

'Oh, that Maeve knew what she was up to, I can tell you that,' said Nicky, decisively. 'There's no flies on that one, my mother-in-law always says. And she'd know.'

'Would she?' Julia thought of the sad woman in the shop. She really felt quite sorry for her.

'Well, my Kev went out with Maeve's daughter, Samantha, back when they were at school. Course, that was before Kev spotted me. Hasn't had eyes for anyone since, I can tell you that. And no one would dare make a play for him, either.' Nicky sounded a bit fierce about this, as if Julia might be thinking of making a play for young Kev herself.

'So who do you think the body is?' said Julia, deftly moving the conversation away from Kev's romantic past.

'Tourist,' said Nicky, with certainty. 'Makes sense, doesn't it? Nobody local went missing in the right time frame, and this place is overrun with tourists in the summer. I'll tell you something.' Nicky dropped her voice, though Julia couldn't think who might be listening, other than Sebastian and Jake. 'You know how it is with tourists. Always up to something. Getting drunk. Out and about, eating scones.' It was unclear how these two activities were linked. 'Mark my words, there's some chap up in London that thinks he's got away with something, and that body under your shed is going to bring him down.' Nicky nodded to herself. Julia wondered if perhaps, in the days before Kev, Nicky had been hurt by one of the tourists. She seemed to bear them no goodwill.

'Anyhow, best I get a move on,' said Nicky, yanking an unsuspecting Sebastian into standing position, and waking Jake in the process. 'Time and tide. Have a good day, then. And good luck with that dog!' she added with a last merry laugh. In a blur of arms and bags, the two of them disappeared down the street.

Julia felt quite exhausted. What a chatterer that Nicky was.

As she walked home, she thought about what she'd learnt about the body in her garden. She hoped that Nicky was right, and that it somehow had something to do with tourists. For some reason, that seemed better than if someone local was involved. But if so, how did it come to be under the shed? And it was all very well that Johnny Blunt didn't think that Bert Steadman was a murderer, the fact remained that Bert hadn't wanted Julia to move the shed. But why would an old accountant have killed a tourist? Or anyone? And then buried her in his own backyard? It just didn't make sense.

'Let's hope the police make some progress soon,' said Julia to Jake, as she let them into her garden. 'Then you and I can get on with the business of being chicken owners. You'd like that, wouldn't you?'

Julia couldn't swear it, but she was almost sure that she saw Jake smile.

10

Julia woke up late on Tuesday. She'd had a disturbed night, filled with strange dreams about finding Toby jugs buried under the shed, and meeting skeletons in the Buttered Scone. The one thing that she hadn't imagined was that country life was going to be more stressful than her life as a social worker in London.

'I think,' she said to Jake, when she woke up, 'that you and I are going to take it easy today.'

Jake was already taking it easy – next to her, in the bed. She had been absolutely determined that he was going to be the sort of dog who slept in his basket in the kitchen. Or, she determined at midnight when he woke her with whining from the kitchen, at the very least the sort of dog who slept in a basket at the foot of her bed. But the reality was that when she'd been tossing and turning in the early hours, the sound of Jake's nails clicking along the hard floorboards, followed by the weight of him in the bed next to her, had been a comfort, and she hadn't the heart to push him off.

'Come on then, Jake,' she said, giving him a nudge. 'You're going out for a wee, and then we've got chores to do.'

Talking to Jake was probably no better a habit than allowing him in the bed, but she was used to years of telling Peter all the things on her mind, even if he hadn't listened quite as well as he might have. Jake, on the other hand, watched her as she spoke, his head on its side, one of her socks hanging out of his mouth. He really was a very satisfying sort of dog.

Julia was surprised by how much she enjoyed the morning's mild activity. She tidied the kitchen. She put the washing on, and hung it out in the sun. Picked flowers and put them in a vase – she managed a poor imitation of Christopher's display. She was rather pleased at her domesticity; it had never been her strong suit.

'Okay, Jake, that's enough housework for one day. We'll go for a walk and some training.' Pippa had told her that Jake had been learning to sit, lie and stay and so on, in preparation for guide dog training. Even though he'd failed the entrance exam, Julia wasn't giving up on him. She was determined to keep up the training, and even improve his skills. She had visions of having him loping alongside her without a lead, behaving incredibly well and not chasing anything or jumping on anyone. It seemed unlikely, but one could dream.

As long as he didn't see any pigeons, Jake was very good on the lead and concentrated nicely when she told him what to do. Julia remembered that Tabitha had told her that people walked their dogs off lead up at the lake. 'We'll go there tomorrow, after my shift at the charity shop,' she told Jake.

The charity shop. She still wasn't quite sure how she'd got herself into that, and despite her peaceful day, Tuesday night was again filled with dreams – this time it involved a skeleton who wanted to trade Jake for a Toby jug at Second Chances. When Jake had once again slipped up onto the bed in the early hours of the morning, it hadn't even been a question. Julia had wrapped her arms around his soft warm body, and finally managed to fall into a deep sleep.

On Wednesday morning, Julia gave herself a bit of a talking

to. She might not have exactly volunteered for this charity shop thing, but it would be good for her. It would help her meet people, and get her out of her rut. *One simply cannot allow oneself to mope,* she thought, as she sipped her morning tea. Besides, she could hardly help but feel content sitting on her little bench, under the overhang of wisteria, with its morning sun and its buzzing bees and its view of the footpath.

The morning walkers were out in full force, even though it was only – she glanced at her watch, a Cartier that Peter had given her for their twentieth wedding anniversary – only 7.30 a.m.! The postman had only just made his way past Julia's house, waving cheerily, but not stopping. Gone were the days when you looked forward to a letter, thought Julia nostalgically, what with emails and messages and Facebook. Good Lord, where did the woman bouncing past on the path to the lake, with an enormous Great Dane, get such energy from, so early? She'd clearly had a good night's sleep. Same couldn't be said for the man heading back in the other direction, hands deep in his pockets, a morning breeze ruffling his red hair. He looked in a right foul mood, so maybe getting up for morning walks wasn't for everybody. Ah – and there was Pippa, with Jake's better-behaved siblings, all walking to heel. Julia glanced to see if Jake had noticed, but he was otherwise occupied, digging a hole under the oak tree.

'Stop it, Jake,' she called, and thankfully, he did. The last thing Julia needed was Jake digging up more bodies. Giving herself a little shake, she stood up, and called Jake inside to have breakfast while she readied herself for the day.

Julia found herself standing outside Second Chances, with no sign of Wilma, even though she could have sworn that the woman had said to be there at nine on the dot. Julia was put out. Getting to the charity shop on time had proven more challenging than she'd expected, because this was the first time that she had left Jake at home on his own. First, she had left him closed in the kitchen, with a chew toy for company. But his howls had made her turn back at the gate. So then she had checked that the garden fence was secure, and moved his basket onto the small covered area near the front door. That way, he'd have the run of the garden and be safe if it rained. She put his water bowl outside, and his toys. Remembering something she'd once read, she filled a plastic bottle, quickly rescued from the recycling, with water, and put it in the hole he had dug under the oak tree. Apparently, that would stop the digging. She left him happily ensconced in his basket, chewing on an old sock that she had donated to the cause of his happiness. She just hoped she would find him equally peacefully occupied when she returned. Although who knew when that would be, because Wilma was late. It was quarter past nine when she finally rocked up, flustered, huffing and puffing and covered in a slight layer of sweat.

'Gosh, you're here,' she gasped. 'Held up. Circumstances.'

With this, she unlocked the door of the shop and marched in, tossing a big gym bag behind the counter. Did she think that she had provided an adequate explanation of where she had been, Julia wondered grumpily, following Wilma into the shop. It wasn't her place to challenge her new boss, even if it was all voluntary and her boss had left her standing, but she couldn't resist asking, 'Everything okay? Just wondering, while I was waiting, whether you were all right.'

'Oh fine, fine,' said Wilma, who was heaving a chalkboard onto the pavement. 'Give me a hand here, won't you?'

Julia took the other side of the board.

'Glad everything is okay. I was just worried because you were late,' Julia said pointedly.

'Yes, I'm fine,' said Wilma, without a hint of an apology. 'Now let's show you the ropes.'

Wilma might have been a bit relaxed about opening time, but she knew her way around a charity shop, and she was determined to show Julia everything, all at once, today. The window display – 'Don't touch that, it's my domain' – and the racks of clothes, the shelves of household items, books and bric-a-brac. The storeroom, where incoming items were sorted – some for repair, some for cleaning, some to go out on display – and where the little tea station was set up.

'People come and drop things off all the time, some of it's good, some of it not worth keeping. You can always do a bit of sorting when the shop's not busy, but whatever you do,' Wilma was saying, when her phone rang mid-morning, 'don't sell anything or give it away without me having had a look at it first. I do all the pricing.'

She answered the phone, and after a minute said, 'Gosh, Diane, I was just talking about you. Didn't you say that you'd be in to help Julia this morning?'

Wilma listened.

'Uh-huh. Uh-huh. Oh terrible, poor you. Uh-huh. Uh-huh. No, of course, stay home.'

'Poor Diane,' she said, finally finishing the call. 'Sick as a dog apparently. Thinks she ate something. Sends her apologies, she did want to help you settle.'

'Not to worry. I'm sure I'll pick it up as we go along.'

Julia had run an entire department of social workers, and spent her time wrangling difficult teens and their parents. She felt she could probably get the hang of Second Chances.

'It's quite busy, lots of people in and out. Never a dull moment. We have our regulars, and some tourists in the season – you know how the young love thrift shopping these days. Some oddballs every now and then, something about second-hand shops brings them out of the woodwork.'

Julia started with the clothes racks, restoring order, putting errant trousers back with their peers, dividing the summer jackets from the winter ones, arranging the shoes by size. Something about it appealed to her problem-solving brain.

'That does look nice and organised,' said Wilma approvingly.

Every so often a customer popped in. To talk, mostly, it seemed. There wasn't a huge amount of shopping going on. But there was a lot of chatting. Wilma seemed to know all the locals and liked a good chat.

A man came in and spent a good ten minutes perusing the books, taking each one out, opening it on the title page, examining it for who-knew-what, and putting it back in its place.

'Anything I can do for you?' Julia asked pleasantly. He gave her a small smile and shook his head.

'That's Dave,' said Wilma in a low voice, her face close to Julia, her mouth hardly moving. 'Comes in every Wednesday. Never worked out what he's looking for. He doesn't speak and he only once bought a book – *Bats of Southern Britain.*'

'Why?'

'It's a mystery...' she said, wide-eyed.

Wilma had just popped out to stretch her legs, leaving Julia 'in charge', when a nervy-looking lady came hurrying in with water splashed all over the front and bottom of her skirt. 'Accident with a water bottle,' she said, grabbing an ugly floral elastic-waisted skirt off the rack. 'I'll change into it, if you don't mind.'

She handed over a tenner as per the price tag – daylight robbery, in Julia's view – and pulled the ugly garment over her head. Then she whipped her damp skirt off underneath and headed out at a pace.

'Was that Tessa Callum I saw leaving?' asked Wilma on her return.

'I don't know her name, but she was rather damp,' said Julia. 'Odd.'

'That's nothing,' said Wilma with a dismissive wave of her

hand. 'Old man Gregory came in once covered in yellow paint. An accident with the road marker, apparently.'

The morning flew by, and Julia felt quite a sense of satisfaction as she gathered her handbag and jacket. She'd helped a few customers, organised the clothes, counted the pieces in a donated puzzle (all there), tested two lamps to see that they worked, and generally been of service.

'I'd better get back to my puppy, see what mischief he's got up to,' she said. 'It was fun, though, thanks.'

'Thanks so much for helping out,' said Wilma. 'Much appreciate it. Can I count on you for Wednesday mornings, then?'

Julia hesitated for just a moment and said, 'Sure. I'd be happy to.'

11

There was no sign of Jake.

Julia slammed the little garden gate behind her and ran to the house.

'Jake. Jakey? Where are you?' she called in a panic. There was an answering rustle behind the wisteria, and she saw the sleepy dog get to his feet, purple flowers dripping off him.

'Oh there you are, you good boy,' she said, rushing over to him. 'I was worried.'

In his wisteria lair she spotted her sock (now Jake's sock), a gardening glove, a potato, a delphinium and three sticks, lovingly whittled and pockmarked by his little teeth. Looking round the garden she could see no major signs of destruction, which was a relief.

He whined in delight at her presence and jumped up, his front paws on her knees.

'Hello, my precious-wecious, did you miss me?' she said, bending down and rubbing her cheek against his velvety head. Then, blushing at her own embarrassing baby talk, she said officiously, 'I'll have a quick sandwich and we'll go and check out the lake, shall we?'

Julia thought that if one were to purchase a jigsaw puzzle of the Cotswolds – say from the Second Chances charity shop, perhaps – the thousand little pieces might form a scene much like the one Julia and Jake were gazing at. The lake reflected the sky above, a pale blue dotted with puffy white clouds. Ducks floated picturesquely on their own reflections. Golden reeds on the far side rustled soothingly in the light breeze. The clear water lapped a sandy beach and a short wooden pier. Around it all was a well-maintained path, and acres of grassland.

'Isn't this gorgeous?' she said to Jake, rhetorically of course, but he answered by bounding across the grass to hurl himself into the mud and water. She sat on a bank and watched him gambol and splash. He could practice his sitting and off-lead walking another time. It was lovely to see him enjoying himself, dashing and splashing.

Julia felt the sun on her back and a deep sense of peace and gratitude. She'd made a good choice. Just look at the place! And look at her dog. She had spontaneously taken on a failed guide dog, instead of her usual deliberate and sensible decision-making, demonstrated flexibility, and made a daring life change. Now she had this darling pup.

Jake ran back to her to shake the muddy water off and throw himself against her chest. Even that didn't dim her good mood and her sense that her life was going in a new and interesting direction. She had a job of sorts, and friends of sorts – acquaintances at least.

And now, it seemed, she would also have James Bond.

Sean O'Connor was walking along the path in her direction, an arm raised in greeting.

'Off, Jakey,' she said, pushing the ecstatic wet puppy off her lap. She noted that she had turned his name into a cutesy diminutive, something that she disapproved of, generally. But this was the new flexible Julia, so there. Jakey.

Jake ran to Sean as if greeting a long-lost friend with a roast chicken dinner hidden about his person.

'Whoa there, well aren't you a lovely chap?' Sean said, deftly deflecting Jake from his trousers. 'Hello, Julia. Lovely day.'

She got up to greet him. 'It is. Lovely park, too. It's our first time here.'

'It seems to have the approval of the canine member of the family,' he said. They both looked at Jake, who had run back to the lake. 'It is nice, isn't it? I walk here every Wednesday. I close my rooms at lunchtime, have a quick bite and then come here, walk round the lake and then up to the woods there. It's a pleasant hour's amble.'

'We are going to do the same,' said Julia.

'Would you like to join me?' he said. 'I'll show you the sights.'

'There are sights?'

'Oh gosh, yes. The old boathouse – very impressive – a family of coots with babies, a tree with a sort of face in the bark. No end to the wonders.'

'Thank you, I accept.'

They moved off, Julia calling Jake. 'I'll put him on the lead,' she said, rattling the chain. 'I don't want him disturbing the coots. Here, Jake!'

Jake was having none of it. He looked her straight in the eye, walked into the lake and set off at a brisk doggy paddle towards the ducks.

'He's an infuriating dog,' she said, stomping down towards the water. 'JAKE, get back here!'

Sean laughed. 'Let's walk round, we'll call him from the other side. He's all right as long as he doesn't go too far.'

'I would not like to have to go and fetch him.'

'You can swim here, you know. I do occasionally, but only in the height of summer. A few of the locals are braver and swim right through the year.'

'I like to swim. But not today, I hope,' she said, eyeing Jake, who was at least hugging the shoreline now rather than heading into the centre of the lake. Maybe he wasn't as dim as she feared.

Julia and Sean joined the path, walking in the direction of the reeds on the far side. The ducks changed direction – presumably to avoid the paddling Jake – and headed to the reeds for shelter. Jake followed, with none of their pace. They were perfectly safe, and he was at least heading to shore. Julia and Sean would head him off, hopefully, and scoop him out.

The ducks reached the reeds and disappeared. Jake crashed in after them, barking.

'Jake!' said Julia, putting on a burst of speed. 'Come here.'

A large goose that had been in the reeds rose to its full height, opened its wings and hissed at him through a huge gaping mouth. Jake yelped and turned away. There was a lot of hissing and whining. Jake was scrambling and pushing and splashing without making much progress. He couldn't force his way through the reeds to shore, or extricate himself to go back to the clear water.

'I think he's stuck,' she said, running round the side of the reeds. 'He's only a pup. Short legs. Idiot. He could drown. I'll have to go in after him.'

'I could,' Sean offered reluctantly, but Julia was already taking her shoes off.

'It's okay, got it,' she said, flinging her jacket, hat and sunglasses onto the ground.

Julia took a deep breath and went in. Her feet sunk in the mud and the water rose to thigh level.

'Damn,' she murmured to herself, parting the reeds with a swimming motion of her arms. They were dense and she couldn't see Jake. 'Jake, where are you?' she yelled, and heard an answering whimper.

She headed in that direction and caught a glimpse of his dark fur amongst the reeds. Now nearly waist deep, she reached out a hand in the direction of the brown. Her fingers touched soft, wet hair. She stretched to her limit, fumbled and grabbed it.

'Got you. Come on.' She pulled hard, dragging him towards her through the reeds and the muddy water. 'Heavens, Jake, you...'

With a final tug, she pulled the wet mass through the reeds.

It wasn't Jake.

It was a woman.

A woman that Julia had seen before.

And she was dead.

12

'Sean, come quickly,' Julia shouted. 'I need help.'

She was still holding the woman by the hair, which felt wrong – cruel or disrespectful – but if she let go, the body might float off again. She reached forward with her other hand and grabbed the woman's shoulder. She had more purchase now and she stepped back, pulling her towards the shore.

'Jake,' she shouted, worried about the dog.

As the reeds parted behind the body, Jake followed, scrabbling and whining.

'Come on,' she said to the dog. 'Come, Jake.'

'Good God,' said Sean, who had waded into the lake behind her. 'That's... Is she...?'

'Help me,' Julia panted, and gave another heave, pulling the body towards Sean. 'Grab her.'

Sean reached forward and held the woman's upper arm. Julia grabbed the panicky Jake. He was too big to pick up easily, and he squirmed and slipped against her, scratching her arms. Sean pulled the woman towards the bank, while Julia pulled Jake, who managed to swim by himself once they were clear of the reeds, his tail wagging happily, oblivious to the drama.

Once they reached the bank, Julia scrambled up, helping Sean heft the dead woman out of the water. She suddenly understood where the term 'dead weight' came from, as they slipped and scrambled, knocking against the heavy body.

Once they finally had the woman on the bank, Julia took a deep breath and surveyed the nightmarish scene. The dead woman wore a black one-piece swimming costume, her body grey and wrinkled from being in the water, her hair full of duck-weed and her legs streaked with algae and mud. Dr Sean O'Connor, almost as pale, wet to his waist, knelt on the grass next to the woman, his fingers on her neck, feeling for signs of life, and his head on her chest, listening.

He looked up at Julia and shook his head slowly.

Jake shivered against her.

'Do you have a phone?' she asked.

Sean had put his phone with Julia's things before he got in the water – a sensible move, in retrospect. He retrieved his phone and dialled. He spoke quickly and quietly into the phone. Julia heard 'Police... Ambulance...' over her own rasping breath and Jake's whimpering.

'On their way,' he said, a moment later. 'Julia...'

'Give me a minute,' said Julia. She felt she might faint, or vomit. She was shaking with cold and adrenaline and shock. She pushed Jake off her lap, where he had settled, and, keeping one hand on his damp shivering back, rested her head on her knees. She took a few deep breaths, trying to slow her heart rate.

Sean came up behind her and put her jacket over her shoulders, and then took off his own jacket and put that round her too.

'Thanks,' she said, lifting her head. She crossed her legs and pulled Jake back onto her lap.

'Do you know this woman? I think it might be...' Julia hoped she was wrong. She'd only seen her that one time, after all.

'It's Maeve Harold,' said Sean.

'I thought so.' Julia allowed a moment of silence. Then she asked, 'Do you think she drowned, poor thing?'

'There's no sign of trauma, so it seems so,' said Sean. 'But she swam here regularly, so it's surprising. Maybe a heart attack or such.'

There wasn't much more to say, while they sat and waited for the police, a dead body lying next to them. Julia kept a tight hold on Jake, worried that he might mistake Maeve's body for a toy. Sean asked her a bit more about herself, and her life in London. She knew that he was trying to distract her, but was grateful. She imagined he must be a fine, comforting GP.

After what seemed like days, but was probably more like half an hour, DI Hayley Gibson came striding towards them, with DC Farmer half a step behind her.

'Mrs Bird?' she said, stopping in surprise. 'What are you doing here?'

'I found the body,' said Julia, realising for the first time quite how utterly insane it was that she, Julia Bird, had been on the scene in the discovery of two dead people in a fortnight.

'Again?' said Hayley Gibson in disbelief.

'Yes, I know. It's... I mean, this is different. The dog... And it was an accident this time. Not that it wasn't an accident before. But a different sort, is what I'm saying.'

'Just tell us from the beginning please, ma'am,' said Walter officiously, pencil poised above his notebook.

'I was walking my dog and he chased the ducks into the pond,' started Julia.

DC Walter Farmer looked sternly at Jake and tutted under his breath. Julia looked the young man over – he hardly looked old enough to shave, and a rash of spots covered his chin. She didn't feel he should be taking such a high-handed tone with her puppy.

Julia pulled the dog to her. 'I know, but he's just a puppy. He's learning not to. I'm teaching him.'

DC Farmer gave a slow nod, as if to say she would be given a chance, but best she didn't mess it up.

'Anyway, he got stuck in the reeds and I went to try and fetch him out and the body was right there, in the reeds,' she said, pointing.

'You moved it?' asked Hayley, somewhat redundantly, given that Maeve Harold was no longer in the reeds but on the grassy bank of the lake.

'I didn't know what it was. I was looking for the dog and I felt something and I just pulled. I couldn't see, really. And so, yes, I pulled her out. Sean and I.'

'All right then. Do you know who she is?'

'Maeve Harold, lived in Winding Lane,' Sean said. 'She worked for the holiday rental agent in town. I believe Maeve liked to swim at the lake.'

'I see. Thank you, Dr O'Connor. How did you come to be involved?' Julia reflected that it made sense that in a village this small, the local police already knew the local doctor.

'I happened to be walking here myself and I spotted Julia here and we walked a bit and then, you know, she found poor Maeve.'

'She was dead when you found her?'

'Yes. I felt for a pulse, and looked for any sign of life. I suspect she had been dead a while.'

'How long is a while?' asked the policewoman. 'Roughly speaking.'

'It's hard to say, but at least an hour, I would imagine. Not more than a day though, the body is quite...' he struggled for the word, 'quite recently deceased. No fish damage, for a start.'

'Understood. A drowning, would you say?'

'It seems so. She was a regular swimmer here, so she was competent in the water and knew the lake. She might have got a cramp, or had a heart attack or a stroke. It does happen. And if she was alone, no one to help her, and well... there you have it.'

'Could she have slipped, bumped her head, something like that, do you suppose?'

'That would be for the coroner's office to determine, but I don't see any obvious sign of trauma. Most likely a simple drowning, caused by some physical crisis, I'd say.'

'So it seems,' said DI Gibson. 'So it seems.'

She surveyed the scene slowly, turning her head from left to right, her eyes bright under a slight frown.

'Where are her things? She must have had a towel, keys, shoes.'

Farmer nodded and set off around the lake at a slow plod, scanning the ground.

'Walter.' He stopped and turned to face DI Gibson. 'Maybe just watch where you're walking. We should get the forensic guys out.'

He raised his eyebrows like two question marks. 'But she...'

'Just in case.'

13

The morning light poured into the little sitting area of the library and glinted off the golden stripes of Too, who was stretched out on a chair, tail twitching in contentment, presenting maximum surface area to the warming rays. Julia stroked her head while she waited for Tabitha to finish helping an ancient tottering lady with a tottering pile of books. Historical bodice rippers, from the look of the covers.

'There you go, Violet, that should keep you going for a day or two,' Tabitha said, stamping the last one. 'Shall I put them in the basket for you?'

'Thank you, dear.'

'Will you manage them? They're quite heavy. I could bring them down the road to you when we close if you like?'

'I'll be all right, thank you, Tabitha. Got to keep going, you know.'

Tabitha saw her out and came to join Julia on the sofa. They picked up where they'd left the conversation minutes before.

'*Another* body?' she said. 'I mean, goodness, what are the chances? And in a village like this?'

'I know. All those years working with troubled folk in the less salubrious parts of London, and I saw precisely one body – an old man who had keeled over on the street, natural causes.'

'Two dead people. Two! In two weeks. And *you* were there when both of them were found. What are the chances?'

She really wished Tabitha would stop saying that.

'Yes. It's crazy. But it's not as if I had anything to do with either of them.'

'Of course not. You'd never even met Maeve, I don't think?'

'Not exactly,' said Julia, thinking of the scene she had witnessed in the charity shop. 'Did you know her?'

'A little, just like you know everyone in a village. But not well. She was a bit of a loner, was Maeve. Lived on her own. No sign of a husband or partner, not as long as I've been here. Not a reader. A daughter somewhere. That's it.'

'Samantha,' came a voice from behind the stacks. Julia jumped in alarm – her nerves were still a little ragged from yesterday's discovery.

Pippa's face appeared in a space between the books. 'The daughter is Samantha. She moved to London, but she lives in Australia now.'

Her head disappeared from the gap and reappeared, along with the rest of Pippa's body, in front of the two friends, having come round the end of the stacks.

'Oh hello, Pippa,' said Tabitha. 'I didn't see you there.'

'Sorry, I was looking for the new Lee Child and I couldn't help but overhear.'

'Well you won't find it here. This is the non-fiction section, as I'm sure you know. Lee Child is...'

'Not to worry about that,' said Pippa airily. She sat herself down on a chair across from them and leaned in, saying, 'Isn't it awful about poor Maeve? And poor you, Julia, what a shock. And after the other thing. Terrible.'

'Yes, awful,' said Julia, stroking the cat's warm fur. 'I'm all right. But terrible for her and the poor daughter of course. Do you know her?'

'I do. Lovely girl, and so pretty and always so well turned-out. Used to do all of our nails for pocket money. Haven't seen her for years, I must say. You know what it's like. Young family apparently – two kids, if I'm not mistaken – and a big career in Sydney. Busy, busy. She popped over from time to time to see her mum, I think, but never stayed long. I'm sure she'll be back soon though. For the funeral. And to sort out the flat. Maeve lives quite near you actually, Julia.'

'Really?'

'Yes, just up Winding Lane. Big white house on the right, converted to four flats. Beautiful. Best views in the village, I think.'

'The one with the blue gate and the fir tree outside?'

'The very one,' said Pippa. 'Maeve was on the top floor, she lived next to Jane, you met her at book club, remember? They've been neighbours forever. Jane will be very upset.'

'Well, time for me to get back to work. Let's see if we can find that Lee Child for you, shall we, Pippa?' Tabitha said.

'Yes, I can't be hanging around chatting,' Pippa said, as if the other two had forced her into it against her will. 'I've got those puppies waiting for me at home. They'll be up to their nonsense. Speaking of nonsense, how's darling Jake?'

'Marvellous,' said Julia, emphatically. 'He's as good as gold. But I'd better get back to him too.'

Jake had been left in the back garden this time, along with his bed and a selection of chewables. Of course, he had ignored them and chewed the spray fitting for the hosepipe and was busy on one of the planks from the old shed. Julia felt a little grumpy that the pile of timber was still there and the shed site still cordoned off, a week after the body had been found. She should have asked DI Gibson about it yesterday, but hadn't thought of it. Besides, not the best timing.

She would just phone her now, thought Julia, rummaging in her handbag for her mobile. No time like the present. She sat on the step with the puppy at her feet and the sun on her shoulders, and dialled.

'DI Gibson.' Not even a hello, what had things come to? Not the village way, at all.

'Hello, DI Gibson. Julia Bird here.'

'Please tell me you haven't found another body.'

'No. It's about the first one, the young woman. Have the crime-scene people finished?'

'The tape's still there? Damn. I forgot to ask.' DI Gibson sounded flustered. 'I was in court giving evidence on a shoplifting, and then I've been busy with Maeve Harold.'

'Could you find out, perhaps?'

'Sure. Sure.'

'Did you get hold of Bert Steadman, by the way?'

'Walter was following up. I must check on that.' She really was not on top of things today, DI Gibson. Julia could hear her typing on her computer while they were speaking.

'Well, I found his email address if you want it.'

'You did? Can you send it to me?'

'Yes. I'll send you the emails we exchanged, too.'

The typing stopped. 'You emailed him?' DI Gibson said in a steely voice. 'After you found the body?'

'Yes, I mean, I thought I'd just feel him out. About the shed. See how he'd react if I said I was moving it.'

'You do realise,' Gibson said coldly, 'that he is a possible suspect. Or at least a key witness or informant. In a murder investigation.'

When DI Gibson put it that way, Julia realised that she

probably should have minded her own business. Her get-things-sorted instinct had made her get ahead of herself. She sighed. This was exactly what had led to the trouble in London. And here she was again, jumping in, making assumptions, muddying things. She felt a wave of shame, and a need to redeem herself in DI Gibson's eyes.

'I was really just dropping them a line to let them know I was all settled,' said Julia. 'I mentioned that I was going to move the shed...'

'Which you had already done.'

'Yes, well, anyway the odd thing is, I mean the important thing as far as you're concerned, is that he was rather cross about the idea of moving the shed, and it made me wonder...'

'Send me those emails. Right away, please. And please do not interfere any further,' said Gibson with an air of finality.

Julia decided not to mention Doug, the shed builder. Hayley Gibson would see it on the email.

'Just one last thing,' Julia said quickly. 'While I have you on the phone. Any more information on poor Maeve?'

'She's with the coroner. No foul play suspected, obviously, just procedure. I expect the body will be released for the funeral in a day or two.'

'How's the poor daughter doing? Samantha.'

'We haven't managed to get hold of her yet. Maeve's mobile was found in the water. It's dead, but the tech guys are trying to get her contacts off it. I'll have to get onto them, too.' There was an audible sigh as DI Gibson added another item to her mental to-do list.

'Well, I can see you've got a lot on your plate, so I'll let you get back to that. And you'll let me know about the shed?'

'Yes. The shed. And don't forget those emails.'

'I'll send them right now.'

Julia did just that. Hayley Gibson was as good as her word, too. Not five minutes later she sent a text message:

Crime scene are finished. You can have your chickens.

'Hear that, Jake?' she said, reaching down to pat the dog. 'We can get our chickens. But first, your walk.'

14

The white house did indeed have a fine position, in the bend of Winding Lane. Maeve's upstairs flat's generous sash windows overlooked the river and the fields and woods beyond. Julia slowed and then stopped at the low blue gate, looking up at the house and trying to imagine the grey corpse she'd pulled out of the river as a living, breathing woman, right now up in her sunny flat, getting the kettle on for tea. Perhaps she would look over the fields, feeling satisfied with her life. But that life had been cut short. It was upsetting to think like this.

Jake had had enough of the wait, and tugged at his lead.

'Okay then, bossy boots,' she said. 'I know you want your walk.'

As she turned to leave, she heard her name.

Jane, from the book club, had come out of the front door, and was heading down the little path to the gate with a shopping basket over her arm. Today she was dressed in a blue velvet top and green plaid trousers. A blue and green tartan scarf brought the whole look together, even if it seemed a bit warm for the weather. Jane smiled widely. 'I thought it was you. And Jake, of course. What brings you here?'

'We were out for a walk and just noticed the house... Maeve. You know that I...'

'You found her.'

'Yes. I'm sorry for your loss. I believe you were neighbours?'

'We'd both been here for ages. More than twenty-five years, can you believe? Back before the village was all smartened up and so busy.'

Julia cast her eyes up and down the lane, noting the sole example of busy-ness – a large black cat sunning itself on a low wall, with a row of hollyhocks bobbing merrily behind it. Jake watched it nervously from behind Julia's leg, glancing up at Julia from time to time as if to say, 'You never know with cats...'

Jane continued, 'Her Samantha used to babysit my Hannah. She even helped her get dressed for her Year 10 dance. Samantha was so good at that. Did beauty treatments for pocket money. Now both of them are all grown up, terrible teenage years over, and off to London. And then Australia, for Samantha.'

'Poor Samantha, must be hard for her, losing her mum so suddenly. And in a freak accident. I suppose she'll be arriving soon?'

'The awful thing is, we can't seem to find her,' said Jane with a frown. 'Maeve's phone fell in the lake, and who has a phone book these days? The police were here, asking. And I can't for the life of me remember the name of the chap Samantha married. I have a feeling it was Alan or Adam or Andy. I know Maeve must have told me the surname, but I can't remember.' Jane knocked her knuckles against her forehead as if to shake the information loose. 'Never met him myself, all these years. He came for a visit over last Easter, Maeve said, with Samantha and the children. But I was away visiting Hannah.'

'I'm sure the police will work it all out.'

'Of course, you're right.'

'Someone will know, for sure. One of Maeve's friends or co-workers.'

'She was a very private person. Always friendly enough, but kept to herself. It was only when this happened that I realised we hadn't even swapped emergency contact details.'

'Not to worry, I'm sure she'll turn up. I was a social worker back in London and I quite often had to find people. We always tracked them down eventually.' Deadbeat dads and druggie mums and reluctant grandparents, unfortunately, although she didn't share that detail with Jane. She was pleased that she never had to do *that* again. 'You'd be surprised. They'll probably find her in a day or two.'

'The landlord will be pleased,' said Jane bitterly. 'Poor Maeve, not even buried and he's making noises about emptying the flat. And we can't exactly do that until we find Samantha, can we? Of course, I should've seen *that* coming.'

'Seen what coming?' Julia was a bit confused.

'The landlord, of course,' said Jane, as if Julia were slightly slow. Everyone in the village just assumed that you knew everything. 'Hasn't he been trying to get the house back for years? Prime piece of real estate, you know. Should never have been split into flats, and that's a fact.'

Julia gave the house another look, and she had to agree. The original house would sell for a fortune in today's market. Some well-off family would snap it up and restore it.

'So why couldn't he just evict you all?' she asked Jane, hoping her bluntness wouldn't offend.

'Well,' said Jane, who seemed in no hurry to get to her shopping. Instead, she put her basket down and leaned against the small stone wall, settling into her story. 'He tried just that. The bottom two flats, young people they were, and he offered them a better deal at one of his other properties – he's got a few. But we weren't just going to leave, and neither was Maeve. Maeve raised Samantha here, didn't she? We moved here a bit later, when Hannah was in Year 8. Graham and I put up a fight when he wanted us out, I can tell you, but we lost eventually. That Will Adamson is a right bully when it comes down to it. We'll be moving at the end of the month. Perhaps all for the best, you know. We've found a lovely little cottage up near the lake, with a bit of a garden.'

Jake gave a loud yawn, as if to indicate his extreme disinterest at Jane's real estate troubles, and flopped down on the pavement in despair.

'And Maeve?' asked Julia.

'Ah well, Maeve had a different lease, didn't she? All signed decades ago, but she was here before us. Nobody's quite sure how she got one over on Will Adamson, because he's as smart a man as you'll find, but somehow, she did.'

'How was Maeve's lease different?'

'My Graham can explain the details better, but what it came down to was that Maeve couldn't be evicted, and her rent stayed almost the same, just a tiny increase each year. My Graham was impressed with the wording, I can tell you.' Jane gave a laugh. 'But Will Adamson was spitting! Got lawyers and everything and they told him the same thing. Good for Maeve. She wasn't going anywhere soon, I can tell you that.'

The two women were silent for a moment.

'And then she died,' said Julia, softly, almost to herself.

'Here's a thought,' interrupted Jane, with a proud grin. 'You said you've found people before for your work in London. Maybe you can help find Samantha. I hate to think of Maeve lying there in the mortuary with no one to bury her. The police are run off their feet with the body under your shed. Maybe *you* can find her.'

Julia thought about it. She wasn't keen to get involved, frankly. Finding people was no longer her business. But she couldn't help but feel that she already was involved, having discovered the poor drowned woman's body and dragged her out of the reeds by her hair. There could be no harm in helping track down her poor daughter.

'I could ask a few people, I suppose,' she said. 'I can't promise. I don't have access to the official databases anymore, but I know people who do. I'm not sure if they'll be able to find information about someone in Australia, though.'

'Well, she got married in London, I believe,' said Jane. 'Not that any of us were invited. But still, maybe you could at least get her chap's name. That should be a big help.'

By this time, Jake had rested up and was whining and pulling on his lead with impatience.

'I'd better be off,' said Julia. 'Write down everything you remember about the family – names and so on – and I'll phone you to get all the details, and I'll see what I can do.'

15

Jake was delighted to be on the move, practically skipping down the road ahead of her. He slowed to a creep when they passed the dozing black cat, averting his eyes and keeping Julia between him and the cat. When they had passed without incident, he picked up speed, tail wagging.

'You're scared of cats!' said Julia with a laugh, giving him a pat. 'That's classic. Now, no more dilly-dallying, I promise. A brisk walk, and home for tea.'

They'd hardly been walking five minutes when they heard a voice. 'Look, Mummy, there's that naughty dog!'

It was a little unfair, as Jake was in fact walking very nicely on his lead and not bothering anyone, but little Sebastian clearly had a good memory. He held no grudges though, falling to his knees to hug Jake, burying his face in his neck.

'Well I never, twice in a week, and isn't it just like the village?' asked Nicky, with what Julia now recognised as her characteristic conversational style of breathless chatter, non sequiturs and rhetorical questions. 'And didn't you just find another...'

She glanced at the child before whispering, 'Body.'

'Yes indeed, awful coincidence,' Julia said shortly.

'Poor Maeve. Drowning. Not even *that* old. And she didn't even have the chance to spend all that money from the Toby jug. Such a shame.'

'And where are you two off to?' Julia asked, eager to change the subject.

'Well, you know, I've just fetched the lad from nursery and we're off to do our errands, aren't we, boy? Goodness me, but wasn't yesterday a big to-do from top to bottom? The postman was late – not at all like Gary these days, I can tell you, although back in the day that was another story – and I was waiting for this letter, a copy of my GCSE certificates, so I could go to the stationers and photocopy them on the way back from taking this one to nursery. I'm thinking of signing up for a course, you know. Never too late, they say. And then that was a whole other mess because my Kev had left early. Some emergency at work, up and out the door at the crack, he was. So he couldn't take Sebastian. In the end, I left without the letter and he was late for nursery anyways, and I didn't get to copy it yesterday, so that's what we're doing today. Off to the stationer's, we are, aren't we, Sebastian?'

She waved a large white envelope, to illustrate the story. Honestly, the woman made Julia's head spin with Gary and Kev and letters and nursery and the stationer's and Sebastian all jumbled into one confusing story.

'Well, good luck with all that,' said Julia, taking advantage of the gap to extricate herself from Nicky's verbal whirlwind. 'Bye bye, Sebastian. I'll see you around, I'm sure.'

As they set off, Julia spotted the familiar figure of Pippa in the distance, coming determinedly towards her. She pretended not to notice, and ducked into the next lane. She realised that if she was out and about in the village, she'd be stopped by each resident, individually, to talk about the drowning accident. That was just the way it was in this place.

'Come on, Jake, we're going back along the river,' she said.

Jake seemed happy with that suggestion, following her down the lane that led to the footpath by the river, and towards home.

It was nice and quiet on the footpath. A jogger passed her at a good lick, earbuds in his ears. A woman sat on a bench by the water, sharing a doughnut with her little girl. Neither of them seemed interested in discussing the body under the shed, or the tragic drowning of Maeve Harold.

Having scanned the area thoroughly for ducks, Julia let Jake off the lead to sniff around, while she turned her mind to Maeve. It was sad that she had lived in the village her whole life and yet seemed to have no real friends. Everyone here was friendly to the point of overwhelming, in Julia's experience. You had to be quite determined to avoid constant interactions, overtures and interrogations. And yet no one knew much about Maeve at all, other than the contentious matter of spotting and snapping up the valuable Toby jug at Second Chances.

Julia thought she might have liked Maeve Harold. It struck her that Maeve Harold had been a clever woman. From what she'd said that day at the shop, she'd played that Toby jug situation smartly and made a good bit of money off it. And she'd got the better of Will Adamson, the bullying landlord, too. Julia felt some respect for the woman. She hadn't seemed like a bad person either, trying to make up with Wilma and Diane and getting rebuffed like that. But still, clever. Good on her, a woman on her own, minding her own business, and getting things done. Rather like Julia herself.

What appeared to be a wraith wrapped in a rug appeared at the end of the path, resolving itself into the old lady she'd seen the other day, the poor thing with dementia. What had Nicky called her? Auntie Edna. Poor woman was very thin, but seemed quite steady on her feet.

'Hello, Edna,' said Julia as they passed, giving the woman a warm smile.

'Oh, it's you,' said Edna, addressing Jake. He grinned up at her, his pink tongue lolling, his tail going madly. She bent over, raised a shaking forefinger to his face, and told him in a school-marmish tone: 'Just remember there's more to it than meets the eye. Except when there isn't. Good day to you.'

And then she straightened up and went on her way, all the while ignoring Julia as if she were completely invisible. Although it was a nice change not to have to discuss either of the dead bodies, it was rather disconcerting. Julia wondered if Edna should be out and about on her own, and then reminded herself that she was a civilian now, not a social worker. And she was no longer in the big city. From what Nicky said, it seemed everyone in the village knew Auntie Edna and kept an eye on her.

The walk had taken a good deal longer than anticipated, what with the stops – first Jane, then Nicky, then Edna. She was looking forward to being home. A cup of tea would be nice, with the last piece of shortbread left over from Peter and Christopher's visit. She should buy some more. Or she would make some! That was a good idea. She had resolved to brush up her cooking skills now that she wasn't working, but she'd made little progress since her success with the oats. It had to be said, Julia had expected to have a lot more free time on her hands. Between the demanding dog, the deaths, the part-time job at the charity shop, and village life, her days were busy.

As she went up the path to her gate, she took a moment to appreciate the heady scent of the roses, and then ran through the rest of the day's errands in her head. Make some phone calls to call in a favour on finding Samantha. Phone Shouty Johnny Blunt to take away the planks and get the chicken run built. Look up a shortbread recipe.

'Hello, Julia,' came the Scottish burr of Sean O'Connor,

interrupting her mental to-do list and making her jump. She hadn't seen him sitting on the bench outside her front door.

'Oh hello, Sean. What are you doing here? Is everything all right?'

She let Jake off the lead. He gave himself a good shake and wandered off into the garden.

'I didn't mean to surprise you. Just wanted to talk to you about something, if you don't mind.'

The doctor looked quite serious, without the twinkle in his eye and the quick witty banter she had come to expect from him.

'Come on in,' she said, opening the door. 'I'll make us some tea.'

Sean sat at the kitchen table and waited while she filled the kettle. In the quiet that followed, he spoke, hesitantly. 'The thing is, Julia, the police just rang me now. Hayley Gibson had some questions about what I'd seen that day, when you found Maeve. The examination of the body on the scene. It's just that...' He cleared his throat, apparently unable to go on.

But Julia, somehow, already knew what he was going to say. She finished his sentence for him.

'It's just that the police suspect that Maeve Harold's death was no accident,' she said.

16

'How did you know?' Sean looked at her in astonishment.

'I didn't *know*. More of a hunch. A feeling,' said Julia, sitting down opposite him. 'There were a few things that felt odd. And then when you said... I knew.'

'Well, you can add a suspicious bump on the head to your list.'

'Really? Goodness me, I didn't see anything when we pulled her out.'

'Neither did I. It wasn't visible, at least not at the scene. The coroner found a bruise when they did the full examination.'

'So do they think she died from a blow to the head?'

'No. She died by drowning. There was water in her lungs. It seems the blow wasn't hard enough to have killed her, but it could have knocked her out.'

'Is the assumption that she was knocked unconscious and then she drowned?'

'Something like that. There's a chance that she banged her head on a rock or a tree trunk when she dived in, or while she was swimming. The police are investigating the possibility, but right now they are treating Maeve Harold's death as suspicious.'

They sat in silence for a moment while Julia processed this new information.

'Shall I?' asked Sean, when the kettle boiled.

'Please,' said Julia. 'Everything's there.' She waved her arm in the direction of the mugs and tea. She felt suddenly exhausted by the day and this terrible knowledge that Maeve Harold had likely been murdered. That meant that a murderer lived in this picture-perfect, friendly village. Julia might even have met him – or her – or passed them on her walks or in the Buttered Scone.

'Milk and sugar?'

'Just milk. Thank you, Sean.'

He put the mug in front of her. 'Here you go.'

'No biscuits I'm afraid, I meant to bake,' she said. She remembered the one piece of shortbread left in the tin, and thought of offering it to Sean. But somehow giving him shortbread baked by her ex-husband's lover seemed inappropriate; she couldn't quite say why.

'Tea's fine. Sorry to arrive out of the blue with this news, I know it's a bit of a shock.'

'It is. A head injury. It's just so... so violent. So awful to think of it.'

'It is. But you seemed to suspect something?'

'Not consciously, no. I had a funny feeling about it all. Working as I did as a social worker all those years, you just get a sense about things. Nothing obvious that you can point to, you just get a feeling that something's not right. Since I found Maeve, I've heard a bit more about her from people in the village, and I got that sense. About her. I can't explain it. Intuition, I suppose. I didn't think, "Oh, she was murdered", not that. Just that something was a bit... off.'

'Well something is definitely a bit off.'

'Oddly, according to the village gossip which I've been

privy to over the last couple of days, there seem to be a surprising number of people with grudges against her.'

'Really?' said Sean, sipping his tea. 'She always struck me as a very private person. Not the sort of person that got out and about enough to really make enemies, if that makes sense.'

'Well,' said Julia, leaning forward, enjoying having someone to talk through her thoughts with. 'There was the whole uproar about the Toby jug.'

'Hardly a motive for murder, is it?'

'You wouldn't think so, but people are strange, especially when money is involved. In my line of work I've seen people do very terrible things for very little money. And when people feel hard done by, things get ugly.'

'So who would feel that angry about the Toby jug?' asked Sean. Julia liked the way he seemed genuinely interested. He wasn't dismissing her ideas.

'Wilma and Diane were both very angry,' said Julia. 'I overheard them talking about it and they were really upset. I was there when Maeve came into the shop actually, and they wouldn't forgive her. Told her they wouldn't be responsible for what happened if she tried to come back.'

As Julia spoke, she heard how damning this sounded. Sean's eyes met hers in a moment of mutual realisation. Sean seemed to think about it for a minute.

'But surely they would have got to the shop too early yesterday to have anything to do with this?' he said.

'That's the thing, though,' said Julia. 'They didn't. Wilma was late in – she arrived at about quarter past nine – and Diane didn't come in at all, she called in sick.'

She sipped her tea.

'But, Sean, that's not even the most worrying thing.'

'Oh dear, tell me?'

So Julia told him about Will Adamson, the landlord, and how extremely well-timed Maeve's death seemed to be. 'It's one thing, a few ladies getting upset about a jug,' she said. 'But this chap sounds much more ominous.'

'I agree with you,' said Sean. 'I think you're someone with a good nose for when things don't fit. I think you should chat to the police about this. About Wilma and Diane, and about the landlord.'

'I've no doubt they'll think I'm a nosy busybody.'

Sean smiled. 'They might. But one has to speak up without fear, wouldn't you say? Rather you tell them too much than too little.'

'You're quite right, Sean,' said Julia. 'And when Samantha comes home, she's going to need closure on what happened to her poor mum. We all need to do what we can to help that poor girl.' Julia was aware that one of the terrible habits of getting older was referring to people in their thirties and forties as 'girls' or 'young' when actually they were fully grown adults. But she felt that Sean wasn't the type who would judge her for this.

'Absolutely,' said Sean. 'She deserves the truth. Now I must be on my way. Evening shift at the surgery. No peace for the wicked.'

Julia felt quite drained by the time Sean left. But at least she had a plan. First thing tomorrow, she would call her friend in London to see if she could help find Samantha's married name, and then she'd call DI Hayley Gibson, and tell her what she'd heard.

Her last task of the day was to call Johnny Blunt. 'Crime scene are done,' she told him. 'We can start on the chickens.'

'Under the plum tree,' said Johnny.

'No,' said Julia. Really, she thought she'd been quite clear about this. Why did the bloody man think they'd pulled down the shed and started this fiasco in the first place? 'Where the shed was.'

'It's just...' Johnny didn't finish his sentence. 'Oh, have it your way, lass,' he said eventually. 'It's your chicken coop.'

At least he hadn't said 'it's your funeral' thought Julia, as she went to feed Jake. That might've been a bad choice of words, in the circumstances.

'And after he's built it, we can get our chickens,' she told Jake, as she dished up his supper. 'Providing we can manage a day without finding a body.' She said it as a joke, but she was glad that only Jake was there to hear the break in her voice. This wasn't what she'd expected from her country retirement at all. The sooner it could be over, the better.

Melanie Houston had been one of Julia's favourite colleagues in the Youth Services; a woman that she had come to call a friend. Melanie did her job thoroughly, with no nonsense and no drama, which wasn't something you could say about anyone. Her job involved tracking down data – contact numbers, police records, tax information – you name it, Mel could find it. And it didn't matter if the query came from a junior social worker new on the job, or the Chief of Police, Melanie's attitude was always the same: helpful, unemotional and solution-driven. Many the errant father had been found and forced to pay child mainte-nance, thanks to Melanie's talents.

'Well, hello! I didn't think I'd be hearing from you. How's retirement? How's the country? Are you bored yet?' asked Melanie with a laugh.

'Funnily enough, no,' said Julia. 'You'd be surprised how much goes on in a village. That's why I'm calling, actually.'

Julia explained the events in the village over the last week, and Melanie immediately snapped into work mode.

'I see what you mean. Far from boring. What do you need?' she asked, and Julia could visualise her with her hand poised, biro in hand, ready to take notes as Julia spoke, as she'd seen her do so often before.

'I'm just trying to track down the daughter,' she told

Melanie, and gave her all the details that she'd got from Jane earlier that morning. 'She was in London, and got married there, but it seems she moved to Australia at some point.'

'Easy peasy, lemon squeezy,' said Melanie. 'Anything else?'

Julia was about to say no, when she had a thought.

'While you're about it, would you see what the system has on one William Adamson,' she said. 'Lives around here. In the property game. Sorry, I don't have much more.'

'I love a challenge,' said Melanie. 'I'll be in touch as soon as I have something.'

Calling DI Hayley Gibson was a more difficult proposition, and Julia decided to have a cup of tea before she tackled it. But as the kettle was boiling, she heard a sharp rap at her door, and when she opened it, DI Gibson herself was standing there, hands deep in her pockets and a worried frown on her face.

'I was just about to call you,' said Julia.

'Really?'

'Yes, about Maeve Harold. I heard you were treating her death as suspicious.'

'Yes. We are investigating the possibility that it wasn't an accident.'

'Well, I might have some information.'

'Just as long as you're not going to tell me she was killed because of the Toby jug,' said Hayley Gibson.

'No,' said Julia, taken aback. 'Well, not only,' she added lamely.

'Good, because you'd be the third this morning. I was busy trying to find someone, anyone, who knows her daughter – can't seem to track her down – but I keep being interrupted by some twit with a theory about *Antiques in the Country*.'

DI Gibson seemed tired and grumpy. Often in Julia's previous work, she had come across fellow professionals in the services who were empty from giving so much of themselves to other people. DI Gibson had that look, and Julia had an idea.

'Tell you what, the kettle's on, and I made some scones this morning. They're a little lopsided, because it's my first try. But I've got some raspberry jam from the farm stall, and some fresh cream. I'd love it if you could join me. I'll tell you what I know and you can tell me why the Toby jug is irrelevant.'

'I really can't. I've so much to get on with,' said DI Gibson with a sigh. She glanced at the sky, which was overcast and threatened rain, and looked through the door into Julia's house with its jug of cheerful yellow nasturtiums on the dresser and its smell of fresh baked goods. 'But you know what? A few minutes won't do any harm. Let's have scones.'

Ten minutes later, DI Gibson – 'Call me Hayley' – was sipping her tea, eating an unconventionally shaped scone topped with jam and cream, and pouring her heart out to Julia.

'The thing with a village,' she said, 'is that no sooner have you breathed a thought on one side of it than the cousin of the woman who lives on the other side has heard all about it. And when it's something as exciting as a dead body under a shed, or a suspicious drowning, well, everyone's got a theory, haven't they?'

'Do they?' asked Julia, feeling a bit silly, because she had a theory of her own.

'The body under the shed, I have been assured on good authority, is part of a satanic burial ritual and we should be sure to check under all the sheds.'

'Could that be true?' asked Julia, aghast.

'Of course not,' laughed Hayley. 'No more than that Diane killed Maeve because of a Toby jug. There's just absolutely no basis for it.' Hayley helped herself to another scone and reached for the jam.

'I have to ask,' Julia said, 'but has anyone mentioned that Diane called in sick to work at the charity shop on the day

Maeve died? Or that Wilma was late in? Or that Wilma threatened Maeve the last time she came into the shop?'

Julia felt foolish mentioning this, for being as annoying as all the other people in the village. Poor Hayley didn't need a whole lot of conjecture from a bunch of amateur sleuths. But Hayley was suddenly sitting up straighter and had taken a small notebook and stumpy pencil from her pocket. 'I am such a cliché,' she muttered to herself, looking at the pencil. Then, to Julia, she said, 'Okay, from the top, Mrs Bird...'

'Julia.'

'...and don't leave out a thing.'

So Julia told Hayley how, on Monday, she had overheard Wilma and Diane talking angrily about how that cunning Maeve had pulled a fast one on them when she'd taken that valuable Toby jug, and how Maeve herself had then come into the shop. And how, on Julia's first day of work at Second Chances – also, as it turned out, Maeve Harold's last day on earth – Wilma had arrived late and flustered, and Diane had called in sick.

'I'll give you this,' said Hayley, once she'd finished, 'you've got more basis than most folk making these accusations. But I still can't see that either Diane or Wilma would have the will to hit someone over the head, or the strength to hold her under the water.'

So, the police believed that the murderer had held the body under the water. Interesting. That would take some strength. 'But what if they did it together? Wilma and Diane between them, they could do it.' Even as she said it, Julia couldn't quite picture this actually happening.

'In theory, yes, they could have managed it together,' said Hayley. 'But just because they could, doesn't mean they did. Two women? And Wilma isn't in the first flush of youth, although she is fit. Still, not the usual profile, even with a motive. If you consider the great Toby jug swindle a viable motive. Which, for the record, I don't.'

She was right. It was not impossible, but perhaps unlikely that Maeve's death was the work of the sort of lady – or ladies – who volunteered in a charity shop. But it could be the work of a landlord; one with a grudge, a need and possibly some hired muscle.

'Hayley, there is one other thing, another lead, a possible...' Julia started saying, but Hayley's mobile rang at just that moment. Hayley answered, and was soon nodding and making noises of agreement. 'Yes... Mmmm... Right ho... I'll be there now.'

'Got to go, Julia,' she said, getting to her feet. 'I have to race. I've been expecting a package from Bristol with the detailed results on the Shed Skeleton, but what with the post running late this week, it's only arrived now. I'd better go and get it before DC Farmer makes a dog's breakfast of it. I'd wanted to ask you if you saw anything suspicious on your walk at the lake, before you found Maeve's body. But have a think, and maybe I can pop by this evening, and we can carry on our chat.' And before Julia could say 'landlord' or 'murder', DI Hayley Gibson was out the door.

17

Julia wrapped four scones in a piece of wax paper and tied the little package with a length of string. Then she called Jake, who was examining the shrubbery for moles or voles or who knows what type of country rodent, pouncing and digging and generally making a mess. When he heard the rattle of his lead, he gave up his foraging and bounded towards her.

'Sit,' she said firmly, and he plonked his behind on the ground and looked up at her. He looked positively angelic, except for the smear of dirt on his snout.

'Good boy. We're going to town to do some digging,' she said. 'Not the sort of digging you've been doing, though.'

Lord, as if conversing with the dog wasn't bad enough, now she was making jokes with him. She popped the package of scones into her basket and set off down the lane, feeling very much like someone in a film – a country lady on a mission of mercy, bringing food to the ailing. She was, in fact, a country lady on a mission of snooping. Before she put her Toby jug theory finally to rest, she would check up on Diane and see if she really was sick. It couldn't do any harm. It wasn't as if Hayley was interested in checking up on Diane's alibi, or

Wilma's. She'd all but discounted them as suspects, and she was run off her feet, poor thing.

Julia's mission was somewhat derailed when, halfway to the village, she realised that she didn't know where Diane lived. Or her phone number. Then she remembered that she had Pippa's number. Julia stopped – Jake pulled irritably at the lead – and dialled his previous owner.

'Hello, Julia,' Pippa said. 'How are you? Everything all right with Jake?'

'Yes, he's fine. I was just wondering...'

'I can't take him back now. It's just not an option. No.'

'No, no. I love Jake!' Julia said, appalled at the thought of giving him back. 'I wanted to drop something at your cousin Diane's, and I don't have her address.'

'Of course,' said Pippa, the relief clear in her voice. 'Just past the post office, turn left into Hillbrow Lane. There's a row of houses – hers is on the right about halfway down, I don't know the number, just look for the petunias.'

Look for the petunias. That didn't sound like much in terms of directions. Oh well, thought Julia as she said her goodbyes, village ways. She continued on her way, enjoying the fresh air and sunshine, the locals going about their errands, picking up a bit of fish for supper, dropping the dry cleaning off. There was a tricky moment with a robin red-breast on a holly bush – Jake lunged at it but got nowhere near – but for the rest of the walk, he trotted obediently at her side.

Diane's house was attached to its neighbours, a row of yellow stone cottages, their roofs swayed like horses' backs between the chimneys. As promised, one of them – halfway down on the right – had a particularly fine display of petunias, pink and white and purple blossoms spilling out of pots on the pavement and on the windowsills.

Julia walked up to the front door and knocked. Diane opened the door, wearing a rumpled tracksuit and sheepskin slippers, her face pale. Behind her, a tumble of children's toys and little jackets and boots filled the hallway. She looked momentarily surprised to see Julia and Jake, and then greeted them warmly.

'I heard you weren't well,' said Julia, fishing in her basket and producing a now rather wonky package of scones. 'I brought you a little something. Scones.'

'How kind!' said Diane. 'Honestly, this is the first day I can even think of eating something. I've been feeling just awful.'

'Those tummy things are the worst.'

'The worst. Gosh, but I must look a sight,' she said, tugging at her sweatshirt and then running her fingers through her red hair, which was lanky and unwashed. 'I've been in bed for two days. Could hardly lift my head off the pillow. But I'm on the mend today. I will have a shower and eat a scone and I'll be a hundred per cent better, I'm sure.'

'I hope so. I won't keep you. Just wanted to say hello. I'll see you at the shop, if you're fully recovered by then.'

'I'll be right as rain. You know how it is, once you've turned the corner.'

'Yes indeed. See you Wednesday, bright and early.'

'Oh, I wouldn't worry too much about bright and early. Wilma has the keys and she's always late on a Wednesday. She goes to a Pilates class. It ends at nine, but half the time she hangs about chatting. I never arrive before about quarter past. I suggest you do the same.'

'Good advice, thanks.'

'You're welcome. And thanks again for the scones,' Diane said, waving her goodbye as Julia and Jake turned to go.

So Diane had been sick, as she'd said. Her alibi looked sound, and it seemed she'd provided one for Wilma too, inadvertently. Julia remembered Wilma arriving with a gym bag, which probably confirmed the Pilates class theory. It was unlikely that either woman had been involved in the murder of Maeve. Julia had hit a dead end, but she was pleased that the two women from the charity shop weren't cold-blooded murderers. Her faith in human nature had been sorely tested in her career, and she had rather hoped the village would restore it, rather than destroy the last remnants.

'What do you want to do? A bit of a walk about, then a pop in at the cafe?' she asked Jake, who smiled at her with his loopy grin. The nice thing about Jake was that he had no ideas of his own, he just went along delightedly with whatever Julia suggested. Today, Julia wanted to explore her new village and clear her head. She set off down the main street, aiming to investigate the far end. She'd never gone much past the few shops she frequented. This time, she'd go and see what lay beyond them.

Her phone rang in her basket, vibrating against her hip.

'Hang on, Jake,' she said, sitting on a bench at a bus stop and digging for her phone.

'Melanie, hi,' she answered quickly. 'How are you? Any news on Samantha?'

'Hi, Julia. Yeah, the Samantha Harold thing is taking longer than I thought. I just did the basic checks, but I can't seem to find anything on her. No tax records. No marriage, no death. No criminal record. Odd. I'm wondering whether she changed her name before she got married, but if that were the case I should have picked it up. Nothing about an emigration either, although there should certainly be a record of that. Anyway, I'm on it. I'll check some of the other sources. I'm sure there'll be some lead soon – people don't just disappear when Melanie Houston is on the job!'

'Thanks, Melanie, I really appreciate it.'

'You know me, no stone unturned. I'm sure I'll find something soon, I always do.'

'Thanks,' Julia said again. 'You're the best.'

'But I was calling about William Adamson, not Samantha,' Melanie said, her voice serious. 'Not a nice fellow. Not at all. He's got a record.'

'Really?'

'Yup. A bunch of charges – harassment and intimidation, forging signatures, and two incidents of assault.'

'Assault.'

'Yes. He did prison time for one of them – a business dispute of some kind; he put the guy in hospital.'

'That's really helpful, Melanie. He was in dispute with Maeve over her lease. He wanted her out.'

'Listen, Julia. He's a guy you don't want to tangle with. I know this kind of record, seen it a million times. What you see on paper is just the tip of the iceberg. A guy like that probably has a bunch of incidents that didn't even make it to the cops, let alone the courts. Sounds like a small-time crim with a nasty streak. Give him a wide berth.'

'I'm not going to have anything to do with him, don't you worry,' said Julia. 'I'll pass the info on to my new cop buddy; she can deal with it. Thanks again. Hey, come visit me in the country some time. I'll buy you a slap-up thank you dinner.'

'You're on. In the meantime, I'll keep digging on Samantha. When I find something, I'll let you know.'

Julia and Jake continued on their exploratory mission, past the supermarket, the off-licence, the shoe shop. The postman, Gary, was sitting on a low wall outside the fishmonger, a worried frown and a faraway look on his face. Julia wondered what postmen worried about. Certainly not missing people, more like missing letters, she thought with a laugh. But Julia was worried about missing people. She thought about what Melanie had said about Samantha. An unusual lack of records, surely? No record of her marriage, and yet Jane had been sure she was married – to Alan or Adam or Andy, she had said, rather unhelpfully. Was Samantha living in sin, and lying to her mother about it? Was Maeve the sort of person who would care, in this day and age?

After the toy shop, Julia passed a small salon with two hairdresser's chairs. She needed a trim. She popped in and noted that the young woman behind the reception had a stylish hairstyle, well cut. Julia asked who had cut it, and made an appointment for the next day.

The shops started to peter out, and there were more small offices. A tax consultant, a physiotherapist, a family lawyer... And William Adamson Property Company.

Julia looked at the frosted glass door, hesitated, and then pushed it open and stepped inside.

18

The first thing Julia noticed on entering the offices of the William Adamson Property Company, was the receptionist's false eyelashes. They reminded Julia of Petunia the cow, her grandmother's prize Jersey. She'd had the longest, thickest lashes, and as a child Julia had loved her slow blink, as if her lashes were too heavy to move. It really was quite unnerving on a human, though. The lashes extended forwards and then swooped upwards and fanned out. Just about as alarming was the orange eyeshadow. Every time the girl blinked, it was as if two tangerine segments descended over her eyeballs.

Julia smiled broadly and tried not to stare.

'Hello,' she said.

'Canny helpya?' the girl enquired.

'I was just passing and I saw your sign. I'm new to the area and am looking for a property rental. What is it you do, exactly?'

'Property,' the girl said, as if Julia herself was a complete idiot. 'Like it says on the door.'

'Buying? Selling?'

'Yeah. And y'know, like, rentals.'

'That's interesting. Do you have any brochures, perhaps?'

'Nah. You'd have to ask me dad.'

'Oh, I see, well not to worry...'

'DAAAAD!' the girl bellowed, in a voice fit to raise the dead, displaying a vibrating tongue-ring.

The sound of doors and footsteps came from the back office.

Butterflies circled Julia's stomach. What was she thinking? She should have heeded Melanie's advice to give him a wide berth instead of blundering into his office on a whim.

William Adamson was a tall, handsome man, nicely turned out. 'Good morning. Will Adamson. What can I do for you?' he asked with a broad smile and a proffered hand.

There was something of the ageing tough about him. Nothing obvious, no tats, no scars, but a steeliness to his smiling blue eyes. And Julia could see from the way his shoulders and chest filled his well-cut jacket that he worked out.

'Pleased to meet you,' she said, shaking his hand. His handshake was firm, and warm.

'Take a seat.'

They moved to two chairs in the reception, either side of a chest of drawers.

Jake settled down quietly at Julia's feet, his eyes moving from Julia to Will as they spoke.

'I recently moved to Berrywick myself, bought a little house down in Slipstream Lane. My daughter is moving back from Hong Kong and she thought she would try village life. Spend time with Mum, work remotely.'

That sounded rather lovely, Julia thought sadly. If only it were true.

'What sort of thing is she looking for?'

'She wants a two-bedroom flat. Preferably in a house. Rental to start with. I heard you do that sort of thing.'

'We do indeed. We've got a number of properties, old

houses converted into very nice flats. I can show you some pictures.'

He took a piece of paper out of the drawer. 'These are our properties,' he said, presenting it with a flourish. 'All well-maintained, good positions.'

On it was a list of seven addresses, most of which were meaningless to Julia. There was no listing on the road where Maeve and Jane lived.

'Do you have anything on the east side of the village? Closer to me.'

'Nothing at the moment.'

'That's a pity. Someone I met said there was a nice house of flats in Winding Lane. I'll ask her.'

'That property is ours.'

'But it's not on the list?'

'There's no rental availability. That property has recently come on the market for sale as a house.'

'Really?' Julia paused, as if she were thinking. 'I mean, perhaps that's an idea? Sell my small cottage and get something big enough for the two of us? Gosh, I'd love that.' The last part wasn't a lie, although she suspected that in the unlikely situation that Jess moved to the village, the very last thing that she would want to do would be to share a house with her mum.

Will, however, had no way to know this and he opened the drawer again, pulled out a glossy, printed sheet of paper and handed it to her.

Julia looked down at professional photographs of the house. One of the exterior, taken at golden hour with its brickwork glowing and its generous bay windows lit from within. Another of the view from Maeve's flat, overlooking the river and the fields beyond.

Once-in-a-lifetime opportunity to own a large period home in Berrywick's most sought-after location. Magnificent river views.

Currently configured as four income-producing flats. Or restore to its original splendour as a family home! Walk to shops and good schools.

Julia read the paper slowly, but her brain was whirring – Maeve had been dead two days, and Will Adamson had a brochure already. He must have been well prepared in advance to get this out so quickly. He must have known that Maeve's flat and its long lease would soon no longer be an issue. She felt a prickle of fear. Was she sitting opposite Maeve's murderer?

Julia looked at her watch and said, in a pantomime of astonishment. 'Goodness, is that the time? I'd better be on my way.'

'Let me take your name and...'

She stood up. 'I really must dash. I'll email you with my details.'

He stood too, looming over her by a good six inches. 'Your name,' he said, coldly. 'Who did you say you were?'

Jake whimpered softly and moved towards the door, tugging at the lead.

'Julia,' she said, and turned to follow Jake.

19

Was there anything quite as nice as a good head massage, Julia wondered, as the hairdresser's fingers worked at her scalp. It was so wonderfully relaxing, head back, those hard fingertips against her skull. She resolved not to think about anything worrying – the two dead bodies, what Jake was getting up to in the garden, a murderous estate agent, what to do about the aphids on the roses, and that she mustn't forget to buy washing-up liquid.

Now she was worrying about the list of things she was telling herself not to worry about!

'All done,' said Molly, the hairdresser, turning on the hand shower to rinse off the conditioner. She reached for a towel and covered Julia's head, gently squeezing and patting her hair dry. 'Come on over to the chair.'

There were three chairs in the Fringe, and only one other was occupied. A very well-groomed blonde was bent over a book of colour swatches – little loops of hair, ranging from blonde, through red and brown, to black, to grey. She and the hairdresser discussed her options in serious tones.

'So what are we doing?' Molly asked, fluffing up Julia's hair, and frowning at her in the mirror.

'Oh, just a trim, I think,' said Julia, surveying the damp mop resting on her shoulders, the fringe hanging to her eyebrows and making her mascara run. She had never quite got used to seeing a sixty-something-year-old staring back at her in the mirror. A healthy, fine-looking sixty-something-year-old, it must be said. But still.

'Well, that's nice, for sure. A trim. But would you think about going a little shorter? I'm thinking less Berrywick and more, y'know, Paris.'

'Paris?'

'Short bob, cheeky, stylish. French.' Molly folded the hair under to demonstrate. 'And then a bit of a side fringe, you know? You could carry it off. Good bones.'

Julia knew herself to be susceptible to a bit of flattery. Not that she was vain, exactly, but she had been a bit of a looker in her time. And she did have good bones, it was true.

'Good to have a change,' said Molly, and then, delivering the kicker: 'Take years off, it will.'

'Well, why not?' said Julia, giving the hairdresser a smile. 'I'm all about the change, these days. Let's do it.'

The groomed blonde loudly announced her intention to go Golden Tan with Ash Blonde highlights, which Julia thought sounded rather lovely. Her own hair had gone from a dark blonde to a mid-brown with streaks of silver at the temples, and she was momentarily tempted by the idea of highlights. But only momentarily.

The blonde had gone on to choosing a nail colour for her manicure. She examined a swatch of colours, like a key ring, with a fan of sticks, each with a different plastic nail at the end of it. She held one against her own nail, extended her hand, head on one side, then dropped the nail, and tried another. They were all the colours of the rainbow, even green and blue and black and yellow and silver and gold.

As Molly swept the cape over Julia's head, the phone rang in Julia's bag. Glancing down, she saw it was Melanie.

'Do you mind?' she asked the hairdresser. 'Work.'

Molly waved her permission.

'Hi,' Julia whispered, cupping her hand over the speaker. She was always very tut-tut about people taking calls in public, because she considered it very rude, but this was important. 'Can't really talk.'

'That's okay. I'll be quick. Bottom line, there's no sign of Samantha anywhere. I've looked everywhere. The last official record I found of her was her A levels.'

'Thanks for trying. I guess the funeral will have to go ahead without her, unless someone else can find her. It's very odd, though. Why would she just disappear so completely?'

'Either on purpose – changed identity, witness protection, criminal, something like that. Or she's a total recluse. Or an unrecorded death.'

Molly made a snipping sound with her scissors to get Julia's attention.

'Gotta go. Thanks, Melanie. Appreciate it.'

While Molly got to work on Julia's hair, Julia contemplated the sad fact that Maeve would be buried without her only child present, and the curious fact that this child – now a woman – was so thoroughly missing from the official record. If Melanie couldn't find her, the police wouldn't either.

The groomed blonde had chosen her nail colour and a manicurist had taken up position on a stool next to the chair, the blonde's hand on a cushion in her lap.

It was oddly mesmerising, watching the careful painting of each nail in turn, the brush running cuticle to tip, cuticle to tip, over each long smooth oval. Julia remembered what Jane had said, that Samantha was something of an amateur manicurist herself, doing the girls' nails for the dance. Everyone spoke about how pretty and well-groomed the girl had been. Julia remembered how back in the day, if you'd wanted those perfect nails, you'd had to get acrylics. Nowadays you could get the effect with gel polish, without having to glue a fake piece of plastic to your nail. She glanced at where the fan was now lying on the counter, like a rainbow of discarded fake nails.

A shocking thought came to Julia, out of the blue, with a rush of adrenaline that made her whole body jerk.

'Keep still, please,' said Molly. 'Unless you want an asymmetrical bob.'

Unless she was very much mistaken, Julia knew where she would find Samantha.

Hayley stared at the four gold ovals lying in the palm of her hand.

'Nails, you say?'

'Yes, false nails. I'm pretty sure of it.'

The DI picked one oval up, turned it over and examined it – the gold upper side of the curve, the once-white underneath.

She held it up to her own fingers. 'I must say, the shape's right.'

Julia looked across her kitchen table at the policewoman, took a deep breath and said, 'Hayley, I think the body under the shed is Samantha Harold.'

'Maeve's daughter?'

'Yes.'

'I don't suppose we could have a cuppa while we talk? I was just about to make tea when you phoned. I'm parched.'

Julia put the kettle on, realising she'd had nothing since breakfast. She was suddenly starving. She fetched a box of chocolate digestives from the pantry. The rustling of paper brought Jake over.

'Not for you, you naughty little thing,' she said, putting the biscuits on a plate. 'Besides, you surely can't be hungry after eating the rose off my watering can and half a bucket of clothes pegs?'

She handed the plate to Hayley, who helped herself to a biscuit before she asked, 'What makes you think it's Samantha?'

'She's completely missing. No one can find any evidence of her. You've tried yourself, and I asked my old London sources.'

'You did, did you?' Julia was pleased to note that Hayley didn't sound cross; more amused, really, and perhaps resigned to Julia's interference.

'Yes. Just trying to help the neighbours, you know. We didn't want her to miss the funeral. Really, I had no idea it would turn out to have anything to do with the police investigation.'

She thought she noticed a slight raising of Hayley's right eyebrow, but the DI just said, 'Go on.'

'And then there's the nails. Everyone mentioned how well-groomed Samantha was, and that she did people's nails and so on for pocket money.'

The kettle whistled and Julia got up to pour the hot water into the teapot. She put it and two mugs on the table, along with the milk in its bottle. Her mother wouldn't approve.

'When I found these ovals in the garden I had no idea what they were, but then I saw some nails, false ones, when I was having my hair cut and it just clicked – same shape.'

'Good cut, by the way,' Hayley said.

'Thanks.' Julia patted her hair, enjoying the smooth, just-cut feeling of it. She had been very pleased with the outcome.

She continued, 'And then there's the body. We know the skeleton was that of a young woman. It's been buried for around twenty years, which is about when Samantha allegedly left the village for London. The timing fits.'

'The timing fits, granted. As for the false nails... well, maybe that makes sense,' said Hayley, nodding. 'But there's one major problem with your theory. Samantha didn't disappear twenty years ago. The friends and neighbours have seen her since she left.'

'Except that they haven't, actually. Not the ones I've spoken to, at least. When I thought about it, I realised that they all told me about her coming to visit, but none of them actually mentioned seeing her. I made some calls to check that I wasn't wrong. The neighbour, Jane, said they last came to visit over Easter when she was away. No one seems to have met the husband or kids. Everyone's just missed them. Or they heard about them from Maeve.'

'We're going to have to interview them all officially, see if anyone's actually clapped eyes on the girl – woman – in recent years,' said Hayley, reaching for her phone. 'DC Farmer, please?' She held the phone away from her face and said to Julia, 'Who have you spoken to? I need names.'

The tea was forgotten as DI Gibson went into full investigation mode, making a list of names in her notebook, and barking instructions at the young copper on the other end of the phone.

'Set up as many as you can for this afternoon. Get them to come down to the station. And, Walter, I'm going to need dental records on that shed skeleton. And a list of local dentists. Yes... See if you can pull in someone to help... Yes, I'm aware it's the weekend... I'm on my way.'

20

Sunday had been, if anything, more stressful than the previous day – which was saying something, as Saturday had featured the identification of a dead body, a conversation with the police, and a message from DI Gibson confirming that the body was indeed Samantha's – not that Julia had been in any doubt.

Having sort of mastered the scones, Julia decided to make her own strawberry jam. Pickling and preserving had been part of her Cotswold fantasy. She imagined the jewel-bright jars all lined up in the pantry – 'Apricot, plum or strawberry – or would you prefer marmalade?' she would ask visitors, as they buttered their home-made scones. 'Take one with you, I have made so many,' she would say, as they left.

Julia had envisaged a relaxing morning with the jam bubbling fragrantly on the stove and Jake napping calmly at her feet while she read the Sunday papers. Who knew jam was so finicky? The recipe was full of mysterious instructions – 'when the liquid has reached the gel stage' and 'push gently and see if it wrinkles' – and further investigation on the internet made the situation, if anything, worse.

After much stressful poking and prodding, she made a call

on the jam. *Done.* 'Ladle hot jam into sterilised and perfectly dry jars...' was easier said than done. Boiling liquid sugar splattered Julia's hand, causing her to drop the half-full, sort-of-sterilised and imperfectly dry jar onto the kitchen floor with a crash.

'Jake, no! Out!' she shouted as the dog came running in, attracted, as he was, to any commotion. He slid to a halt in the patch of hot jam, surrounded by shards of glass. With a yelp, he lifted his scalded forepaw and rolled onto his side, distributing the sticky mess across the entire right-hand side of body. His fur protected him from the broken glass and the worst of the heat, but still it had to be uncomfortable. Jake looked at her as if hurt, and she saw him position his four paws, readying himself for a good shake.

In her mind, Julia saw it as a slow-motion movie scene, the dog's rippling chocolate hide hurling splatters of jam in all directions, his tongue and face jiggling from side to side, her outstretched arms and her horrified face shouting, 'Noooooo, Jaaaaaake...'

In real time, and real life, her kitchen looked more like a murder scene than either of the two murder scenes she had seen in the last two weeks. Red splatters covered the counters, walls and floor, with blobs of strawberry quivering horribly all over the room. Jake slunk stickily out of the door, which she slammed behind him, shouting threateningly, 'I'll deal with you later!'

The clean-up took an hour. When it was done, Julia went outside to find Jake, who was lying in his little lair with leaves and grass and soil stuck to the cooled jam, and playing host to quite a few bees. Waving the buzzing bees away from her face, she rinsed him with a hosepipe and then shampooed him with the expensive lemongrass and coconut oil shampoo she'd been talked into buying at the salon yesterday. Another hour.

She managed to salvage a single large jar of strawberry jam which she put in the pantry, where it did glow somewhat jewel-like, but would always, and forever, be a solitary example of her jam-making.

She was so exhausted by the horror show that she spent most of the afternoon on the sofa with her book. But her concentration was interrupted by thoughts of Will Adamson and the professionally printed brochure. Had he planned to kill Maeve Harold, and got the brochure all ready? It just seemed so... premeditated, so brutal. *Will Adamson was spitting!* Jane had said. But still, spitting was one thing, murder was another. Maybe he'd got his hands on the place some other way. The lease?

What else had Jane said? *My Graham was impressed with the wording, I can tell you.* Jane had seen the lease! Julia reached for her phone and dialled Jane's number. It turned out Jane did indeed have a copy of the lease, she'd email it over. Julia's next call was to Peter, who was properly alarmed at her involvement in *two* murders, but agreed to take a look at the lease. 'Only if you promise me you won't do anything rash with the information,' he said. 'Honestly, Julia, I don't know what's come over you since you moved there. You're like a different person.'

Julia perked up rather at the idea that something had 'come over' her, just as she'd hoped, when she moved here. That was rather the point, wasn't it? To be, if not a different person, at least a somewhat changed one? With a different life? It struck Julia as ironic that the changes that perturbed Peter, had been set in motion by Peter's own marriage-ending change – falling in love with another man.

'Thanks, send my love to Christopher,' she said.

Peter was deaf to irony at the best of times, and just said, 'Will do,' before ending the call.

She took an evening walk with Jake, who smelled of lemon and coconut with a faint whiff of strawberry, and was subdued after his difficult day. He didn't chase a large mallard duck which any court in the land would agree had provoked him terribly with its tuneless quacking and its beady eyes. He simply sighed and gave a tiny shudder, as if he'd seen terrible things and didn't want more trouble.

'Good boy, Jake,' she said, and they turned for home.

Julia was done with cooking after the jam massacre. Monday morning saw her bright and early at the Buttered Scone, tucking into a full English breakfast – eggs and bacon, a fried tomato, mushrooms, a sausage, baked beans and toast – glancing at the front page of the *Berrywick & Surrounds Gazette* while she awaited the arrival of Johnny Blunt. Her jam-making fantasy might have gone out of the window, but her henhouse was going to make up for it. The crime-scene team had been and had another look, embarrassed, Julia thought, by the fact that they had missed the little oval discs. They had found a few more – triumphantly – and declared that the area was now the most thoroughly checked piece of ground in the UK, and she could go ahead with her coop. Julia wasn't going to argue.

She was only halfway through the ginormous grease-fest, and similarly halfway through the front page of the local paper, when Johnny arrived.

'Morning,' he asserted loudly, causing Jake to look up and see what the fuss was about.

'Hello, Johnny,' she said. 'I was hoping to run into you. I wonder if you could start on the chicken coop this week?'

'All such a rush. Are you sure the police are done?' he bellowed, causing the elderly couple at the next table to shrink into their sensible water-resistant outerwear, their eyes wide with horror.

'Yes, like I told you, that's all taken care of,' said Julia to Johnny.

'I hear it was poor Samantha Harold that was buried under

your shed,' said Flo, who was passing by. News certainly travelled fast in Berrywick. 'Dental records,' said Flo authoritatively, and leaned over to give a table a cursory wipe.

'Samantha Harold?' asked a woman in the far corner. 'I remember her from Brownies. Good heavens, poor thing.'

'Indeed,' said Flo. 'A shocker.'

Johnny Blunt tutted, and shook his head sadly. He looked quite shaken, poor chap.

'Bill please,' called the woman at the next table, waving her arm to Flo while her husband crammed the last half piece of toast into his mouth. They hadn't come to the picturesque Cotswolds to eat breakfast amongst murderers.

'Saw that young copper, he told me,' Flo continued. 'Terrible really, isn't it? Imagine, her and her mother, both found dead in the same week.'

The elderly tourists looked appalled. *Two* dead bodies.

'Come on, Jeffrey, we're going,' said the woman, throwing a handful of notes onto the table and making for the door.

'But some twenty years apart,' a voice piped up from across the room.

'Yes of course. Not connected at all. What a bizarre coincidence. So very sad,' said Diane, from the table by the door.

'So, the chicken coop,' said Julia firmly, bringing Johnny back to the subject at hand. 'When can you start?'

Johnny gazed into the distance and drew his remarkable eyebrows together beneath his blue cap, as if mentally consulting his schedule.

'I'm not sure,' he said, uncertainly. 'I'm thinking, um...'

'Tomorrow?' Julia asked.

'Ah no, not tomorrow. I need a few days.'

'Wednesday, then?' asked Julia, trying to keep the irritation out of her voice. She would just need to get used to the slower pace of life here.

'Well, I could get the timber tomorrow, I suppose. Get things sorted on Wednesday, start on Thursday.'

'Perfect.'

'Ah no, Thursday won't do, the cricket's on.'

Julia felt her London impatience rising to the fore.

'It only starts at four, they're playing in India,' said Flo helpfully from across the room. 'Different time zone.'

The woman had the hearing of a bat.

'Well then, I suppose I could get the frame up in the morning. Leave in time for the match.'

'That would work.' Flo nodded, although quite what the coop-building arrangements had to do with her was unclear.

Julia tried not to drum her fingers on the table while Johnny mulled over the options.

'Well then, I might come by Thursday, bring Brendan along to help.'

'Nine o'clock?' asked Julia.

'Let's not get carried away, shall we, City Miss? I've got to have me brekkie first. Can't do carpentry on an empty stomach now, can I? Ten a.m. or thereabouts, I'll be there.'

Julia picked up the unread paper, stuffed it into her tote, called Jake to heel and went to pay her bill.

'Terrible about poor Samantha,' said Flo, ringing up her English breakfast and her coffee. 'Such a pretty thing, and clever too. She was in the same class as my Fiona. Did so well. Won the English prize. Who would do a thing like that to a young girl? I don't know, I really don't.'

21

The Buttered Scone was the perfect place for a fry-up and a gossip, but it was not the place to gather your thoughts and consider weighty problems. For that, Julia headed to one of the benches along the path by the river where no one would bother her, and Jake could have a bit of a sniff around.

Julia chose a bench in the sun, which was pleasantly warm, rather than hot. She freed Jake from the lead and took her phone and her newspaper out of the basket.

As she opened the paper across her knees, she heard a message arrive on her phone. It was a voice note from Peter. She still wasn't used to the idea that she and Peter were friends – just friends. It was hard, this business of ex-husbands. But he was the perfect person to ask about the contract that Maeve had with Will Adamson, and whether it was really so watertight. Hopefully this voice note would shed some light.

'Hey, Jules. Look, the contract is well drawn up, but because it's so old – over twenty years – your chap's lawyers should be able to get it dismissed. It's unfairly onerous on him if he wants to sell. I can walk you through it if you like, but bottom line – there's been a recent change to the law and while it might've held up before, the lease definitely wouldn't hold up in court now; he could almost certainly get out of it. Chat soon.'

Julia typed a quick thank you. Looking down at her phone, she saw, on the open newspaper below, a picture of the man himself. Will Adamson. BERRYWICK BUSINESSMAN HONOURED read the headline.

Julia read the article out loud to Jake:

'Berrywick property developer Will Adamson was awarded "Small property developer of the year" by the Property Association of Southern England. He received the award at a breakfast in Bristol on Wednesday. Mr Adamson said...' But she never read what Mr Adamson said, because she suddenly realised the implications of what she had just read.

'Jake! Wednesday morning. Will Adamson was in Bristol for breakfast, which means he wasn't at the lake, killing Maeve Harold. And it seems he didn't have the motive either, if the lease isn't watertight. The Toby jug theory seemed unlikely – and Hayley certainly wasn't buying it. So who killed Maeve? And why?'

'Who killed Cock Robin?' Edna asked from behind the bench, causing Julia to jump and Jake to give a small yelp of surprise from amongst the reeds. '"All the birds of the air fell a-sighing and a-sobbing..." Just like the girl. Poor lass. Or the mother. Not the man, though. No sobbing for him, no.'

'What girl?' asked Julia.

'What girl?' asked Edna.

'What man?'

'Who knows, now, rose? The nose knows,' Edna said, tapping her own rather elegant nose as she shuffled off down the path.

Did Edna have some deeply buried wisdom or insight, or did she just emit random thoughts and phrases? There was the occasional string of words that seemed pertinent, even profound. But overall, her utterances sounded like gobbledygook. There was no way Julia was going to solve the vexing problem of these two deaths by listening to an old woman. She needed to work things out properly.

There were so many questions. They bubbled to the forefront of her brain in a rather random order.

Question one, thought Julia, wishing she had a piece of paper, was how on earth Samantha's body had come to be under the shed. Whoever had hidden it there must have had access to the Steadmans' garden, and must have known about the work on the shed.

Julia's phone beeped, and she glanced at it. Tabitha:

Such good news that you're able to start building the coop!

Well, that sort of answered the second part of the question – or made it wider, depending how you saw things. In a village like this, news of Julia's chicken coop had reached Tabitha in the library within half an hour of her making the arrangement with Johnny. The building of the Steadmans' shed might have similarly been local gossip at the time it was built. Anyone, really, might have known about it. But who would have had access to it? The Steadmans, and a builder who was dead in the graveyard. And pretty much anyone who chose to stroll in under the cover of darkness. It wasn't like the garden was locked.

Question two, thought Julia, grabbing Jake's collar before he could notice a mother duck and her ducklings swim past, was why had nobody known that Samantha was missing? Or, as it turned out, dead? It really was very strange. She watched the mother duck herd her ducklings up the bank on the other side of the river, keeping them safe from any predator, like a certain large chocolate Labrador. Maeve Harold had failed to keep her duckling safe, and she'd lied about it. But why? Why had she made up stories of a husband and children and a job –

and all the while the poor girl had been lying dead under Julia's shed?

Julia checked on the ducks. They were out of sight, and she considered it safe to let go of Jake's collar. He immediately began sniffing along the edge of the river, knowing that he'd missed out on something, but not sure what.

Surely if Maeve had known that her daughter was missing, she would have gone looking for her? Alerted people? Filed a report with the police? Unless...

Julia felt a chill in her veins as she thought it. Unless Maeve had killed her daughter. Julia couldn't imagine making up such elaborate lies – Australia, for goodness' sake! – unless one had something to hide. Maybe she hadn't wanted anyone looking for Samantha, because she knew full well that they'd never find her. Because she'd murdered her.

And now Maeve herself might have been murdered. It made a horrendous type of sense; Maeve would have kept Samantha's death a secret if she herself had caused it. Almost clever, one had to admit. But if Maeve had killed Samantha, then who had killed Maeve, and why?

Julia jumped as a loud bark indicated that Jake had spotted the ducks again, and was about to leap in the water.

'Come here, you lump head,' she called, and to her amazement, he did.

'Jakey,' she told him, as they headed home. 'I need to find out more about Maeve and Samantha.' She couldn't be sure, but Jake seemed to get a little bounce in his walk at the suggestion.

Julia had settled Jake with a bone, and switched on the kettle to make tea, when her phone rang again. She had no idea why she had believed for one minute that life in the country might be lonely, she thought, seeing Wilma's number on the screen.

'Julia, it's a nightmare,' said Wilma, as soon as Julia answered. Now, perhaps a few weeks ago, this might have thrown Julia. But she was wily to the gossip of Berrywick now, so she knew that Wilma must be talking about the identification of Samantha's body.

'It is certainly very bad news,' said Julia. 'Not what I expected at all.'

'And so inappropriate,' said Wilma.

'Yes,' agreed Julia. She supposed that that was one way to describe the death of a young girl twenty years ago, missed by no one. 'Certainly, inappropriate.'

'Plus, I have nobody available to help.'

Julia thought about this for a minute. 'I don't think you need to help, Wilma,' she said eventually. 'I'm sure the police have it all under control.'

'The police?' said Wilma, sounding perplexed. 'I don't think this is the sort of thing that the police deal with at all.'

'I'd think it would be exactly the sort of thing that they deal with,' said Julia, in what she hoped was a decisive voice. She really was starting to wonder if Wilma was a full box of chocolates. She knew from experience that these excitable sorts just needed a firm voice and a plan of action.

'Perhaps in London the police have enough people to help,' said Wilma, 'but I just don't think that here in Berrywick I can ask poor DI Gibson and that useless boy to help me clean up Maeve's flat, Julia. I don't think that would go down at all well.'

Julia took a deep breath, and poured the boiled water over the teabag in her mug. Her heart sank slightly. Would she ever learn not to jump to conclusions?

'Perhaps you should start from the beginning again, Wilma,' she said. 'I seem to have got hold of completely the wrong end of the stick.'

The issue, it seemed, was that in the absence of Samantha, someone needed to clean out Maeve's flat. And, because of Will Adamson applying pressure, it needed to be done soon. The charity shop often helped out in situations like this, explained

Wilma, but she was so short-staffed these days. She had no idea what to do, she said.

'I wonder,' said Julia, as she guessed she was expected to, 'I wonder if perhaps I could help?'

'Oh, Julia, would you? That would be marvellous,' said Wilma, as if that hadn't been the whole purpose of the call. 'The police have been in and had a look around. They've given the go-ahead for the place to be cleared. Mr Adamson has given Jane the spare keys, and she'll meet you there at ten tomorrow. She's got her daughter, Hannah, there, and they'll help you.'

'Tomorrow? Oh, that's rather soon. But fine. Should I let them know to expect me?'

'Oh, they're expecting you at ten tomorrow,' said Wilma, already forgetting to act like she was surprised by Julia's offer. She added firmly: 'And don't be late. It reflects badly on the shop.'

22

The flat was neat and sparse, thank goodness. Julia was rather disturbed at the idea of going through a dead woman's things and when she left her house that morning she had a moment's panic that it would be like something from that television programme, *Hoarders*. Old newspapers and broken appliances and dust bunnies and rat droppings.

On the contrary, Maeve's sitting room had an almost sterile quality, with few personal effects. There was a sofa in front of a TV, with a coffee table and a rug between them. The table was bare, except for an empty teacup on a side plate scattered with crumbs. Maeve's last meal, Julia thought sadly. Next to it, a library book. Jodi Picoult. There were no family photos on the walls.Everything about Maeve felt a little sad. The way she'd died, of course. And her dead daughter. The soulless efficiency of her house.

The absence of family.

'There's only an elderly aunt in a home, and a cousin in Glasgow,' Jane said, as if reading Julia's mind. 'He couldn't come down. Busy, he said. He asked that we pack up any personal items, jewellery and suchlike, he'd pay for shipping. Sell the furniture. The rest can go to the charity shop.'

Jane pursed her lips, but didn't offer any comment on the cousin or his request.And now, sadly, Maeve's neighbours and a complete stranger were packing up the dead woman's belongings. Julia tried not to focus on the layers of sadness. She was here to do a job, and that was what she'd do.

'Where should we start?' she asked Jane, deferring to her as a neighbour and friend.

'Let's do something easy to start with, shall we? Do you and Hannah want to get going on the bookshelf? I'll do the rest of the bits and pieces in here. We won't get it all done today, but we can at least do the sitting room, and maybe start on the bedrooms if we have time, and get those boxes off to Second Chances.'

'Sounds like a plan.' Julia smiled at Hannah and brought over two of the empty cardboard boxes that Wilma had delivered, along with masking tape and a thick felt-tip marker. 'Fiction and non, I suppose?'

'Okay, and there's some CDs and DVDs. I'll box those up.'

They got going, barely looking at the titles after a while.

'It's been years since I was in this flat,' said Hannah, taking a stack of CDs off a shelf and giving them a cursory wipe with a cloth. 'I must have been about fifteen the last time. Poor Samantha. Can't believe she was murdered.'

'I'm sorry. It must be a terrible shock, and after all these years.'

Hannah sat back, her head tipped as if she was looking into the past. She was a pretty woman, with the same sense of style that Jane had. Julia imagined that she must've been a lovely teenager.

'Samantha was so... alive. Full of life, you know. Had a spark. The boys liked her, I'll tell you that much. Very kind to me, she was. Used to babysit me, and I always loved that. She would make up stories while she played with my hair, and tickled my back. She always had perfect nails. So clever with words too, was Sammy. Then when I was too old for babysitting she just let me hang out sometimes.'

'She sounds lovely.'

'Oh, look at this!' Hannah held up a Radiohead CD. 'She loved them. Remember, Mum?' she called out, waving the CD at her. 'You used to say, "Not that bloody album again!"'

Jane squinted at it. 'Goodness, yes. Heard it ten times a day for a while. These walls are not exactly soundproof, Mr Adamson being an absolute skinflint. You could hear a dropped glass or a raised voice.'

'Were there many of those?' Julia asked, casually, taping up a full box and writing NOVELS on the lid. 'Raised voices?'

'Oh you know, just what you'd expect with teenagers, the occasional shouting match. They got on well, but I must say towards...' Jane paused. 'Towards the end, before she, well... when Sam was off to uni... I must say they did have words when she came home on the weekends. My impression was that it was about boys. Men, I suppose. Sammy would have been about nineteen. But you know what mums are like, we do worry, even when the kids are a bit older.'

'Like thirty-five,' Hannah said with a laugh.

'Right you are.'

They worked in silence for a while, Jane taking the pictures off the walls, and wrapping the few knick-knacks in newspaper, the other two finishing the bookshelves.

'I've been round and round with it in my head and what I don't understand is, why would she tell us that Samantha was visiting her when she wasn't?' said Jane, turning to Julia with a frown. 'And the stories about the husband and the children. She made them up. It makes no sense.'

'I can't make sense of it either,' said Julia, truthfully. 'Unless she knew Samantha was dead, but wanted to pretend she wasn't.'

Julia waited to see how Jane reacted. The more Julia thought about it, the more convinced she was that Maeve must have killed Samantha. It was so obvious really, when one looked at the facts. Keeping Samantha's disappearance a secret, even telling lies about it. And now that Jane had told her that Samantha and Maeve had fought towards the end, that made it even more likely. She waited for Jane to reach the same conclusion, but to her surprise, Jane had a completely different idea.

'You mean, like, had a breakdown? I saw a documentary about that once, a woman who had a stillborn baby, but she couldn't accept it. Still behaved as if it was alive somewhere.' Jane sighed and shook her head. 'Perhaps... Still very odd though, to keep it up all those years. And she really was a very normal person in all respects. Quiet, sensible, kept to herself.'

'Was she always that quiet and reserved? When you first knew her?' asked Julia.

'Come to think of it, perhaps not. When I first moved in she'd ask me round for tea or a glass of something. She came over to ours a bit. Not, like, in each other's pockets, but you know. A pop in every now and then. And she had a few people in and out. Even a man once, he was around for a bit. What was his name, now?'

Jane frowned. Julia waited hopefully. It was a horrible thought, but a strange man in the picture might be a clue to Samantha's death. Although it still wouldn't explain why Maeve had lied. Nothing would really explain that unless she had killed Samantha. Or maybe the man had, and Maeve had helped him hide the body People did the most terrible things in the name of love, as Julia well knew from her work.

'Can't remember it. Anyway, he was long before Samantha... left. And Samantha had friends, girls would come round. Yes, it was livelier before Sammy went off to uni, that's for sure.

I didn't notice really, that things had gone quieter. Just seemed like, I don't know. Age. Time of life. Kids gone.'

'Or maybe she was sad for a reason. Like because her daughter had... disappeared.' Julia hesitated to share her theory of Maeve as a possible killer. The thought had clearly not occurred to Jane.

'I suppose,' said Jane. She gave a deep sigh. 'Let's get back to work, shall we? Idle hands and all that,' she said, snapping back to efficient mode. 'Julia, shall we make a start on Maeve's bedroom? I'll do the clothes, you do the rest?'

'I'll just finish here and then I'll do Sam's,' said Hannah, who was closing up the last box of old-tech music and forgotten movies.

Maeve's bedroom was neat, with the same rather impersonal quality that was evident in the rest of the flat. Except that next to the bed there was a framed picture of Maeve and Samantha, the girl in her mid-teens, her arm around her mum's shoulders, them both laughing. The only picture of Samantha on display in the house. Julia felt a jolt of sadness, looking at the two of them. How Maeve must have suffered when she'd looked at it first thing in the morning and last thing at night.

She picked it up and put it in the box with the few personal items to be sent to the cousin in Glasgow. She added a book of inspirational verse and a pretty antique candlestick, both at the bedside. Not that he'd want any of it, by the sounds of things.

'Oh, Mum, look at this!' Hannah called from the passage.

The two women followed her voice into what was clearly Sam's old bedroom. 'It's exactly how it was before she left!' said Hannah. 'I remember it all so well. The posters. Oh my word, her collection of Beanie Babies. Even her little jewellery box, the one that played that song... Ooh, I envied it.' She opened the lid and the tinny sound of 'Clair de Lune' filled the room sadly until Hannah snapped the box closed.

'What do you think happened to Samantha?' she asked her mother. 'Really, Mum, who could have killed her?'

'A man?' Jane said, more as a question than an answer. 'That's what usually happens to a young girl, isn't it? Some awful man with a temper.'

'And he just shoved her under the shed? Left her there for twenty years?'

'Honestly, love, I don't know. How can we ever know why people do these awful things?' It was true, in Julia's experience, that there was usually a man involved. But her mind kept going back to the bedroom, left untouched all these years. As if Maeve was waiting and hoping for the nineteen-year-old Samantha to walk right back in after two decades.

Or was it a shrine to a dead daughter, the daughter she had killed?

23

Julia took Diane's advice and didn't rush to be at the shop for opening time. Wilma would be late, and besides, Maeve's boxes were only being collected at ten. Instead, she took her tea and toast at leisure and thought about things.

The night before, she had made a case file for Maeve and one for Samantha, just as she had when she'd been a social worker. She felt a little ridiculous taking out two cardboard folders from her desk, writing a name on each. After all, she had no official interest in the matters. No jurisdiction. She was no longer Head of Youth Services for her area. She was just a rather nosy retired person now. A nosy retired person who happened to have stumbled into a situation involving two dead bodies.

She had started by making a list of everything she knew about the person in question. Each cardboard folder contained one piece of A4 paper, with her handwriting on it. Julia was quite surprised at how much she knew about the two women she'd never met.

She had started with a list of all the words and phrases used to describe Samantha – pretty, lovely, lively, kind, good at English, clever with words, did girls' hair, the boys liked her.

Her suspicion that Maeve had killed Samantha just wouldn't go away, as much as she hated to believe it could be true. Something that stuck in her mind from yesterday's discussion was that there had seemed to be a change in Maeve and Samantha's relationship when Samantha had gone to uni. More conflict, raised voices. Perhaps something to do with a boyfriend? Jane had suggested that might be the case. Could something have happened, a fight that went too far? Julia had seen all too often how an otherwise balanced person could be pushed to act irrationally by a difficult teen. Julia herself had been lucky with Jess, who had weathered the teen years fairly peacefully. But even calm Jess had been known to have a fit of rage about something that seemed completely random to the people around her. But could Maeve have lost her temper? A struggle gone wrong? An accident, of course. It was the only thing that Julia could think of that would explain why Maeve had pretended Samantha was in London, and later Sydney, with her imaginary happy family.

At around the same time that Samantha had disappeared, Maeve had become more withdrawn, more private. Depressed, perhaps? That would happen if you'd killed your child in anger, that's for sure. Julia could hardly stand to think about what that would do to a person.

'Gosh, look at the time!' she said to herself, or to Jake, or to the jug of sunny yellow tulips on the kitchen table, or just to the universe at large.

She got up and rattled Jake's lead, a sound that always woke him from a doze or brought him in from whatever mischief he was up to.

'Good boy,' she said, absent-mindedly, as she attached the lead to his collar. 'We're going for a quick walk and to practise sitting and staying. And then I'm going to go out to the charity shop and you are going to stay here and have a nice nap and not eat or dig.'

Jake looked delighted about all that, and she hoped he had got the bit about not eating or digging.

Julia enjoyed walking Jake around her new home village, which was now starting to feel quite familiar. She'd come to look forward to seeing particular vistas – this magnificent oak, that fine bed of peonies just come into bloom, a fat marmalade cat that seemed permanently affixed to a gatepost a few blocks down. Jake was sitting and staying and walking at heel like a champ. He really was quite a good boy, when he wasn't a little terror.

Wilma and Diane and a pile of boxes awaited Julia when she got to the shop.

'Oh *there* you are, Julia,' Wilma said a little pointedly, glancing up at the cuckoo clock which was both time-keeper and merchandise.

'Good morning,' Julia said pleasantly, offering no explanation for her tardiness. Diane gave her a small smile of complicity.

'Well, now that you're here, we can start with the boxes. Thank you for helping out yesterday, by the way. Anything good?'

'I did the books mostly. Quite a lot of fiction, most of it not too old. Some self-helpy sort of things. A few cookbooks. I didn't look too closely, I was mostly just packing, but I reckon there are some books that will sell.'

'Oh good, we are rather short. Lots of readers in Berrywick, and lots of folk who like a bit of a bargain. Why don't you get the books out and start pricing them and we can pop them straight out? Just make up a price and write it in, in pencil. We start at fifty pence for older books, going up to two or three pounds if it's something new, or a hardback. If there are any V.F. Andrews, mark them up a bit – there's a huge market because he's local. Other than that, just do what you think, it doesn't really matter. Or ask me if you want to. And anything very old or damaged, keep it aside and we send it to the recycling.'

'Righty ho,' Julia said, in a cheery can-do sort of voice. She didn't exactly relish the prospect of going through all the same items again, but she was a volunteer, which did rather mean doing what needed doing.

'Good, I'll go through the odds and ends, price those, and see if there's anything nice for the window display. Diane can help the customers.'

Of which there were currently none, Julia didn't say. She just picked up a pile of books out of a box and got to work. It was quick and painless if you didn't stress over whether each one was a fifty pence book or a one pound book. She finished a box of novels in no time and picked a few of the newer, better ones for the display on the top of the bookshelf near the door. She hoped this didn't count as stepping on Wilma's toes.

A group of youngsters came in and went through a rack of second-hand coats and jackets. Clothes that would have looked old-fashioned on Julia, at sixty, somehow looked funky on them. Was that a word still? Funky? Or was it 'cool'? Or something else altogether? She missed having Jess around to keep her up to date with these things. At least her own daughter was still alive, and just far away, unlike poor Maeve's.

Julia turned her attention to the box of non-fiction books. As she worked through them, she noticed a pattern in the books that Maeve had owned. A couple on grief – including the classics by Elisabeth Kübler-Ross – and others on family, relationships and loss. Julia picked up one titled: *Rules of Distance: Mending Fractured Families*. She read the back cover: '*Dr Fredericks offers empathetic advice to help you move away from blame towards understanding and healing, and even resolution...'*

Maeve had definitely been looking for answers, or help, or comfort, as far as her family was concerned. As Julia flicked through the pages, something fell out. A folded piece of paper in a rather childish handwriting. Julia opened the envelope and saw the words: *Dear Mum*. Slipping it out further, she read the first sentence.

Julia knew what she had to do. She slid the letter into her bag as she reached for her phone.

Hayley arrived at Julia's house at 3 p.m. on the dot, as arranged. As a punctual person herself, Julia appreciated punctuality in others. Especially when there was a mystery to be solved.

The detective had hardly fought off Jake's effusive welcome and sat down before Julia pushed the letter into her hand. She waited impatiently while the younger woman read the sparse sentences. And then read them again, out loud:

Dear Mum,

I'm going to London.

I know you think I'm crazy or a terrible person, but I have to follow my heart.

I can't stay here, obviously, and I don't want to go back to uni.

I'll get a job and see what happens. Please don't try to contact me for a while. I need space.

I'm sorry we fought.

Love you,

Sammy

'What do you think?' Julia asked.

'Well, it looks like Samantha did go to London like everyone thought,' said Hayley, with a frown.

'Except that she's been dead under the shed all this time. So when did she send this?' Julia looked at it again. She looked up at Hayley. 'It makes no sense, does it?'

'We can't date the body precisely, and the letter isn't dated. One possibility is that she wrote the letter, left it for Maeve, and was killed before she left for London. Or she was killed sometime later, on another trip home.'

'And poor Maeve never realised, thinking she was in London?'

'It's a theory,' said Hayley non-committally.

'I must say, I had Maeve as Suspect Number One for Samantha's murder,' said Julia.

'I had no idea you were making a list,' Hayley said, with a hint of humour in her tone. 'I would have thought that was our job.'

'I'm not, it's just that the neighbours heard arguing around that time, a lot of conflict, which was unusual...'

'And you know this how?'

'I was helping Jane and her daughter, Hannah, pack up Maeve's flat and they mentioned it.'

'Oh, well go on. What else did they say?'

'That when Samantha went off to uni, and came back for visits, there was conflict. Possibly about a man, a boyfriend, although it seemed to be more a theory than hard evidence.'

Hayley thought for a moment, and seemed to make a decision. 'Look, Julia, I'm going to tell you something, but this is confidential information from a police investigation. I need you to promise me that you won't tell anyone what I tell you.'

'Of course. Promise. Believe me, in my line of work I learnt to keep my mouth shut.'

'Maeve filed a missing persons report on her daughter a few

months after she supposedly left for London. It's on file. No progress. It seems the police didn't take it very seriously. Sammy was an adult, and she'd clearly gone of her own accord – Maeve would have told them she'd left a letter. But she was worried about her, and filed the report.'

Julia took a sharp intake of breath. This was big news. Game-changing news.

'So that means that Maeve didn't kill Samantha,' she said. 'She wouldn't have drawn attention if she had.'

'I agree. Although it doesn't explain the stories she made up about where the girl was.'

Julia thought about the broken families she'd seen over the years. 'Maeve must have been very hurt by her disappearance. And ashamed. What kind of mother is just cut off like that by her only daughter? She might have started with a few small fibs – Sammy's doing well, too busy to come and visit right now, but I'll see her soon, that sort of thing. Just to avoid the gossip.'

'Gossip? In this village? Surely not!' Hayley said in mock astonishment. And then, more seriously, 'What you say makes sense, though, Julia.'

'After all, she expected Samantha to come back before long. And once she'd started with a bit of a fantasy life, it would be hard to admit otherwise. Hard and humiliating. Poor Maeve.'

'Poor Maeve.'

'Poor *dead* Maeve,' said Julia.

'That's the next question, isn't it? How does Maeve's death connect with Samantha's?' Hayley said.

Julia nodded. 'It's too much of a coincidence – we find Samantha's body and a week later, her mother dies in mysterious circumstances. There must be a connection. Which means that the killer is almost certainly someone in the village.'

24

The two women sat in silence for a moment, considering the implications of that thought. Someone in Berrywick was a murderer. But who?

Julia ran through all the pleasant, wholesome folk she'd met in her short time in the village, and tried on the thought that each one was a killer.

Flo, the waitress? Pippa, the dog walker? Dr Sean '007' O'Connor? Demented Auntie Edna?She stopped right there: it was inconceivable. Each more unlikely than the next.

'Let's go back,' said Hayley. 'Instead of thinking about who killed Maeve, let's think about why. Why, just days after the discovery of the first body, would someone kill Maeve?'

'Revenge,' said Julia, after thinking for a moment. 'When Samantha turned up dead, someone reckoned that Maeve must have killed her, and they killed Maeve in return.'

Hayley flipped open her notebook and checked something, shaking her head.

'Except that Samantha hadn't been identified when Maeve was killed. It was only because of the false nails that we worked it out at all, and you only had your hair done after Maeve died.'

'True. Gosh, this detective business is hard.'

'Yup.'

Julia wasn't giving up. 'Okay, so here's another possible reason – Maeve was killed to stop the police from identifying the body as Samantha. Think about it. Mystery Person kills Samantha. Everyone, including Maeve, thinks Sam is in London or Sydney. Only Maeve also knows that she hasn't heard from her daughter in twenty years. No one else knows that she hasn't been in touch, no one *except* the person who killed Samantha. Once that body turns up, it's only a matter of time before the age and sex is identified, and Maeve will start to wonder if maybe it's Sam, and goes to the police and says, "I was lying about the visits, my daughter disappeared years ago, I think this might be her..."'

'Right, and we do DNA testing or dental records and find out it's Samantha...' Hayley nodded slowly. 'And Mystery Person knows that once we know it's Samantha, we're a whole lot closer to finding him or her.'

They sat for a moment with their own thoughts.

'If the same person killed both women, it means Doug Harrison, the shed builder, wasn't Samantha's killer,' Hayley said. 'Not that I thought him a good suspect. Farmer checked it out, there seemed to be no connection between them.'

Jake had had more than enough of this chatting. It was time for his afternoon walk, and then his supper. In short, the highlight of his day. He nuzzled his muzzle under Julia's hand and, when she ignored him, flopped down on her feet with a dramatic sigh and a pleading roll of his brown eyes.

Hayley could take a hint.

'I'll be off. Let's think about it. Give me a ring if you come up with anything useful,' said Hayley. 'And thanks for the letter.'

She flapped the folded sheet of paper against her thigh as

she stood up, and then put it into her bag. 'I'll keep it for evidence, if you don't mind.'

'Of course,' said Julia. 'I'll get Jake's lead and we can walk out together.'

Julia had had a long and busy day, but she knew by now that an afternoon walk with Jake invigorated rather than exhausted her. And she was right. They took one of their preferred routes, along the river towards the little playground, enjoying the slight chill in the air.

'There's naughty dog!' came Sebastian's delighted cry. 'Hello, naughty dog.'

Nicky and a man that Julia presumed must be her husband followed the little chap as he rushed towards Jake, burying his face in the soft fur. Julia slipped Jake off the leash so that he could play with the boy.

'Goodness, but doesn't he love that dog, even after the ice cream and all? You wouldn't think, but there you go, that's children for you, isn't it?' said Nicky, by way of greeting. Julia realised what talking to Nicky reminded her of – a waterfall. That rushing feeling as the freezing water cascaded over your head, overwhelming your senses and rendering you curiously numb.

'Hello, Nicky.'

'You know my hubby, Kev? Finished work early, so here he is in the park with us, wouldn't you know.'

'We haven't met, but you mentioned him. Hello, Kevin, nice to meet you.'

Kevin barely had time to insert a polite, 'Hiya,' before Nicky resumed her flow.

'Of course, yes, I remember now, I was telling you about the village and my Kev. Well goodness me, speaking of, isn't that the news about poor Samantha? And there we were all those years thinking she was off in London and Australia, doing all sorts of things, with a family and all, isn't that so, Kev? And instead she's been lying here dead. No family. No fancy career. Cut down in her prime, wasn't she, Kev? Poor thing.' She added the last as an afterthought, perhaps noticing that her delivery had been rather too eager. She paused for a nanosecond, to illustrate her feelings of loss and sympathy, but quickly resumed.

'Remember, Kev? I told you I met the lady who had the body under her shed? And then she found another body! I don't know how you sleep.' She shuddered.

'I'm sorry about Samantha,' said Julia, smiling kindly at Kevin. 'I know she was a friend of yours. It must be horrible.'

'Thanks,' he said glumly. 'School friends. It's a sad thing. A very sad thing.'

'Long time ago though, wasn't it?' said Nicky, rather dismissively. 'He's been right thrown by it, though, our Kev. Who'd have thought she was under the shed? First girlfriend, can you believe? Can't say they were well-matched, even so. She always was rather, well... Anyhow, gave him the boot when school finished. Her loss, my gain. Isn't that right, Kev? Wouldn't have Sebastian now, would we? Not that I'm glad she... you know...'

'Now, Nicky, that's enough,' Kev said calmly. 'The woman's dead, and her mother besides.'

'Oh now, I wish her no ill, poor thing,' said Nicky in a placating tone, although Julia would have said that the time for wishing Samantha ill or not had long passed. 'She wasn't the angel you make out, Kev. She came asking to borrow money at the end, remember? So's she could go off wherever it was... That wasn't exactly nice, was it? That was the last time you saw her, now I think about it. Wouldn't that be right? She certainly lacked tact, that's the truth.'

'Nicky!' Kev said, almost shouting. 'Would you stop that? It's not right to speak of the dead like that.'

Jake, who didn't like loud voices, came running over to sit at Julia's feet. If there was to be any trouble, he'd rather she be close by. The child followed, and started wailing. 'Daddy shouting... Want the doggy.'

He hurled himself onto Jake, who wriggled out of his grasp and ran around them in a large circle, Julia shouting and lunging at him as he passed her.

Sebastian fell to the ground in a full-on tantrum. It was quite astonishing, actually, like a cartoon of a tantrum, little heels drumming on the ground, fists clenched, tears and snot spewing, and a bellow... Good Lord... A bellow that would wake the dead. Which would be handy, come to think of it, given the circumstances.

Nicky scooped up the writhing child and held him tightly to her chest.

'I'll see you at home,' she said coldly to Kevin, and stomped off. Julia could see bits of Sebastian emerging from her grasp – a foot, a hand, the top of his curly head – as they set off across the park.

As the yelling faded from earshot, Kevin gave a deep sigh – of despair or relief, Julia didn't know – and sat down on the bench. Jake, now safely returned to the leash, echoed with a sigh of his own and lay down. It was beautifully quiet and peaceful without the wailing and the incessant talking.

'Sorry about that,' Kevin said, reaching into his pocket.

'Don't mention it,' said Julia. 'Kids...'

'I meant Nicky,' he said, pulling out a crumpled pack of Camel. 'She was always funny about Samantha. Jealous, I suppose.'

'Well, those early romances can be very powerful.'

'True, right?' said Kevin, turning towards her. 'And Samantha. She was great. I mean, just, y'know, really pretty and nice. Had a spark.'

Julia nodded, gazing ahead of her, allowing him the space to speak – something she suspected he didn't often have, with

Nicky's endless yammering. He lit a cigarette, politely blowing the smoke away from her.

'And clever, too,' he continued. 'So clever. Don't know what she was doing with me. Never did. Solid C's all the way through school, and her being this straight-A student. English prize every year. She could write. And maths. I mean, who's good at maths? But Sammy was.'

His voice was tinged with pride, after all this time. Julia could see why Nicky would be irritated. She gave an encouraging 'hmmm'.

'Out of my league, she was. Everyone could see it but her. That's why Nicky gets a bit... funny about her.'

'Well, Samantha obviously saw something in you,' Julia said kindly. 'When did you break up?'

'After school. She was going off to uni, and we decided to make a clean break of it. Well, she decided really. I didn't have much say,' he said sadly. 'She didn't even come and see me when she was home for the weekend. Said she wanted to give us both a chance to get over it. But I think...'

He hesitated, inhaling deeply and then exhaling a big cloud of smoke.

'I think she'd met someone. I ran into her once when she was home and I asked her, but she wouldn't talk about it, just said it was early days, a bit complicated and it wouldn't go anywhere. I wondered if it was someone, y'know, inappropriate. Like a lecturer at the uni or something. Or even someone who was, like, maybe with someone else, or married? Although I'd be surprised about that. But it wasn't like her to be so cagey. She wasn't one to spare a fellow's feelings. Nicky has that part right.'

I have to follow my heart... thought Julia, remembering the letter.

'You're very easy to talk to,' said Kevin. 'I don't have many people to talk to. 'Specially not about Sam.'

'I like to listen. So what happened? With the money? The last time you saw her?' Julia said, keeping her tone casual.

Kevin took another desperate pull of his smoke and answered, 'Funny thing. She came round one afternoon. Hadn't seen her in a while and she arrived on the doorstep, crying. She'd had a big fight with her mum. Wouldn't go into it. Just that Maeve didn't understand, she was so hard on her.'

'Did they get on, usually?'

'Yeah, think so. They was close. But, y'know, mums and daughters. Anyway, Sam was really upset, said she couldn't stay there after what was said. Must have been bad, to see the state of her. Anyway, Sammy said she needed to get away for a bit, she wanted to catch the train to London, and could she borrow a hundred pounds. I was working by then, down at the off-licence, saving up, so I suppose she figured I was good for a hundred. But I didn't have it on me. Nothing in my wallet, and the bank was closed. I even checked the money tin my parents kept for emergencies, but there wasn't more than a few pounds in it. I offered her to stay the night and I'd get it in the morning. She said she couldn't wait.'

'Why, do you think?'

'I dunno. Said she couldn't stay in the village another day. Couldn't face it. Had to get out right away.' There were tears in his eyes when he looked up at her. 'Anyway, she said she'd find the money, whatever it took. Said goodbye, said she'd be in touch, and that was the last time I saw her.'

He dropped the end of the cigarette and ground it into the grass with the toe of his boot. Julia wondered if, perhaps, that was the last time anyone saw Samantha – anyone other than her killer, of course.

25

Julia did not sleep well on Wednesday night. She kept going over the conversations of the day – with Hayley and Nicky and Kevin, trying to untangle the threads, and then weave them into a clearer picture of what had happened, and how Samantha had wound up under Julia's shed instead of safely in London, where she had been headed.

Julia tossed and turned until Jake abandoned the bed. With much huffing, he jumped down, finally settling himself on the mat next to the bed with a deep reproachful sigh. At about 4 a.m., Julia also gave up trying to sleep, and went to the kitchen to make tea and think. She could almost hear Hayley telling her that she should leave this to the police and not worry, but Hayley wasn't the one with a body under her shed. Julia would bet her bottom dollar that Hayley was still fast asleep somewhere, unbothered by any of this.

The truth was that the pieces of information she played over in her head, didn't quite gel. Kev had talked about his breakup with Samantha as if it was something that he had accepted as inevitable. He had spoken in a matter-of-fact way of her request to borrow money, but maybe at the time he'd been less phlegmatic about having an ex-girlfriend demand his hard-earned cash. Had Kevin mellowed with the passage of time, or was he presenting a calm, unemotional persona so as not to draw attention to himself as a murder suspect?

As for Nicky, well, her input into any conversation inevitably made it murkier rather than clearer. It was just so hard, the way Nicky threw information all over the place every time she opened her mouth, to separate out what she was actually saying, to sift out what was relevant and to follow any thread.

Julia sipped her tea, remembering an earlier headache-inducing conversation with Nicky. The day after Julia had found Maeve's body, that had been, and there Nicky had been carrying on about the postman being late the day before and Kev being at work early and unrelated nonsense like that. Like Julia had had time for that sort of chit-chat, Maeve not even chilled in the morgue.

Julia took another sip of tea, trying to shake off the annoyance, and then choked and spluttered, as she realised exactly where her thoughts had led her. At the noise, Jake poked his head around the door, as if to ask if everything was okay.

'I'm fine, Jakey,' said Julia, 'but I think I've just put two and two together.'

A few hours later, when Johnny Blunt arrived to get started on the chicken coop, she realised that she had an audience on whom to test her theory. She'd picked up her phone to call Hayley at least three times, but each time had chickened out. Hayley was friendly enough and had welcomed Julia sharing her discoveries, but Julia didn't want to overstep that boundary. She was only too aware that Hayley regarded Julia's efforts with a sceptical amusement, and was only just starting to trust her intuition. The last thing she wanted was to go to her with another baseless idea.

While Johnny did seem a little surprised when Julia hustled him inside and insisted that he definitely needed a cup of tea before he even thought of hammering a single nail, he didn't object. 'I never say no to tea,' he said. He wasn't shouting today, which meant that his hearing aid must be nestled in there beneath the grey curls and the blue cap. 'God did a good job the day he invented PG Tips.' Julia decided not to get involved in a debate about the origin of teabags, and settled for making Johnny and herself a good strong cup.

'This way we can wait for Brendan, before we start,' said Johnny, pleased. 'Now, what's on your mind, lass?'

Lass? Julia decided to let that pass too.

'How do you know something's on my mind?' she asked.

'You're just like my Gloria when you're worried, and my Gloria was often worried,' said Johnny. 'Now you tell me what's bothering you, and I'm sure I can help you sort it all out, good as new.'

But when Julia finished setting out her story, Johnny looked less sure of himself.

'You're sure that the morning that Maeve died was the same morning that Nicky said Kev was early to work?' he asked.

'Absolutely,' said Julia. 'And then she told me how Samantha asked him for money, and how tactless that was. What if he got angry, so angry that he killed her? You hear about things like that all the time.'

'That you do. Young men with tempers. God knows, I've seen enough of that in my lifetime.' Johnny paused for a moment, a faraway look in his eyes. Then he said, 'But Kevin, I don't know...'

He looked sad, and old, and a little shaken. Julia felt sorry for him. It must be awful to imagine that someone you'd known their whole life might be a murderer.

'Well, it's just a theory of course. But he does seem the most likely suspect – the love interest, Sam's rejection. He might have killed Sam in a crime of passion as a young man. And then when the body was discovered, he killed Maeve to avoid it being identified as Samantha's. He would have known that if Sam was identified, the ex-boyfriend would be the first in line for a visit from the detectives. He was protecting himself.'

More tutting and head shaking from Johnny. 'Kevin's a good chap... He works hard there at the hotel; he could have been on early shift,' he said uncertainly. 'But I don't know... I suppose you never know people...'

'So should I go to the police with my idea?' asked Julia, pushing her tea away. She felt like she'd been drinking the stuff for hours, and was starting to go off the taste.

Johnny crossed his arms and looked up at the ceiling, as if for confirmation, and then gave a decisive nod.

'Yes, of course. That's the thing to do. Leave it to the authorities.'

Their discussion was cut short by Jake's excited barking.

'Hello, Grandpa, hello, Mrs Bird.' Brendan greeted the excitable Jake with a good scritching of the ears, setting off a mad whirring of his tail. Johnny smiled weakly at the boy.

'Oh hello, Brendan, come in. Tea before you get to work?'

'Just had a cup, thank you. I'll get started unloading the wood and such shall I, Grandpa?'

'You get started unloading the wood,' said Johnny bossily, as if Brendan hadn't just said exactly that. He seemed to have rallied after the conversation about Kevin.

'Right ho, Grandpa,' said the boy, giving Julia a little smile. He really was the sweetest chap. 'You got your ears in, I see.'

'That I have. Not that it's an invitation to be yammering at me all day, mind. I want to be able to hear Mrs Bird so we can decide about the chicken coop. Now you run along, I'll be out in a minute, just finishing up my cuppa here with Mrs Bird.'

Johnny downed his tea before joining Brendan in the garden.

Julia agreed with him about Kevin. He did seem like a decent chap. She didn't want to make the young man the subject of a police investigation based on hearsay and twenty-year-old anger. But on the other hand, her theory was compelling. It made sense.

It came to her that she might investigate his whereabouts on the morning of Maeve's death. If he had been at work as he'd said, then he was off the hook for the murder.

Julia asked Johnny and Brendan to keep an eye on Jake, who seemed delighted with the company. She put on some lipstick and brushed her hair – the hotel where Kevin worked was considerably posher than her kitchen table, and required a bit more effort on the grooming front.

'Popping out,' she said, waving to the men. 'I've got an errand to run. Won't be long.'

'Oh aye, all right then,' said Johnny, giving her a knowing nod and a wink, and wiggling his audacious eyebrows. The sequence made him look like he was having some sort of seizure. She didn't tell him that she was going to the hotel, rather than the police.

Julia drove her small Peugeot to the hotel, feeling pleased to be back behind the wheel. Since arriving in Berrywick, she'd walked to most places, and felt like she'd neglected her little car. It had had a lot more outings when Julia had had a job and a life in London. 'Don't worry,' she found herself saying to the car, as they careened down the narrow roads of the village, 'when things calm down, we'll go exploring.' First talking to the dog, and now to the car. At this rate they'd have to lock her up by the end of the month, she thought with a laugh.

The Swan was at the far end of the village, its entrance on the main road, and its garden backing onto the river. It was an ivy-covered picture postcard of a place, popular with tourists, but with a pleasant restaurant that locals frequented for breakfast meetings and special occasion suppers. Julia herself had never been – the name suggested that it was not a Jake-friendly zone.

The drive gave her time to consider how she would find out whether Kevin was on early shift a week ago. Nothing came to her, and in the absence of an idea, she parked, walked into the hotel restaurant, and asked for a table on the terrace. With a quick glance at a large diary set on a small table, the woman at the front told Julia to make herself at home at any of the open tables on the terrace. 'Nothing booked,' she said with a smile. Julia walked through the restaurant and out the glass doors, chose a table, and settled down to look at the rather lovely view of the river, the grassy bank and the eponymous swans.

A waitress, dressed in an over-the-top black and white uniform clearly designed to please the tourists, brought her a menu and Julia ordered a coffee and a Chelsea bun. The waitress was back in a moment. The coffee smelled delicious and the Chelsea bun was the size of Julia's head.

'Gosh, that'll keep me going!' Julia said, hoping to start up a chat that might lead somewhere. Although *where*, she wasn't quite sure.

'Famous for our bakery,' said the waitress, cheerfully. 'No one leaves here hungry, I'll tell you that much.'

'It's my first time here,' said Julia. 'I moved to Berrywick quite recently, and I've been meaning to come. It's lovely. Tell me, what time do you open?'

'Seven, on the dot,' the waitress grinned. 'For the hotel guests.'

'That's early. You must have to get here at the crack of dawn!'

'The chefs and kitchen staff do, but the wait staff scoot in ten minutes before opening. Unless of course there's something special on to set up. Then a team might have to get in extra early. We pride ourselves on our customer service, I can tell you that.'

'What sort of special functions do you host here?' Julia sipped her coffee, relieved to be released from the endless round of tea she seemed to have slipped into at home.

'There might be a conference that wants to start early. Or a wedding party. Then they write a note in the book, and best you check that every day, I tell you, in case they've changed your shift for the next day. Learnt that the hard way, I can tell you that much.'

When the waitress talked about the book, she indicated inside with her head. Julia suspected that the book that the waitress was referring to was the same one that the lady at the front had checked when Julia arrived. She tried hard to think of a way that she could ask if one of these special events had happened last Wednesday, but she just couldn't come up with anything that didn't sound insane in its specificity. 'Where was your colleague Kevin last Wednesday when a woman was murdered?' just wasn't the sort of thing that you could slip into a conversation with ease, as it turned out.

'Give me a wave if you need anything more,' said the waitress. 'But otherwise, you can pay at the front. Cash or card, but be patient if you need change. They never fill up the kitty properly, and she'll have to go and find it.'

Julia smiled. 'Thanks for the warning,' she said. 'I only have cash. But it's fine, I'm a patient woman.' She was able to enjoy the rest of her coffee and Chelsea bun, safe in the knowledge that she had at least a bit of a plan. She'd pay with the fifty-pound note that she always kept stashed in her bag for emergencies, and they'd have to go to find change. In that time, she could quickly leaf back through the famous book, and see if anyone was on duty early the day that Maeve died. Really, she thought, this detectiving business wasn't nearly as hard as Hayley made out. Plus Hayley had the power to just stroll in and demand information.

Indeed, the plan went just as intended. Julia apologetically proffered the fifty quid and the lady at the desk took it with a deep sigh.

'I'll have to find change,' she said. 'Are you sure you don't have anything smaller?'

'So sorry,' said Julia. 'I usually do. I don't know how I wound up with just this. But there we are. And my bank card expired, too.'

The lady sighed again. 'I'll go and see what they've got in the office,' she said, and then muttered, 'Tourists,' under her breath as she walked off, but Julia was too focused on the task before her to take offence. Glancing around, she checked that no one was watching her. The dining room was empty but for one old man nursing a hot drink and reading the newspaper. Most people were on the terrace, thanks to the lovely sunny weather that didn't seem to be ending this year, and as a result, the waitresses were all outside too.

Julia slipped behind the small table, and opened the book, leaving back to the previous Wednesday. There it was. In red.

HIGH-TEK SALES CONFERENCE. 40 PAX. 8 A.M. START. 6 A.M. SET UP. TEAM LEAD: KEVIN. TEAM: AMY, JANINE, TALLULAH.

'Bingo,' said Julia, under her breath, and looked up.

Straight into Kevin's eyes.

'Something I can help you with, Mrs Bird?' he asked, his voice cold, as he took in the page that she was looking at.

26

'Kevin!' she said, in an Oscar-worthy impression of surprise. 'I'm just waiting for my change. What are you doing here?'

'I work here. Didn't you know?'

'I didn't. I don't think we talked about your work. What a coincidence. Lovely place, isn't it? I had the idea to pop in and give it a try. Trying out all the local spots. Don't tell Flo down at the Buttered Scone, but I think your coffee's a cut above theirs.'

Kevin smiled, bearing out Julia's long-held belief that a touch of flattery never went amiss, and could distract a person from all sorts of things. He leaned in and said confidentially, 'Our own special blend. Italian. We get it direct from the importers. Organic, fair trade, hand-picked and roasted. You won't get better in Berrywick, I promise you.'

'Well, I did enjoy it. The bun too. I'll certainly be back. Ah, here comes my change!'

She smiled at the woman bustling huffily in from her trip to the office with a fist full of notes and coins. 'Thanks so much. Sorry for the inconvenience. No small notes,' she explained to Kevin. 'Always one of those customers, hey?'

'That's what we're here for, isn't that so, Brenda?'

'No trouble at all,' said the desk lady, who had hitherto behaved as if she had been asked to donate a kidney. 'Here you go.' She gave Julia a big smile along with the money.

Kevin walked Julia out to her car. 'Goodbye, then. Will you be at the memorial? It's tomorrow at three.'

'Yes, I'll be there.'

'You and the whole of Berrywick,' muttered Kevin, bitterly. 'Couldn't keep them away with a stick.'

'There's a lot of local interest, I'm sure. Two murders. And a mystery,' said Julia mildly. 'And of course Samantha and Maeve were two long-time village residents, well-known and well-liked. People will want to pay their respects.'

'I suppose.' He looked away into the mid distance, his jaw tight. He swallowed.

'I'm sorry for your loss, Kevin. It's very hard, even twenty years later, to lose someone you loved. And in such a horrible way.'

When he looked at her, his eyes were misty. 'Yeah. Yeah it is. Hard.'

She laid a consoling hand on his arm.

'I can't stop thinking about it,' he said. 'How she died, who could have killed her. If I ever find him, I swear...' As he spoke, his eyes narrowed and his fists clenched.

'Now, Kevin, the police are on it. Justice will take its course,' Julia said. 'You just take care of yourself now, see?'

'Yeah,' he said, opening the car door for her. 'I'll see you tomorrow, Mrs Bird.'

He closed the door firmly behind her.

When Julia got home, Johnny and Brendan had erected the four poles that would form the corners of the frame of the chicken coop and were starting to hammer in the planks that were piled nearby. The sight of it filled her heart with a little flutter of joy.

Julia might not have entirely succeeded as a country lady – she kept forgetting to deadhead the roses as instructed by Christopher, her scones were misshapen, and the jam-making fiasco was still fresh in her mind – but she was well on her way to having hens and her own fresh eggs. And she had a dog, she reminded herself, looking lovingly at Jake, who was lying on his back and wrestling a stick.

'Looks good. I'll get you some tea, shall I?'

She brought out a tray of tea and biscuits – she had learnt her lesson and stocked up in advance of their arrival.

'How did the mission go? What did the police say?' asked Johnny, who clearly watched too many spy movies.

Julia blushed slightly, caught out on her lie of omission. 'I didn't go to the police, I went to check on Kevin's alibi for Maeve's murder. Kevin was at work early on Wednesday as Nicky said. He got there at 6 a.m. for a function, and worked his usual shift, so he was not down at the lake knocking Maeve on the head and drowning her.'

'Pleased to hear it. I wouldn't like to think that young Kevin was a murderer.'

'Well, he might be ruled out for Maeve's murder, but he's still a possible suspect in Samantha's. Although somehow, I doubt it. My impression is that he really loved her, and not in some horrible, jealous way that would lead him to kill her.'

'Can't say I disagree,' said Johnny, nodding sagely, for all the world as if he were an actual police detective. 'He doesn't seem the type. Never been anything other than a good chap. Believe you me, if he was the sort to murder a person, he'd have killed that yammering Nicky just for some peace and quiet. No, if you ask me, Kevin's not a violent man.'

'Noted. But I'm afraid when it comes to the murder of young women, the boyfriend or the ex-boyfriend are the culprits, most of the time.'

'Sad world. I'll be getting back to work, then. Should have

those walls up by the end of the day. And we'll finish it off tomorrow.'

'That's wonderful! I'll let Farmer Chuck know I'll be along to fetch the hens in a day or two.'

'Now don't get carried away, Miss Impatient. Things have got to dry and there's a fence to put up. Can't trust that little bugger...' He nodded in Jake's direction. 'And even if we could, there's the foxes to think of.'

'Right, and the hens will need some bedding, I suppose.'

'Oh aye, a few pillows and a nice blanket.' He laughed heartily at his joke.

'I'll be sure to get pure cotton,' she said, playing along. 'Only the best for my girls. Will they be needing a bedside lamp?'

He gave a laugh that turned into a cough and made his eyes water. 'Oh, you city people, you'll be the end of me. Just some nice hay will do it. But your Farmer Chuck will sort you out with that, and some feed, too.'

Johnny went off chuckling, and Julia fetched her secateurs. She would deadhead the roses as instructed by Christopher. He'd even shown her how to do it, cutting above a joint at an angle. It was a satisfying job, once she got going. The smell of the blooms on a warm afternoon was overwhelming – rich and sweet. The buzzing of the bees and the snip-snip of her secateurs provided a pleasing soundtrack to her thoughts. The growing pile of dead flowers on the lawn at her feet was gratifying. The rose bushes looked healthy and well-cared for without the stragglers, the new buds waiting to burst into their velvety selves. Out with the old, in with the new. Improved vigour and fresh growth and so on. Like her life, really.

She couldn't keep Samantha out of her mind. It was true, what she'd said about the boyfriends and the exes. What did she know about Sam's post-Kevin relationships? Only what Kevin had said – that he'd thought she was seeing someone, and that she was secretive about it. She had said it was complicated.

What did that mean, Julia wondered. Had the guy been seeing someone else? Had he been married? Or her tutor?

A thorn dug deep into her thumb, driving other thoughts out of her mind.

'Blast!' she said, pulling her thumb off the rose bush and sucking it. 'Stings like heck.'

Jake, who had come over at her exclamation, wagged his tail happily at her.

'Enough gardening for today, Jake. Come on, I'll take you for a walk. But before I do, I need to phone Hayley.'

27

After a week of bright and warm days, the weather turned, as if to provide a suitably dramatic backdrop for the double memorial. Heavy clouds moved in across the fields and hung low above the gravestones, crosses and statues of angels. The little grey stone church where the service had been held seemed to skulk in the gloom, its stained-glass windows giving a soft glow of colour on the grey day. A light breeze rustled the branches of the dark yew trees and caused the mourners to pull their coats around them with a shiver.

Half the village had turned up, much as Kevin had predicted. He was with Nicky and a group of men and women in their late thirties, who Julia assumed were Samantha's friends from school. Julia had noted them greet each other enthusiastically when they arrived at the church, as if they hadn't seen each other for a while, then remember the solemn occasion and quieten down to whispers, falling silent as the priest got up to give her sermon. The poor woman had stumbled awkwardly through euphemisms like, 'tragic circumstances' and 'sadly taken', and moved on to a rather touching reflection on the mother and daughter being reunited in heaven. Soft-hearted

Tabitha sniffed into a hanky and whispered, 'Poor dears. After all those years...' Julia put an arm around her shoulders and gave her a squeeze.

Julia saw pretty much everyone she knew in Berrywick milling about, waiting to go into the church. The whole book club was there. Jane, Maeve's neighbour, wiped her eyes and gave her nose a good blow. Diane and Wilma were there together, having shut up the shop for the afternoon. Julia presumed they'd forgiven the Toby jug incident. Sean O'Connor caught Julia's eye and gave her a nod and a quick smile. Pippa was there, looking strangely unfinished without a brace of dogs. Flo from the Buttered Scone seemed similarly out of place without a cloth or a tray in hand. She did have her daughter, Fiona, with her, though – or Julia assumed it was her daughter; she was the spitting image of her mum, a kind, round face with surprised eyebrows and a button nose. Jess looked about as dissimilar to Julia as it was possible for a daughter to be – taller, darker and bigger boned than her mother, more like her father's family. Their personalities were even more different than their appearances. Julia wished, momentarily, for a like-minded, familiar sort of daughter with whom she could have an easy affinity. Much as she loved Jess, she always seemed to be making an effort with her, and suspected that Jess felt the same. Julia put that out of her mind.

There were a few faces she didn't recognise, but no one who seemed to be family, or even a very close friend. In fact, with the exception of Jane, Kevin and a few of the younger school friends, the funeral was a strangely emotionless affair. Everyone was shocked by the murders, but no one seemed to be mourning Maeve or Samantha deeply and specifically. Sad, Maeve keeping herself to herself all those years, waiting for a sign of her daughter, and spinning a fantasy life for the girl.

In the graveyard, Julia saw where Maeve and Samantha would lie, side-by-side, once the bodies had been released for burial. Julia noticed the older graves, some with fresh or wilting cut flowers, others worn by the weather and covered in years of moss. It was oddly comforting to know that although every one of the graves had started with a fresh and painful loss, they had weathered into a quiet, peaceful history.

The mourners started to move into the church. Julia followed and took a place near the back. A tall man came in and stood at the back of the church. Julia had seen him before. She recognised his lanky build and distinguished air, as well as his red hair greying at the temples, but she couldn't place him. Probably, she had passed him on one of her many walks on the roads and paths of Berrywick. As Julia looked at him, wondering where she knew him from, a woman arrived late and joined him. Julia recognised her too, and she remembered where from – she had come into the charity shop on Julia's first day. She was the woman who had bought a skirt and put it on immediately after an accident with a water bottle.

The water bottle woman did not look happy. She said a few terse words to the man under her breath. He put his hand on her forearm as if to calm her, but she pushed it away angrily with a few more whispered words. The two of them sat down, not speaking. Julia wondered what that was all about. It had the look of some marital disagreement, a husband and wife in a domestic spat. Perhaps he'd forgotten to pay the electricity, or take the leg of lamb out of the oven. Julia was not convinced that a church was the place for this type of disagreement.

Outside, gravediggers were at work. Julia wasn't sure if this was in preparation for the eventual burial, or if some other poor village soul was going to their final rest. The sounds of their spades rode the breeze into the church, punctuated by the occasional grunt of exertion. Julia wondered about the first time Samantha had been buried, tossed under a shed and covered with a shallow layer of soil and rocks. Even such a perfunctory burial would have taken some time, especially for a man working alone.

There was some awkward milling about outside the church after the service. Tabitha wandered off to speak to some people that Julia did not know. Sean came over to greet her. Julia was pleased to see him. They were joined, after all, in the awful discovery of Maeve's body.

'Well, that's that,' he said, which seemed about right. The usual platitudes, 'Lovely service,' or, 'She lived a good life,' or even, 'She will be missed,' didn't seem appropriate under the circumstances.

Julia nodded.

'I'm not sure if this is the time...' Sean cleared his throat. 'But I was wondering if you might like to, um, go somewhere with me. And Jake, of course. I mean. I was thinking of a walk along the canal path. We can walk as far as Edgely, have lunch at the canalside pub, and take a boat back. I've always wanted to do it and I thought...'

'I'd love that, thank you.' Julia hoped she sounded calm, but inside she was shaking. It had been a good long while since a man – let alone a good looking one – had asked her out. She hoped Sean couldn't tell how unexpected it was. 'Sunday?'

'Sunday is good.'

'It's a date then.' He hesitated and blushed, and then said firmly, 'Yes, it's a date.'

'Sunday, then.'

'Good.'

And he turned heel and left.

Julia took a deep breath. A memorial and being asked on a date all in one afternoon was certainly a lot for a person to chew over. She thought she'd get going too, and be home before Johnny and Brendan left. She still didn't quite understand why Johnny hadn't wanted to come to the memorial, but he'd muttered something about wet cement and cross bars, and really, she hadn't wanted to ask anything more.

Walking out of the small churchyard, Julia passed Flo and her daughter, who were heading towards the tall redhead with the disgruntled wife.

'Hello, sir,' the daughter said to the redhead. 'How are you doing, sir?'

'Very well thank you, Fiona. Sad times, though. And please, you don't need to call me sir.'

'Habit, sir. School. Sorry, sir, I mean, Mr Callum,' she said, blushing.

'Or Patrick,' he said.

'Well now, I don't know if I could!' She laughed. 'And you being the head now, and all.'

'I'm going,' Patrick's wife cut in abruptly. 'I'll see you at home.'

'I'll be right behind you, Tessa,' he said, seemingly unperturbed by her manner.

If Patrick Callum had taught at the school where Samantha had been such an outstanding student, then he might have some useful insights. Julia edged closer.

28

'I don't think we've met,' Julia said, offering him a hand. Fiona and Flo had dispersed, following Tessa out of the churchyard gate, leaving Patrick and Julia, an odd pair, rather thrust together. 'Julia Bird. I'm new to the village.'

'Ah, welcome. Patrick Callum, far from new to the village.' He gave a little smile at his own joke. 'Long-time resident. Sorry about the circumstances. Were you a friend?'

'Samantha was found under my shed. And, er, I found Maeve.'

'Oh, yes, I heard. Mrs Bird, well, what a strange and awful coincidence. Two bodies.'

'Awful, yes and very strange. So I didn't know either of them alive, but I have a sort of... connection, I suppose. Which is why I'm here. I'm very sorry for your loss, though. Sad to lose friends in such a terrible way.'

'It's very sad, but we weren't particular friends. It's a village, so everyone knows everyone to a degree. But really, you couldn't say friends.'

'Yet here you are, at the funeral,' said Julia, hoping she didn't sound rude.

'Member of the community and all that,' said Patrick, puffing up his chest slightly. 'I try to come to any event that touches on the lives of my pupils, past and present. Right thing to do.'

'So did you teach Samantha? I thought I overheard...' Julia blushed a little at her nosiness, but Patrick didn't seem bothered.

'For a little while. When I was the English teacher.'

'Oh, well then, you must have known her well. I'd love to hear more about her.'

'Not well, no. My goodness, it was such a long time ago, and I have had so many pupils.'

'I heard she was a good student. English especially.'

'You seem to know a lot about her.'

'Just village chatter. I was curious, given our connection.'

'Well, you probably know more than I do. I'm embarrassed to say I can't remember much about her. And then she moved away, you know.'

'Well, yes. Or people thought she did.'

'Yes, people thought she did,' he said, and something passed over his face momentarily. Perhaps sadness?

Patrick Callum seemed to pull himself together, saying briskly, 'I'd best be off. I'm sorry I don't have more for you, Mrs Bird, but as I say, so very many students. Only a few stand out, I'm afraid. Goodbye.'

Julia looked for Kevin and the school gang, thinking she might get some more reminiscences about Sam, but they'd left already, perhaps decamped to some wake of their own. She should be getting home, anyway. It was getting chillier by the minute and looked like it might rain. She didn't want to be caught in a downpour.

As she made her way to the gate, she met Hayley Gibson, coming in.

'Damn, missed the whole thing,' the detective said, by way

of greeting. 'I got caught up in... Well, never mind what. How was it?'

'Okay. Sad. But also, not very. A bit odd,' said Julia, putting her hands into her pockets against the chill.

'So no one offered a graveside confession, I take it?'

'No.'

'Pity. I made some inquiries after your call yesterday. The people up at Gloucester Uni are going to find Samantha's student records. The file would have been put into storage. It was all paper back then, so someone will be spending their weekend digging through files in dusty boxes in a warehouse somewhere. Glad it's not me. Hopefully they can locate it.'

'Okay, good. If we can find a housemate or someone, maybe we can get a lead on the mysterious man she was seeing.'

'I'm not sure I'm liking the plural pronoun, Julia.' Julia took a moment to work out what on earth she meant, but before her brain had clicked in, Hayley said, '*We*. Just to be clear, there's no *we* in the investigation. I'm investigating, and you are...'

'A concerned citizen,' said Julia, brightly. 'Not investigating, obviously. Of course not. Just helping the police with their investigations where I can.'

'That's it. Exactly,' said Hayley, in a more conciliatory tone. 'I mean, I appreciate what you've done so far, and your social work background is quite handy, your instincts are good. But, you know how it is.'

'Absolutely. Understood. No problem at all.'

'No questioning of possible witnesses, suspects, anything like that.'

'We don't even have any suspects. We've crossed off the Toby jug murderers and the landlord and...'

'We?'

Julia laughed, and after a moment's hesitation, Hayley joined in.

'Don't worry, Hayley, I hear you. I'll be off, try to get home before it starts to rain. Good luck. I hope you get something useful back from the uni.'

'We'll see,' said Hayley, not sounding very hopeful.

The chicken coop was all but finished when Julia got home. The fence was up and the door and ramp had been put in. The nesting boxes were ready for a handful of straw and a clutch of eggs under a fat, broody hen. Brendan was touching up the varnish and sanding any rough spots, Jake at his feet, watching adoringly.

'Johnny, Brendan, it's perfect!' Julia said. 'Look, Jake, this is where the chooks are going.' She stroked his silky ears.

'Hang on a mo,' bellowed Johnny, reaching into his pocket for his hearing aids.

'He doesn't put them in for just anyone, you know,' said Brendan quietly, while his grandfather fitted the aids into his ears. 'He likes you. Or at least, he doesn't think you're a "damn fool with nothing sensible to say."'

Julia smiled at the boy's imitation of Johnny's brusque insult. 'I like him, too,' she said.

'There we are. What was it you were saying?' Johnny asked at a perfectly reasonable volume.

'I was saying that it's perfect! I love it. Just like the picture.'

'Better than the picture. See here, I used these special hinges. Stainless steel. Lasts forever. And look at the nesting boxes. Did my research. Adjusted the height, you see? More comfortable for the gals, and for you when you collect them eggs. Added the wire on the roof, too. Safer all round.'

He grinned proudly at her, his eyes shining and his blue cap bobbing as he nodded his head in approval at his own work. 'Not a bad job, though I say so myself.'

'It's perfect!' said Julia, for the third time. 'I'm going to get the hens on Tuesday. Once they're settled in, we'll have a housewarming for them. A little garden party. The three of us, and maybe one or two of the neighbours. To celebrate.'

'A housewarming party for a henhouse? Whoever heard of such a thing?' Johnny sounded gruff but looked pleased. 'But, if that's what you want, then, that's what we'll do.'

'Sounds good,' said Brendan.

The men packed up, promising to come back in the week to fetch the last of the tools and materials and drop off the invoice. Julia went inside to feed Jake and pour herself a glass of wine. She felt she deserved it, after the funeral. And it was Friday, after all. She took herself out to the front bench where she could enjoy the last rays of sun slipping below the horizon and the evening sounds of the birds and insects. The clouds had lifted and the evening was mild. The air smelled of wisteria and cut grass from her neighbour's mowing. Jake was calm, having enjoyed the company all day.

Julia took a sip of the chardonnay, enjoying the slight woodiness on her tongue and the peaceful scene around her. The evening rush hour on the footpath – such as it was – was just about over. A few dogs had passed, walking their owners. She recognised some of them – an ancient spaniel with a limp, a Jack Russell with a particularly bouncy manner, the Great Dane. You could hardly miss the great speckled thing. She remembered she'd seen the dog before, him and his owner, the day she'd walked down to the lake. The day she'd found Maeve.

She took another sip and remembered someone else she'd seen that day. Patrick Callum. That was where she'd seen him! He'd been one of the people on the footpath, walking away from the lake towards the town; she'd noted his red hair. She felt that odd sense of satisfaction you get when you've solved a tiny mystery, or remembered a forgotten detail.

The path had emptied entirely now, leaving her in a state of calm contentment. Her village experience had got off to a rocky start, what with the body. Bodies. She had wondered if it had been a rash move. But what progress she'd made! A dog and a new chicken coop. Acquaintances who might be friends. And a date – of sorts – with a dishy doctor with a Sean Connery burr. To be honest, she'd hardly thought of Peter in days. And while she'd heard Hayley's caution, it must be said that her amateur dabbling in the crime investigation was certainly keeping retirement boredom at bay.

Yes, things were shaping up well for Julia Bird at Berrywick.

29

Julia's sense of contentment continued through the weekend, and she woke on Monday morning with a smile on her lips.

Sunday with Sean had been, well, interesting. First off, it had to be said that the towpath along the canal was absolutely lovely, tracking the water at a precise distance, through little villages, under picturesque bridges, past brightly painted barges, alongside barrels of petunias striped purple and white. Sean and Julia had walked close together, but not touching, Jake between them like a cheerful brown velvet chaperone with poor impulse control.

It was so very pretty, and so very charming, that Julia felt as if they were in a movie, or perhaps one of those advertisements for some product – health insurance, hair growth supplements, modern dentistry – aimed at fit and healthy 'mature' folk. Sean would have been cast, for sure. He really was a fine-looking man, and he had the whole 007 thing going for him. Julia liked to think that she was an ad-worthy companion, trim and reasonably well groomed in her elegant semi-athletic country wear. They made a good couple. Not that they were a couple. Just friends, although this was after all a date. So maybe they weren't going to be just friends forever.

The conversation was easy – they chatted about the passing scenery, Jake's antics (nothing too alarming, he was on his leash), the progress of the chicken coop, the double memorial, the weather, politics, what they were reading. By the time they reached the riverside pub at Edgely there hadn't been an awkward moment; even the silences were companionable. They ordered two ploughman's platters, and the conversation turned – or, to be more accurate, Sean turned the conversation – to his wife, who had died five years previously of cancer, and his two young adult children, one in Vietnam teaching English and the other in London, studying (said with invisible quote marks) music.

Julia countered with a very brief overview of her own history. 'No really, it was for the best, and Christopher is very nice...'

Once that was all out in the open, there was nothing more to say except, '*Jake!* Put that down...'

Which was exactly what Julia did say when the dog – who had slipped from the leash, unnoticed – ran by with a Scotch egg in his mouth like a delicious porky tennis ball. An older gentleman – definitely too old and snaggle-toothed for the modern dentistry advertisement – came hobbling past, brandishing a stick.

'Ye dastardly canine!' he shouted. 'Unhand me lunch!'

Julia caught Sean's eye, and saw his face begin to dissolve into reluctant laughter. Her own cheeks tightened and her mouth pursed, even as she launched herself from the bench at the trestle table.

Sean snorted.

Julia giggled.

The old man raised his stick and shook it in the direction of the dog, shouting, 'I'll have ye for breakfast if ye don't release my lunch, ye scoundrel.'

That did it. Julia collapsed back onto the bench, weak and laughing. Sean was puce and coughing. Jake clearly thought better of facing down the furious armed man and ran under Julia's bench, where he cowered, while also taking the opportunity to swallow the Scotch egg before it could be removed from his possession. As he finished the last bit of sausage in its golden breadcrumbs, its erstwhile owner caught up with him.

Julia calmed the man with grovelling apologies and additional Scotch eggs and he went off in a huff muttering about 'foreigners', which, Sean explained, meant anyone from further away than the next village over.

The trip back on the boat had been pretty and uneventful. Jake was full, tired and shamed, and hadn't even made a mock charge at the swan which came paddling cheekily close by. Sean and Julia had sat in companionable quiet, occasionally remarking on some aspect of the landscape, and had parted with a kiss to the cheek which had lasted perhaps a moment longer than a casual peck.

Yes, thought Julia, as she sipped her Monday morning tea, life was good.

Julia's happy ruminations were interrupted by the sharp ring of her mobile phone. *DI Hayley Gibson*, said the caller identity. Julia did love the way that you knew who was calling before you answered (or didn't) these days.

'Thought I'd let you know, the file's arrived,' said Hayley, with no preamble, as soon as Julia answered.

The file from the university that would hopefully give them better insight into Samantha's last few months. Julia wasn't sure if Hayley was going to tell her more, but she thought the fact that she'd phoned was a good sign.

'Oh good, and...?' she ventured.

'Took a quick look. Not much in it, but there's a housemate.'

'That's fantastic. They might know all sorts of things, right?'

'Possibly,' said Hayley. Her voice indicated that she wasn't convinced. 'I'm going to do my best to look into it but I've got a lot on and DC Farmer is off sick. Bunions or bulimia or beriberi... It was a bad line when he called. Possibly he said bilharzia, but I don't think we get that here. Anyway, one of the other lads is trying to locate where the housemate is now. Oh, hang on a mo. That's him. Other line.'

And she put the phone down. Not three minutes later, she rang back and continued where she left off.

'Housemate's a local, still lives in Gloucester. I'm thinking, I have to go to Gloucester anyway on another matter, should be quick, so I'll see if I have time to pop in on her. Was hoping to get there today but it's turning into a wreck of a day, what with the interminable paperwork the department requires for the least little thing, and a hundred phone calls to return, so I just don't think that today is realistic. A pity.' Hayley allowed herself a small sigh. Julia thought for a moment.

'Tell you what, I'll drive you,' she said. 'You can use the time in the car to do your paperwork, make your calls, read your emails, whatever you need to do. A nice forty-five minute break to get that all done. I won't bother you at all.'

Hayley was uncharacteristically speechless for a moment, and then said, 'Well, I mean, thank you, that would... It might be really useful... The other thing is a bit urgent...'

Julia could hear her wavering. Everyone liked a bit of help, especially busy can-do people who don't seem to need it, and are thus never offered it. She added a sweetener. 'You won't even have to find parking. I'll drive you straight to wherever you need to go and wait in the car. Then there should be time for us to see the housemate.'

'*Us.*' Julia could almost hear Hayley's raised eyebrows.

'Yes.' Julia hoped her tone made it clear that she was not open to argument or negotiation on this point. If she was going to drive Hayley all that way, well, she deserved a bit of an inside track. But would Hayley go for it?

Hayley paused, sighed and then decided, 'Fine. Thelma and Louise go to Gloucester. I'll be at your place in an hour. But we're taking my car.'

As promised, Julia drove silently to Gloucester while the detective answered emails and made phone calls, all of which seemed to involve deathly boring administrative queries and follow-ups about noise complaints. Julia was slightly disappointed. She had hoped for some juicy real life crime stories as they drove. But so boring was the content of Hayley's calls that Julia was quite relieved when they pulled up outside the address she'd been given.

'Thanks,' said Hayley, opening the door. 'That was really helpful. I got a lot done.'

'My pleasure.'

Hayley looked at Julia, as if weighing her up.

'Here,' she said, having apparently found in Julia's favour. She handed her a small sheaf of papers tucked into a cardboard folder. 'Samantha's file. The people at the uni sent scans. I printed them out. Keep you busy while I'm gone.'

Julia grinned at the detective, and Hayley tried to frown, but failed.

'Don't get too excited, it's slim pickings. Back in ten.'

Julia started at the top of the pile, and scanned Samantha's university application. Her training and experience had taught her to read – or listen – with an open mind. There was often something telling in between what was actually said.

Except in this case, Samantha's file was dull as ditchwater. Excellent school results, a prize for English creative writing, no discipline issues. But the school stuff wasn't of interest. Julia flipped over a few pages, hoping for something more about

Samantha's life at uni. Some admin and receipts related to university housing – that must have been how they had tracked down the housemate. The poor girl had only been at uni for a few months before she disappeared, so it was hardly surprising that there wasn't much record of her time there.

It was all rather disappointing, thought Julia, going through the papers one last time. She was about to close the file, when she spotted one she had missed, as she had skipped through in search of more university-related info. A letter of recommendation from Samantha's school. She ran her eye over it. It certainly was gushing.

> A rare talent... Seldom in my teaching career... The sensibili-
> ties of a writer... Passion and precision... Highly recommend...

She lowered the letter, feeling sad about all the promise and possibility that had been cut short when Samantha was murdered.

Julia looked down at it again, and this time, read the signature at the bottom of the page: *Patrick Callum, English Teacher*.

30

'You've got to admit it's very strange,' Julia insisted. 'Patrick Callum claimed he barely remembered her, and yet he wrote her a personal recommendation. And not just any old recommendation, a positively glowing endorsement – seldom in his career has he had a student with such rare talent, et cetera et cetera. Yet somehow, no recall of her.'

Hayley looked thoughtful, her brow furrowed in concentration. 'I agree it's odd. What was he doing at the funeral, for that matter? If he hardly remembered her.'

'Well, I actually asked him that at the funeral.' Julia felt a small glow of pride that she had this covered. 'He said that because he's the headteacher he feels an obligation to attend things that affect the school's students. Past and present, I remember him saying.'

A waitress came over. They had stopped for tea and to discuss the new developments around Patrick Callum. With their orders in – they decided on a slice of pound cake, too, given the circumstances – they resumed their conversation.

'That *might* be true,' Hayley said. 'In a village, people do tend to turn up at every event. And he is a prominent person, as headteacher. Maybe it's true that he felt he should show his face. But even so, it's odd about the letter.'

The two women paused for the arrival of the tea and cake, and tried to untangle the implications of the letter.

'What does it mean?' said Hayley. 'Are we saying he killed her, based on the fact that he thought she was good at English but then denied knowing her? That would be a stretch.'

Julia nodded. 'Yes, I have to say it's a stretch. The letter and his lapse of memory hardly add up to evidence of murder.' She paused, wondering what Hayley would make of the thought she had had as they sipped and chewed. 'Kevin said that she was having a relationship, and he thought it was maybe with an older man. Maybe married, he said. Do you think it could have been Patrick? Do you think maybe they were having an affair?'

'It's not a totally impossible theory, I have to say. And they would have kept that very hush-hush. Young woman, older teacher, married man,' Hayley said, her face distorted with disgust. 'Very dodgy. And very risky for him if it got out.'

'So it *could* be that when he denied knowing her at the funeral, he was simply covering for the affair. If it got out, he could lose his job, even face charges depending on when it started, how old she was.' Julia looked at Hayley and added, tentatively, 'Or it could be more ominous than that. Maybe back then, he needed to stop her talking.'

Hayley's eyes met hers. 'And maybe now, he needed to stop Maeve remembering.'

The two women felt a frisson of excitement. Had they cracked the case?

'Maybe the housemate remembers something,' Hayley said. 'It was a long time ago, but perhaps she saw something.'

Julia smiled and knocked back the last of her tea. 'Only one way to find out,' she said.

With tea and cake inside them, they drove to Sharon Miller's house, a modest-but-nice two-storey, with a small garden out front, and a low fence. They had phoned ahead and she'd said she would be there all morning. True to her word, Sharon was outside hanging up a selection of small, very small and tiny clothes on a line in a little yard alongside her house.

'All done,' the woman said, putting in the last peg and wiping her hands on her apron. Appraising the line, she shook her head and said, 'It's a wonder how they manage to create so many dirty clothes. You'd think there were ten of them, not three.'

Sharon Miller was a pretty, if rather harassed-looking blonde, heading to forty, as Samantha would have been, and showing the signs of wear and tear that Julia remembered from her own early motherhood.

'Thanks for making the time to chat; we won't take too much of your time. I'm DI Gibson and this is Julia Bird, a social worker.' Julia noted that Hayley was phrasing it as if Julia was a social worker actually on the case, rather than a retired social worker with a newly discovered gift for coming across dead bodies. It felt like a small victory.

'Well, I'm sorry to hear about poor Samantha,' said Sharon. 'Lovely girl, or seemed to be. I mean, we didn't know each other well, just four or five months. Until she... she left. Only I suppose now, she didn't just leave, did she?' The question was rhetorical, and Hayley did not answer.

'What was she like?' Julia asked.

'A good housemate. Considerate, tidy, friendly. A clever girl, she was. Always had her nose in a book. Loved her novels, she did. Writing, too.'

'Did you socialise together at all?' asked Hayley.

'Not really. The occasional trip to the pub. Once or twice we went to the Saturday morning flea market down in the square. I was already going out with Bill.' She gestured to the full washing line, the inevitable result of her romance with Bill. 'I was with him most weekends. And Samantha and I, we didn't have classes together, and she was quite a private person, not one of those best-friend-on-the-first-day sort of girls.'

'Did she have a boyfriend?' Hayley tried to make the question sound routine, but Julia could hear the curiosity in her voice. This was the real question.

'Not someone here at uni, as far as I know. But I have a feeling there was someone. Maybe someone from home? Ooh, it was all so long ago.'

'I know, and thank you for trying to help. Do you remember anything about the chap from home? A name? What he looked like?' Julia and Hayley both held their breath, waiting for the answer.

'I don't think I met him, which is a bit odd, come to think about it. I mean, it's a quick train trip, so the fella could have come to visit if he was that keen, couldn't he?' Sharon looked up at the sky, as if for inspiration. 'I wonder if... Now, I think about it, I seem to remember he was older, so maybe he had a busy job or some such and couldn't get away. And she often went home on the weekends, so she would have seen him there. But I never saw him. Not even once.'

Julia deflated with disappointment. But she wasn't prepared to give up that easily.

'That's very helpful, thank you,' said Hayley, while Julia busied herself with her phone, finding the website she wanted. There it was – a picture of the headteacher on the school's website. Bingo.

'Do you recognise this man?' Julia asked, holding it up to Sharon.

'Oh yes, now *him* I recognise.' Sharon sounded pleased to be able to help at last. 'I don't know the name, but he was her cousin. Quite a bit older than her. Used to come and fetch her sometimes, to give her a lift back home for the weekends, I think. It was a long time ago, but I never forget a redhead. I always thought it was sweet, the way they were so close, the cousins. Lovely.'

The two women said hasty goodbyes to Sharon, walked to the car, and got in, Hayley in the driver's seat this time. As soon as the doors slammed behind them, they turned to each other, eyes wide.

'Cousin?' said Julia, at the exact same time as Hayley said, 'Never forget a redhead.'

They smiled.

'Well, we know that Patrick isn't her cousin,' said Julia.

'And so they must've had a reason to be lying about it.'

'Kevin said he thought she was seeing an older man.'

'And Patrick lied about how well he knew her,' said Hayley.

They both thought, seeing if the direction of their thoughts was wrong. Julia could only see one reasonable conclusion.

'So Patrick the so-called cousin was Samantha's lover?'

'Seems so,' said Hayley. 'I'm thinking that he wasn't taking her back to her mum's at Berrywick. He came to fetch Samantha every now and then for a weekend tryst somewhere out of town. And then something happened between them, something that led him to kill her.'

'That's a bit of a leap, isn't it?' asked Julia, who tried hard to give people the benefit of the doubt. 'Just because he was sleeping with her doesn't mean he killed her.'

'Granted. One certainly can't be killing every ill-considered lover,' said Hayley, with a small laugh.

'But it's looking likely, isn't it?' said Julia. 'The timing works, for one thing. And it makes sense. I know you've seen your fair share of the dark side of life, as have I. When it comes to violence, it's usually the loved ones handing it out.'

'That's true, and Patrick Callum had a lot to lose. Starting with his marriage. Could be Samantha was getting too attached, wanted to come out in the open with it, wanted him to ditch the wife,' said Hayley.

'And his job. Maybe they had a falling out, and she threatened to tell the school, get him sacked.'

'Could have been a lot of things. A surprise pregnancy, perhaps? Or maybe she'd found someone else at uni and he was in a jealous rage. But we're getting ahead of ourselves.' Hayley sighed.

'I think it's time for a visit to the headteacher,' said Julia.

DI Hayley Gibson nodded and turned the key.

Julia realised that she knew Patrick and Tessa's house. It was not far from her own, and on one of her and Jake's regular walking routes. She had admired the blossoms on their cherry tree when she had first come to town, and noted the carefully tended hedges and the well-cut lawn. They had a friendly beagle who always ran to the gate to greet Jake.

Hayley and Julia received a somewhat less effusive welcome than Jake would have, but plenty of cheerful tail wagging, nonetheless. Patrick came after the dog calling, 'Come on, Buttercup.'

'Hello, Mr Callum,' said Hayley pleasantly. 'I'm DI Gibson, I wonder if I could have a word?'

'Hello. Everything all right, I hope?'

'Just a few questions about a student, if you don't mind.'

'Of course,' he said, deftly holding Buttercup back with his foot while he opened the little wooden gate and let the women in.

'This is Julia Bird, a social worker.'

'We've met,' he said, nodding towards Julia. 'Hello.'

'Yes, at the funeral, wasn't it?' Julia said.

They were at the front door now, and Patrick seemed undecided as to what to do. 'Should we sit in the garden?' he said. 'It's nice out, and I think my wife's having a lie-down.'

They agreed, although it was in fact a little chilly, and

turned to follow him round the side of the house, where an iron garden table and chairs were set up under a tree.

Hayley got to the point. 'It's about Samantha Harold,' she said. 'I'm looking into her murder and speaking to people who knew her. I believe you were her English teacher.'

As Patrick gave Hayley exactly the same story he'd given at the funeral – lots of students, poor recall – Julia looked up at the house and saw a woman's face appear in the kitchen window. It was the same woman who she'd seen having words with Patrick at the graveside, his wife. Not having a lie-down, then.

'Maybe this will jog your memory,' Julia said, handing Patrick the printout of his recommendation letter.

'Goodness me, how could I forget!' he said, putting a hand to his forehead in an exaggerated show of surprise. 'Of course, Samantha *Harold*. You know, I think I was mixing her up with someone else. You won't believe how many Samanthas there were in the 2000s. Yes, a very good student she was. A reader, which is not something I can say for most of them, sadly.'

Julia was interested in his quick recovery, and his easy charm. In her experience, a red flag where reliability was concerned.

'So you knew her, then?'

'Yes. She was in my English class. For two years, I think. Yes, that's right.' He gave a good impression of it all coming back to him. 'A-level English, Samantha Harold. There you go,' he said, handing the letter back to them as if that settled things, and the interview was done, but Hayley pressed on.

'Did you know her personally at all? Anything you could tell us about her? Her friends, boyfriends, family life?'

He shook his head. 'Nothing, I'm afraid.'

'Did you ever see her outside of school?'

'No.'

'The thing is, Mr Callum...'

Patrick's wife appeared at the back door, and called anxiously, 'Patrick? Who's here? What's going on?'

'Nothing, Tessa, just school business.'

'The thing is, Mr Callum,' Hayley resumed. 'We have witnesses who say otherwise, that you did see her outside of school, that you visited...'

She stopped when she saw Tessa walking across the lawn towards them, Buttercup trotting behind her.

'Aren't you the detective?' she asked, and Hayley nodded.

'Detective Inspector Gibson,' she said, offering a hand.

Tessa kept her own hands firmly in the pockets of her dress. 'Well, anything you have to say to Patrick, you can say in front of me.'

31

'Now, Tessa, there's nothing for you to concern yourself with. Just something to do with a student,' Patrick said, sounding completely unperturbed. He was a smooth one, that was for sure. 'You go and put the kettle on, I'll be up for tea in a mo.'

'Which student?' Tessa asked.

'Samantha Harold,' said Hayley. Julia kept her eyes on Tessa, looking for a reaction. Tessa knew the name, that was certain. There was a passing expression, almost a wince – of pain, perhaps? – on her face.

'What about her? She's dead, isn't she?' the wife asked. She had a nervous air and a slight tremor. She kept glancing at her husband.

'Tessa, the kettle,' he said firmly.

She turned to her husband and spat out: 'I am waiting to hear what the police have to say about Samantha Harold.'

Hayley intervened, calmly, 'I'm hoping Mr Callum can help us with some information about her. It seems that he knew her quite well, as a teacher and...' she paused. Julia could almost see her brain ticking over, deciding how much to say, what to reveal when. 'And outside of school.'

'Happy to help, Detective Inspector,' said Patrick, trying for – but now not quite achieving – a casual tone. 'Although I'm certain that nothing that I can tell you will be of any use to you in your enquiries.'

'Let me be the judge of that,' said Hayley, rather sharply. 'How about we start with your visits to her at university? Tell me about those.'

'You must be mistaken,' he said.

'There's a witness. Her housemate. Sharon. Remember her? Because she remembers the red-haired older man.'

'Plenty of red-haired men about these parts. All that Irish blood from over the channel,' he said, with a chuckle. He really was quite annoyingly slick.

'It was you, Mr Callum. Sharon recognised you in a photograph. We're following up on other people who lived and worked in the residence at the time. I'm certain I can find other witnesses too. Why were you there, Mr Callum? What was your relationship with Samantha Harold?'

'I was her teacher, as I said.'

'The housemate seemed to believe that you were a cousin,' said Julia.

'Well, you see,' said Patrick, his easy smile returning, 'it's the cousin you should be looking for. Not me. Wrong red-headed man. Happens to me all the time.' He beamed around the group of women listening to him, as if he had solved a very difficult problem for them.

But Tessa Callum had reached some sort of breaking point. 'Oh for the love of God, Patrick, just tell the woman the truth, why don't you? She's a policewoman, for Pete's sake. Not one of those women you can just pull the wool over, tell them any damn thing you please, and smile, and they'll believe you. She's going to see through your lies and nonsense. Just tell her the truth.'

The poor wife was shaking, with adrenaline or anger or both.

'Tessa! I do apologise, Detective, she's not well...'

'Stop that!' shouted his wife. 'Stop saying that.' She turned to Hayley and Julia and said in a perfectly polite voice, 'My husband was having an affair with Samantha Harold.'

'Tessa, what are you talking about? I think we'll have to pick this up some other time, Detective, my poor wife isn't in the best of health. Goodness, Tessa, what a thing to say. Where are your pills?'

'Maybe I'm not well, but I'm not crazy, whatever you say. I can't live with this any more. I can't live with your lies.' Tessa reached into the pocket of her dress and pulled out a little pill bottle. She opened it and shook out two pills, which she put into her mouth. 'There, I've had my pills and I still say you were sneaking around with that poor girl. I still say you are a liar and a cheat. TELL THE WOMAN THE TRUTH!'

The beagle cowered at the outburst, and then slunk back to the house for safety. Tessa's anger dissipated as quickly as it had arrived, and she gave a heartbroken sob. Julia put a comforting hand on her shoulder.

Hayley held her hands out, palms up, and said calmly, 'It's over, Patrick. We know about the affair. So here are your choices. You can admit it now, and tell me everything you know. Or you can make me run around Gloucester looking for corroborating witnesses, putting me into a *very* bad mood, and then come down to the station in cuffs next week.'

'Cuffs? What? *Hand*cuffs? No. I mean. I did... We did... I admit that we did, um, see each other. Briefly,' he said, the cocky man deflated at last. 'I did visit her in Gloucester. But she had already left school, I wasn't her teacher. And she was of age. There was nothing illegal. I'm not some paedophile, I want you to know that.'

'Noted.' It was clear from Hayley's cold tone that she considered this to be a technicality, rather than a comfort.

'It was wrong, I know. Something I deeply regret, as I told my dear Tessa at the time, when I begged her forgiveness for this unforgivable slip,' he said. He had recovered some of his poise – or pose. He brought his hand to his heart, the very picture of contrition. He was back in the game, manipulating his audience with his wiles. 'It was a mutual attraction that should never have been acted on. A mistake, on both our parts.'

'And what about the murder, was that a mistake too?'

Patrick, it had to be said, looked genuinely confused.

'What? Oh no. No, no, no. I didn't *kill* Samantha.'

Tessa let out a brief hysterical burst of laughter, which ended abruptly with her hand over her mouth. Julia suspected that the pills – whatever they were – were kicking in. The woman had seemed somewhat unhinged even before the pills – a man like Patrick Callum would do that to you. But what else would a man like Patrick Callum do? Would he kill? Julia couldn't say. That was the trouble with a murder investigation, as she'd recently discovered. Just because someone was a narcissistic fool and a bully didn't necessarily mean they were a killer.

'Where did you think she was then, when she disappeared? Didn't it seem odd to you that your lover had left town without a trace?' said Hayley. 'Or did you already know full well what had happened?'

'Well, no. I was surprised, to be honest. She said that she was going away for a while, to London. She said she would contact me, but I never heard from her again. I suppose I thought that she'd decided it was time for us to part. We'd both realised, on some deep level, that it wasn't right. I was suffering terrible guilt...' He looked around as if he expected sympathy for his pain. Honestly, the man was insufferable.

'Terrible guilt? That would be a first. Guilt,' snorted Tessa, rolling her eyes. 'You lying psycho bastard.'

Patrick continued as if she hadn't spoken. 'I asked around, discreetly, and heard that she had indeed gone to London. Even her mum said so. She didn't go back to uni. Her mum told people that she was settled and doing well. I just assumed... And then later, I heard that she was married, and had moved to Sydney and even had a kid or two. I couldn't believe it, when her... her body was found.' For the first time, Julia thought she saw a look of genuine emotion on his face. The problem was, it was almost impossible to tell which genuine emotion it was – grief, guilt or fear.

'Where were you on the morning of Wednesday last week?' Julia asked suddenly. It was a toss-up as to whether Patrick or Hayley looked more surprised at her outburst. She was tired of hearing Patrick's self-serving nonsense.

'Wednesday?' he frowned, working back through the week. 'Wednesday, Wednesday... I took the car in I think, or was that Tuesday? I can't remember.'

'Let me help you. It was the day Maeve Harold drowned,' said Hayley.

'Oh good God,' said Tessa, in anguish.

'Oh, come now, you can't be serious.'

'Answer the question, Mr Callum.'

He glowered at the DI, his fists clenching at his side like he wanted to hit her.

'I'll prompt your memory for you,' said Julia helpfully. 'You were on the footpath. You passed my cottage. You were on your way back from the lake. The lake where Maeve died.'

'On the very morning that Maeve died,' added Hayley.

'Oh, Patrick...' Tessa moaned.

'I can explain...' said Patrick.

'Well, best you do.' Hayley's voice was icy stern.

32

Julia and Hayley had decamped to Julia's house, which was less than a mile from Patrick and Tessa's, with the intent of discussing the day's discoveries. They were now sitting at the kitchen table mulling over Patrick's explanation: that he had set off to find Maeve, knowing that she swam in the lake every Wednesday, but she wasn't there.

Patrick's story was that he had woken in the night gripped by a horrible, horrifying thought – that the body found under Julia's shed might be Samantha's. The police had released a statement that the body was that of a young woman, and that she had been buried some twenty years before. His unconscious had done the work while he was asleep, and at 3 a.m. had woken him with a shocking hypothesis – that Samantha didn't just disappear to London and cut off all communication with him; that she had been murdered and buried less than a mile from his house. He had tossed and turned through the early hours, and then got up as soon as it was light. He would go and speak to Maeve first thing. Everyone knew she swam on a Wednesday morning. He would go to find her at the lake and tell her his fears. And then they would decide what to do. The trouble was that Maeve hadn't been there.

'The thing is, Maeve *was* there,' said Julia now. 'I can vouch for that, seeing as I personally found her dead body.'

'I suppose it's possible that he didn't see her,' said Hayley. 'He was looking for a swimmer, not a body.'

'Yes, it's true he wasn't scanning the area for hidden bodies, and I suppose she was in the reeds. I only saw her because of Jake. And Patrick was in a terrible state, if he's to be believed.' It was possible that it had all unfolded as he claimed – he had gone to talk to Maeve and failed to find her – but the fact remained that Julia didn't trust Patrick. He seemed like a slippery character in all respects, and he'd lied about knowing Samantha.

'Killing Maeve only makes sense if he killed Samantha. Maeve was the one most likely to link the body to Samantha's disappearance. And that would, potentially, bring the girl's lover into the spotlight and lead you to him.'

'Well, there's not enough evidence to bring him in on Samantha's death. But he was seen at the lake on the day of Maeve's murder, so I'm going to focus on that. I'll get DC Farmer to follow-up on his story and the witnesses tomorrow. He said he saw some lady with a big dog and the postman and Auntie Edna. Whoever they are.'

'Auntie Edna is away with the fairies, poor woman's got dementia, so she's not likely to be of any use to you. I've seen the Great Dane lady, she's one of the regular walkers, but I don't know her name. I actually saw her that morning too. You can ask Tabitha about her, she'll be here soon. She's coming for an early supper. You're welcome to stay.'

'Oh, I don't want to be in the way...'

'No trouble, I'm just going to make some pasta. You'll like Tabitha, and she's a font of local intel. Everyone comes past her desk at the library.'

Speak of the devil, and Tabitha appeared, a huge basket on her arm. She deposited it on the table with a thump and a sigh, and turned to Hayley with a friendly smile, while Julia made the introductions.

'Ah yes, I have seen you around. Good to meet you,' she said, and proceeded to remove items like a magician conjuring rabbits from a hat.

'The new Epiphany Bloom mystery by Katie Gayle. It's hilarious, I checked it out for you,' she said, handing Julia a book. 'And honey from my neighbour, he harvested the beehives on Saturday.' She deposited the golden jar on the table. 'Oh, and a cabbage.' She thumped the pale green beauty, as big as a bowling ball, down next to the honey. 'From my garden, last of the season. That'll keep you in coleslaw for a while. Now where's my shawl?' said Tabitha, digging around some more, and pulling it out with a flourish. 'There we go.'

She flung the crimson shawl around her shoulders and sat heavily in the chair.

Julia was charmed. 'How wonderful, thank you. Village produce! You don't get *that* in London. People bring wine. Or chocolates. Bought. This is so much nicer.'

Julia offered everyone a glass of the home-made lemonade she'd made over the weekend. Admittedly, it wasn't a home-grown cabbage, but it was a good start. 'I'll soon have eggs for you. The chickens are being delivered tomorrow. And my plum tree is absolutely covered in tiny fruit, so we'll be eating those in a month or two's time,' she added, unsure quite how many weeks or months it would take for the hard green stones to transform into juicy purple globes.

'It's delicious,' said Hayley, taking a long gulp of the lemonade.

Over a bowl of pasta topped with a simple tomato sauce, Julia and Hayley filled Tabitha in on what was happening with the investigation. It was hardly as if it were confidential, given that everyone in the village knew everything within minutes anyway. Julia concluded, 'So Patrick admits to the affair, but he's adamant that he had nothing to do with Samantha's death, or Maeve's. He says he couldn't find Maeve and didn't kill her – which he would say, of course.'

'Oh, do you know the lady who walks the Great Dane?' Hayley asked Tabitha. 'Patrick saw her on his way to the lake. My DC is going to follow-up, but I thought you might know...'

'Oh yes, Yvonne Gaylar. She and her husband own the gift shop in the village. They bought it a few years back. If you pop in there tomorrow you'll probably find her.'

'Thanks. Auntie Edna is the other witness, but Julia says she's...'

Tabitha shook her head.

'You'll get no sense out of old Edna, poor dear.'

'And the postman?'

'Gary Butler? Well he's easy enough to find. Constant as the sun is our Gary, you can set your watch by him. Wasn't always the case apparently. People say he was a wild one back in the day, but these days he's very reliable. Great dad too, after a shaky start.'

'Thank you. I'll get DC Farmer onto it tomorrow. Speaking of which, I'd best get myself home. I want to brief Walter tonight. Departmental meeting starts at nine, and goes on for eternity, or noon, whichever comes first.' Hayley rolled her eyes to the heavens. 'Police work is big on admin these days. Thanks for the supper and the lemonade. Nice to meet you properly, Tabitha.'

She started to clear the table, but Julia stopped her. 'Not to worry, I'll do it. It'll be quick. You go along.'

'Thanks a mill. I'll see myself out.'

Julia and Tabitha got up from the table, picking up the pasta bowls and the empty glasses. Julia stacked the dishwasher while Tabitha gave the table a wipe. It was a companionable sort of

activity, clearing the supper table, and Julia felt a fleeting
melancholic stirring, thinking of the many years she'd done the
same with Peter. The familiar little dance between table and
sink, dustbin and dishwasher, brushing past each other,
exchanging the odd observation. The sadness didn't stay. She
was resigned and resolved, as far as her marriage was
concerned, and happy with her new life in Berrywick. She put
the sentimental moment behind her.

Something else niggled Julia, a stray thought that was
imprecise but felt important, but before it could present itself
for scrutiny, Tabitha addressed her, her voice sad and
sympathetic.

'Poor Tessa must be in a state. She's such a fragile thing
even at the best of times.'

'She was distraught. And then angry. Actually furious. If I
was Patrick Callum, I'd sleep in the spare room tonight. Popped
a couple of pills too, I noticed. Can't say I blame her. Married to
that man.'

'She's not a well woman. I've seen the deterioration since
I've been living here. She's very withdrawn. I see her about the
village, but she hardly greets anyone. She comes into the library
from time to time and she always seems on edge and anxious.'

Julia remembered Tessa coming into the charity shop on
Julia's first day, how she'd struck her as a flustered, anxious sort
of person. Julia had thought what a bunch of oddballs the shop-
pers were. The silent man perusing the books that he never
bought, and then the jittery woman buying a skirt to change
into there and then.

The skirt. Julia felt the blood rush to her face.

Tessa had bought the skirt because the skirt she was wearing
was wet. On the very day that Maeve Harold had been
drowned.

33

Julia had rather more sympathy for Patrick's nocturnal anxieties, having spent a night similarly tossing and turning, mulling and worrying. She was awake at six, more tired than when she'd gone to bed.

'No point in lying in bed,' she said to herself, out loud, in her dead mother's voice. She swung her feet to the floor and sat for a moment, exhausted at the thought of the long day stretching ahead of her, after what felt like about two hours of sleep.

'Nothing else for it,' she said, again channelling her mother.

Standing up with a grunt, she padded to the kitchen and put on the kettle for tea. It was too early to phone Hayley with her latest theory – that Tessa Callum was a viable suspect for Maeve's murder, and perhaps even for Samantha's. Her motive for Samantha's murder was clear and simple – probably the oldest in the book, in fact. The young woman had been having it off with Tessa's husband.

And what about Maeve? Well, her motive would be the same as Patrick's would be – to try to avoid the identification of Samantha's body, which would lead the police to the Callums' door. In addition, Tessa was clearly disturbed, and on some fairly strong meds. She might have just flipped.

The kettle whistled and Julia poured the boiling water into the pot, savouring the smell as the tea leaves released their perfume. She put the lid on the pot and left the tea to steep.

'Come on, Jake,' Julia said, rather to his surprise. It was a little early for his Good Boy Exercises or his morning walk, but he was not one to quibble about the details. He bounded out of his bed, sat, and did his endearing little bum shuffle at her feet while he waited for the lead. Julia clipped it on and took him into the garden and they practised walking at heel, sitting, staying. He cast a side-eye to the shrubbery from which the dawn chorus was coming in full throat, but resisted the urge to head in there and extricate a robin or two. Excellent boy!

Next, she unclipped him from the leash and they did the same exercises, walking at heel, sitting, staying. His attention was a little less impressive, what with the incessant chirping and twittering, singing and whistling coming from the birds. Suddenly, it was too much temptation for Jake. He had had enough of their cheery morning larks and was going to do something about it. He bounded into the flower bed to investigate, flattening a little patch of pansies under his bear paws, and crashed through the rhododendrons, scattering petals and alarmed birds in his wake. Bad boy!

'This is exactly why you failed guide dog school,' Julia said grumpily, once she'd wrangled him to heel. 'Some sight-impaired person dodged a bullet there, I tell you. They'd be in a bush or under a bus by now.'

He looked at her with his adoring eyes and wagged his tail happily, as if she were showering him with compliments. She brushed dirt from her thighs, deposited by Jake while he'd jumped up at her in delight at his successes.

'Let's go in for tea,' she said, wondering whether she should be concerned that her most regular conversational partners were her dead mother and a badly behaved chocolate Lab. And a police detective, she reminded herself. 'Then we'll phone Hayley and tell her my theory about Tessa. And don't forget the chickens are arriving this afternoon. I'll be expecting best behaviour. Now, heel.'

Jake smiled angelically, and trotted beside her into the kitchen.

Julia changed her trousers, drank her tea and waited impatiently until 8 a.m., which she considered a reasonable time to phone a busy police detective.

At 8 a.m. on the dot, she phoned Hayley and went straight to voicemail. She left a voice message, and then typed a text:

Call me! I have information about Tessa. It's important.

Annoyingly, there was no reply to either message, which left Julia in an antsy state of anticipation that seemed to preclude her doing any other task. She forced herself to empty the dishwasher, while keeping a sharp eye on her mobile. She filled Jake's water bowl at the outside tap, with her phone gripped precariously in one hand. The closer it edged to nine, the less she expected to hear from Hayley. She knew that her dreaded departmental meeting would be starting any minute.

She sent another message:

I think it could be Tessa, not Patrick.

'This is ridiculous,' she said to Jake, when Hayley still didn't respond. 'Let's go for a walk.'

Julia chose the route that would take them past Patrick and Tessa's house. She hoped – well, she didn't quite know what she hoped. Perhaps that she would spot Tessa on the path and have a chat in which Julia's training as a social worker would miraculously draw her out. Even encourage Tessa's confession. Or that some clue would fall into Julia's lap. She would overhear a secret conversation or an informative marital argument, like in the movies. She had enough sense to laugh at herself. But still, as she drew up to the Callums' house she slowed down to a snail's pace, Jake walking sedately by her side.

Buttercup came running out of the open gate when she saw Jake, dashing about in a frenzy of excitement and running into the road. Jake bounded after her with such force that he pulled his lead out of Julia's hand. It was a country road with precious little traffic, but still, you couldn't have dogs running about. Which was why the Callums' gate was usually closed.

'Buttercup! Come here! Get inside! Jake! Stop it! Heel! Now!' Julia shouted, chasing the mad dogs around. The beagle finally obeyed, dodging past her into the garden. Jake followed. He had no intention of listening to Julia's instructions now that he had a frisky partner in crime. The two dogs ran through a small gate in the hedge that led to the back garden.

'Bloody dogs!' she muttered to herself. Now she would have to go in and fetch the evil beast. She contemplated just going around the back, but imagined how embarrassing it would be if one of the Callums emerged in their pyjamas to find Julia chasing a Labrador around their garden. She had better let them know she was there, she decided.

She walked to the front door, knocked and waited. No answer. She knocked again and shouted, 'Hello! Tessa? Patrick?' while peering through the glass windows on either side of the door. There was nothing to see, and no sign of life.

The Callums must be out. Having done the polite thing and tried to raise the owners, she was now at liberty to enter the property and haul her disobedient hound out by the scruff of his neck. She followed the yapping and cheerful growling of the playing dogs and walked round the side of the house, following a path along a deep green box hedge, and through the gate to the garden she had been in just the day before.

But something was different. Horribly, terribly different.

In the middle of the Callums' perfectly mown, weed-free lawn lay Patrick Callum, a pair of garden shears protruding from his chest, his eyes open and staring at the sun as his blood seeped from his body to the earth. The two dogs chased each other in wide circles around his body, yapping with the pure joy of being alive.

'Well, he's definitely dead,' said Sean, rather unnecessarily.

The three of them looked down at the body.

'How long?' asked Hayley, brusquely.

'An hour or so.' He turned to Julia. 'I'd say you narrowly missed the killer.'

'I just can't believe that you've found another body, Julia,' said Hayley, sounding quite annoyed by it. 'We've been happily jogging on with a petty crime here and a white-collar crime there, and then you move in and wham, there are bodies all over the place.'

Julia had phoned Hayley as soon as she'd seen Patrick's body, and thankfully, Hayley had answered. Hayley had called Sean, unclear of the exact status of the body, and the two of them arrived together.

'It's hardly my fault about the bodies,' said Julia, feeling wrongfully accused, although of what she couldn't say. 'It's not exactly what I wanted from a quiet retirement in the country, I can tell you that.'

'I suppose not,' conceded Hayley. 'Now explain to me again what happened?'

'I was just walking past with the dog,' began Julia, when Hayley interrupted.

'I suppose you'd have me believe that you just happened to stroll past, after leaving a message on my phone that you suspected the lady of the house of murder?'

'Okay, so maybe it wasn't a complete coincidence. But I was jumpy and you weren't returning my calls.' Julia gave Hayley an accusatory glare.

'Okay, so you're strolling past, and then?'

'Buttercup came running out the gate, which was open.'

'The dog?'

'Yes. She got Jake completely worked up and then the two of them ran into the garden. I had no choice but to come after.' Julia paused. 'I did try to knock, but no one answered.'

'Where is Tessa, that's what I'd like to know?' said Hayley, looking back down at poor Patrick, the shears still protruding from his chest.

'I expect she ran off after she did it,' said Julia, who didn't have a doubt in her mind about how Patrick had died.

'After she did it?' said Hayley, lifting her eyebrows.

'Think about it, Hayley,' said Julia. 'One. Tessa knew that Patrick was having an affair back then. She killed Samantha in a fit of jealousy. Two. She knew that Maeve would tell everyone that Samantha wasn't really in Sydney. So she killed her. I saw her that morning and her skirt was wet. She must've got wet at the lake, drowning Maeve. And now, she knew that Patrick would be able to point the finger at her to get you off his case. Or she was just plain furious at him for putting her in this situation. So she's killed him too.' Julia felt triumphant, having set out her theory. And to her satisfaction, Hayley was nodding, her finger against her cheek.

'Makes sense, as a theory, I have to say,' said Hayley. 'The crime-scene chaps will be here soon, let's see if there's hard evidence to support it. The priority now is to find Tessa.'

'The thing is,' said Sean, sounding more tentative than the two women, 'I'm not entirely convinced that Tessa Callum is strong enough to drown a woman or stab a man. I've been her doctor for many years and I don't think it's breaking confidence to tell you that she suffers terribly with her back. Amongst other things.'

'Either way,' said Hayley, 'we have some questions to ask her. And it looks like we'll be asking them soon.'

As she spoke, Hayley indicated the gap in the hedge, where Tessa Callum stood, her hands over her mouth in a silent scream.

34

The silence was momentary. As Tessa stepped over the wicker basket and bright yellow secateurs she had dropped, she let out a shriek that would shatter glass.

'Patrick!' she screamed, rushing towards him. 'Get up...'

Hayley intercepted her, her arms firmly around Tessa from behind, pinning her arms to her sides. The heaving woman stared at the dead man, panting in shock.

'Mrs Callum, I'm sorry but you can't go any closer. It's a crime scene.'

Tessa struggled against her, hysterical now, as Hayley led her away from her husband's body, to sit on the chair under the trees.

'Oh God, oh God, oh God...' Looking over towards Patrick's body, Tessa reached into her coat pocket for a vial of pills. She shook two into her hand. 'My nerves,' she said by way of explanation, and tossed the little white pills into her mouth. After a moment's hesitation, she shook out a third pill and – in the seconds while Julia was deciding whether she should intervene – sent it down the hatch after the other two. Tessa swallowed dryly and turned to face Sean, who was still looking intently at the dead man.

'Is he dead, Dr O'Connor?' she asked.

'I'm afraid so,' he said in his calm, steady burr. 'He's gone, Tessa. Patrick is dead.'

'What happened?' she asked Hayley. 'I don't understand.'

'That's what we're trying to piece together, Mrs Callum,' Hayley said. 'I'm sorry to ask you at a time like this, but would you be able to talk to me, just for a few minutes? Any information you could give us now would be very helpful in the investigation.'

'I don't know...' Tessa said, her voice slow, as if she were speaking underwater. 'I mean I wasn't here, so... I don't know.'

'Just a few general questions, if you could. It would be very helpful,' Hayley said again. 'When did you last see Mr Callum, um, alive?'

'When?' asked Tessa, blinking. 'You mean, the time? O'clock?'

'Yes. Did you see him this morning?'

'Oh yes, this morning,' said Tessa. Her voice had started to slur.

'And was he... I mean, he was alive?'

'Of course he was alive,' Tessa said crossly. 'What else would he be at seven o'clock in the morning?'

Hayley had no ready answer for that one. She soldiered on, 'So you woke up, and he was fine, and then...'

'We had tea. He was very alive when we had tea. Very. But now he's dead.' She looked over to the body, as if checking that she'd got this part right.

'And after tea?'

'Alive, I'm sure.' Tessa's forehead creased in confusion. 'He went to put the bins out, so he'd have to have been alive, wouldn't he? So, still alive. I was picking the flowers.'

Hayley and Julia exchanged a glance at that, thinking of the garden shears in the dead husband's chest.

'Right, tell me about the flowers. You picked...'

'It's for the church. Wednesday,' Tessa said, perplexed at Hayley's ignorance. 'I cut the flowers. And leaves. The same as usual, but the roses weren't good. The heat, you know. But the dahlias. Good.'

'So you picked the flowers and then?'

'I took them to the church, of course. Gave them to Reverend...' Tessa stopped mid-sentence and moved her hands as if she were trying to entice birds from the sky. She'd forgotten his name. 'Reverend Jason. Jacob. J... J... J...'

'Johnson?' Sean said, helpfully.

'Reverend Johnson. He was there. I put them in the bucket. Jilly is going to do the arran... orange... the... the... the *arranging* today, we take it in... in...'

There was another pause as Tessa struggled for the word 'turns'.

'Anyway, you know...' she said. By now her eyeballs were practically rolling back in her head.

'Tessa, have you taken anything? Any pills?' Sean asked.

'It's just the medication you prosecuted... prescript... prescribed...' she said. 'I took one of those.'

Julia held up three fingers behind Tessa's head, and gave Sean a meaningful look, eyebrows raised. She wiggled her three fingers. He nodded in understanding.

'Tessa, it's been a shock, I think perhaps a nap is in order, if the detective is done with you.'

Hayley looked intensely irritated at the quality of the information she was getting from this particular witness, but managed to respond quite professionally. 'One last question, if I may, Mrs Callum. When you left the house to go to the church, did you see Patrick?'

'Oh yes. He was reading the... Espriss. Espers. *Express*,' she said, sounding satisfied at having nailed down the tricky word.

'He was alive? When you left, Tessa, was Patrick alive?'

'Yes,' she said, and gave a little sob. Tears sprang to her eyes. 'Alive.'

Sean helped the barely ambulatory Tessa upstairs to her bedroom, leaving the two women staring after them. Hayley sighed. 'Well, that wasn't the most helpful interview I've ever conducted.'

'No. Although I'd be surprised if she killed Patrick. She doesn't seem together enough to murder him, or to make up a story.'

'Agreed. And too frail, from what Dr Sean said. Her alibi for Patrick is easy enough to check out, though,' she said, reaching for her phone. 'I'll get some uniforms down from Gloucester. Someone can go and see Reverend...'

'Johnson.'

'Johnson, and a couple more can go door-to-door in the road. Ask if anyone saw anything.'

'I'll be getting home,' said Julia, looking at her watch. 'I'm expecting a delivery. My chickens. Let me know if I can help with anything.'

'Thanks. And I'll let you know if anything turns up.'

35

It felt like months since she'd last done charity shop duty, Julia thought as she walked briskly into the village. So much had happened. Death, mostly. She shuddered, recalling the sight of Patrick impaled by the shears. Death and detectiving.

It wasn't all bad though, she reminded herself. There had been a date with Sean, which had been lovely. And dog walks. And a darn fine chicken coop, now populated by six sweet, speckled hens. She racked her brains for more good things on her alliterative theme.

'Diane!' she called warmly, coming up behind her on the main road. She was easy to spot with her height and her long red hair.

'Oh hello.' Diane slowed down so they could walk the last stretch together. 'Lovely day, isn't it?'

It seemed both women had deliberately arrived ten minutes late, with the result that they got to the door just as Wilma was unlocking it.

'Oh *there* you are,' Wilma said, as if she'd been pacing around, concerned, for hours. 'Do come in.'

Diane and Julia shared a smile.

Wilma bustled around officiously, opening blinds, switching on lights, and handing out directions. Diane continued with her ongoing task of sorting new donations into piles – display, storage, cleaning, chuck out, and so on.

Wilma had made it clear last time that this was considered too high-skilled a job for the newbie. Even though the newbie had two degrees and a decades-long career in which she was responsible for decisions that affected actual peoples' whole lives.

Instead, Julia was given the job of trawling through the stock to find suitable clothes, accessories and knick-knacks for the spring-themed window display which Wilma was creating, a job which was, right now, infinitely preferable to being responsible for decisions that affected actual peoples' whole lives.

'Ice cream colours,' Wilma said, flinging her arms about dramatically as she expounded on her creative vision. 'Strawberry, pistachio...'

Julia considered adding, *Rum and raisin, chocolate chip...* but instead said, helpfully, 'Apricot, mint.'

'Exactly! Bright and cheery, without being garish,' Wilma beamed. 'I'm seeing whimsical. Optimistic. Playful. Arresting to the eye, of course.'

She appeared to be channelling Andrew Lloyd-Webber.

'Got it,' said Julia, heading for the stockroom.

It was rather a pleasant activity, and Julia found she had a knack for it. In the same way that she picked out odd connections, it seemed she had a sort of magpie eye for funny and unusual items. A Japanese paper parasol with pink blossoms. A set of yellow and green polka dotted soup bowls. A photographic book of rare orchids. Toddler-sized pink wellies. It was astonishing, the things people bought, and then tossed out. Or predeceased. She pondered a little on who might have bought the paper parasol and why. Was it a romantic whim on a visit to Japan? A prop for a play? An ill-advised gift?

'Marvellous!' said Wilma, startling Julia out of her imaginings. Probably for the best; the possible histories of the objects had made her a little sad. Wilma beamed at Julia's stash of goodies. 'You *are* doing well. Shall we break for tea?'

'Lovely, I'll put the kettle on,' said Julia. The back room served as tea station as well as storage facility.

While the kettle boiled, Julia took her phone from her bag and checked her messages. She'd missed a call from Hayley Gibson, but there was no voice message.

She sent her a text:

Looking for me? Working at Second Chances today. Chat later.

As she put the mobile phone back, her hand found the folded paper invoice that Johnny Blunt had left on her kitchen table that morning. Julia hadn't had time to look at the bill, she'd just tossed it into her handbag to deal with later.

Noticing it now, she shook her head in wonder at village behaviour. The man had literally walked into her house and left a handwritten invoice on the table. He'd put three lemons on it, to stop it blowing away, presumably – and he had previously promised her lemons, a gift from his garden. Had he never heard of email? Or privacy? She wondered if he had even given her a bank account number, or whether she had to leave a bag of farthings and florins at the post house. She unfolded the paper.

It said CHICKEN COOP and an amount. The amount, she had to admit, was even lower than agreed, which she found surprising, especially given the excellence of her chicken coop. And look – he had indeed scrawled his bank account details, and the account name – *John G Butler*.

'Well that's weird,' she said to herself, putting it back in her handbag to deal with later.

'What is?' asked Diane, who had wandered in to check on the tea-making.

'Well, village life generally. It seems that I am now a person who doesn't lock the front door, for one. But more specifically, names. Is Johnny Blunt really called John Butler, do you know?'

'Oh yes. Blunt is a nickname. Because he's so blunt. We've all called him Johnny Blunt for years.'

'Yes, not one to mince his words, is Johnny. Calls me City Miss when I ask him what time he'll be arriving to work on my chicken coop.'

'That's our Johnny,' said Diane. 'I was at school with his son, Gary Butler. You must have met him, he's the postman. Gary used to dread his dad coming to the school. Once said to our teacher, Mrs Harris, "Must be a good life, the teaching, innit? You've put on a bit of padding there, haven't you?" He wasn't even trying to be rude.'

Julia laughed. 'No, he's just forthright.'

'It got even worse after Gary's mum died. I think Gloria kept Johnny in hand a bit, but when she passed he was let loose on his own and there was no stopping him. One time he said to one of the parents who was worrying about her daughter, "Don't you fret so, there's not everyone can be bright you know. Someone's got to clean the lavatories."'

'Poor Gary must have died at that one,' said Julia.

'I don't think it helped poor Gary, you know, having such a blunt father. Gary went right off the rails, didn't he? Drugs and women and fights. Wasn't a week that went by that people weren't talking about him. But then he had Brendan, and got the job as postman, and he seemed to settle right down. You never hear a bad word about Gary these days, but old Johnny is as rude as ever.'

This entertaining litany of Johnny's blunt faux pas was

interrupted by the tinkle of the bell, indicating that someone had come into the shop.

'Julia!' called Wilma, a note of panic in her voice. 'You'd better come. There's a policeman. Looking for you.'

'Morning, ma'am, nothing to worry about,' said DC Farmer. Wilma looked relieved at that, given Julia's well-established reputation with dead bodies. 'I'm checking the timeline for the morning of Mr Callum's death, and I hoped you could fill in the details.'

'Yes, of course,' said Julia.

DC Farmer flipped open his notebook and held his pencil at the ready.

'You arrived at the house at what time?'

'I left my house just after nine, so it would have been about twenty past nine when I got to the Callums'.'

'Right. And you found the body when?'

'Within about five minutes, maybe ten. I called for a bit, tried to raise someone, and then went in to get the dog.'

'Nine thirty?'

'Thereabouts.'

'And no sign of Mrs Callum?'

'No. She definitely wasn't there. She was at the church, apparently.'

'Yes, confirmed by three witnesses. Got there at eight thirty, delivered the flowers, had tea with the vicar.'

'And did they say she seemed her usual self? No sign of stress?'

'No, quite normal. She...' DC Farmer stopped himself short, realising, apparently, that his job was to ask questions, not answer them. 'The timeline, Mrs Bird. What happened after you found the deceased?'

'I called Hayley, DI Gibson, and she called Dr O'Connor. I could check the phone record, but it was pretty much immediately. And they were both there very quickly. Being in the area.'

'Not to worry, ma'am, I have DI Gibson's timeline on that. I'd like to go back to the time before you arrived at the Callums'. Did you see anyone on your way there?'

Julia tried to remember, but couldn't. 'I don't know, there are usually some walkers out and about, but I can't say I remember anyone.'

'Milkman? According to the neighbours, he'd been round.'

'I don't think so. I think I would have noticed, but I can't say for sure.'

'Postman?' he looked down at his notepad. 'Witnesses say he's always there at 8.45 a.m., and as far as anyone can remember, yesterday was no different.'

'Sorry, again, I don't remember. But if the neighbours' timing is correct, and the postman – Gary, isn't it?'

He nodded.

'If Gary is as reliable as everyone says, then he would have been round before I got there.'

'Amazon delivery fellow?'

'No. Honestly, I don't think I saw anyone in the road or thereabouts.'

DC Farmer looked mildly disappointed in her, as if she could have tried a little harder, snapped his notepad closed and said, 'That's all for now, ma'am, thank you for your time.'

Julia fetched her cup of tea, now only lukewarm, and considered what she'd learned. The witnesses at the church seemed to have Tessa off the table as a suspect, leaving – no one. Who would want to kill Patrick Callum? And why? One thing Julia knew was that Patrick's death had to be related to Samantha's and Maeve's. The question was how?

In her head, she ran through the usual reasons that one person might kill another. Jealousy was a perennial favourite. Well, Tessa would have fit the bill on that score – the spurned wife – but she was increasingly unlikely as a suspect. Revenge? Kevin, or someone else who loved Samantha might have had that motive. Silence? Could someone have killed Patrick to keep him quiet, to protect themselves or someone else?

She went back to work, picking up a box of random accessories. That pair of heart-shaped sunglasses had potential.

36

The good news was that the coop had proved safely Jake-proof. The chickens were happily pecking and scratching in their new home when Julia returned from her stint at the charity shop. The less good news was that the hosepipe was not as resilient to the dog. Jake seemed to have spent quite a chunk of the morning chewing it with his sharp little teeth, leaving a scattering of holes.

'Naughty Jake,' Julia said, pointing at it. He wagged his tail, pleased she'd noticed his handiwork. 'Oh well, I suppose it's a sprinkler now.'

She returned her attention to the chickens. They had been sold as 'point of lay', which meant, apparently, that she could expect an egg any day. She was tempted to go and check the nesting boxes, but decided to do it last thing this evening, to give them another few hours to get going.

'No rush,' she said, in a friendly tone. 'You girls get yourselves settled in. Make yourselves at home. Enjoy the facilities. Plenty of time for eggs.'

She was talking to chickens now, as well as dogs. The fowl regarded her with their beady eyes, and continued their scratching and low clucking. It was a peaceful, contented sound, and Julia herself felt peaceful and contented on this pretty summer's day in her exuberantly flowering garden. She would put the murders out of her head, and enjoy the rest of the afternoon in the garden. There were tomatoes to be watered – the plants had popped up in the compost heap, with no help from her, which she appreciated – and the pots full of pansies could do with a good soaking. Yes, a nice quiet afternoon of gardening was just the thing.

'Well that's a fine coop,' came a man's voice behind her, causing her to jump and Jake to bark sharply and the chickens to rush into a huddle at the back of the pen. 'Sorry, didn't mean to startle you.'

It was Mr Steadman, followed closely by Mrs Steadman, both of them rather more tanned than when she'd met them to sign the transfer deeds for the house. Mrs Steadman was wearing a jaunty straw hat with a red ribbon on it, a cheerful hat which would have been more at home on the Mediterranean than in the Cotswolds, perhaps.

'I hope you don't mind us popping in,' said Mrs Steadman, whose first name Julia was struggling valiantly to recall. 'We were in the neighbourhood, visiting our old friends and neighbours, and thought to say hello. See the old place.'

'Not at all, it's nice to see you. Annie.' *Got it, Annie. Bert and Annie.* 'How was... Sardinia?' *Got that too.*

'*Bellisimo,*' said Annie, closing her eyes in blissful remembrance. 'The food was divine. And the sea. It's the colour of cornflowers.'

'Oh, that sounds lovely.'

Annie smiled, and adjusted the straw hat. 'Life-changing,' she said. 'My spiritual home, I feel. Can't wait to get back. I'm having Italian lessons.'

'You got rid of the shed, then,' Bert said, having had enough of the holiday conversation.

'Yes, I did,' Julia said firmly. She wasn't going to defend her home improvement choices to the previous owner of her house.

'We heard about what you found. The body. The police contacted us,' said Annie. 'I'm shocked. I can't believe that we lived all those years here with a body buried in our garden.' She gave a shudder.

'Terrible business,' said Bert, nodding. 'Terrible. I always said the shed had a strange feel, didn't I, Annie?'

'Ooh, you did, Bert. You did. I thought it was just the dust, your allergies playing up, you know. But now we know, it must have been the body. It might have been there since the shed was built.' She shuddered some more.

'We went away a lot in those years. Caravanning, every weekend. I suppose someone could have...' Bert tailed off. 'Doug. I mean. He was a good chap...'

'It's a shock, I know,' said Julia. 'But he's dead and there seemed to be no viable connection between him and the victim. And everyone seemed to agree he was a good chap. So, a dead end.' She paused, and blushed slightly at her choice of language. 'I mean...'

'Sad business. Anyway,' Bert said, keen to change the subject, 'it's a fine-looking coop.' He gave it a few good smacks, as if testing its strength. 'Well built.'

'I love it. I looked at lots of designs online.'

'Online, hey?' He sounded astounded that the internet should accommodate such things as chicken coops.

'Yes, there are loads of ideas and plans and pictures and so on. I found a few that I liked and Johnny Blunt worked it all out.'

'He's all right, Johnny Blunt,' Bert said grudgingly. 'Shouts a bit, but he's all right. Knows his wood.'

'Quite a coincidence, isn't it? Johnny Blunt building the coop,' said Annie.

'Why's that?' Julia asked, readying herself for some convoluted village story.

'Well he helped Doug Harrison build the shed, back in the day. Then twenty years later, he tears it down and builds your coop.'

'You're right,' said Bert. 'I'd forgotten Johnny helped him out.'

'Johnny helped build the shed?' It was a piece of information so astonishing that Julia wondered if she'd misheard or misunderstood. 'Johnny Blunt?'

'Yes. Surely he told you?'

'No, he didn't mention it,' said Julia.

A little while later, having heard more about the Steadmans' trip and their reminiscences about the village, Julia waved them goodbye. She'd barely been able to concentrate as she spoke to them – her mind returning again and again to what they had just told her about Johnny.

As soon as they left, Julia retired to the sitting room and collapsed onto the sofa in shock. Her head was spinning. Johnny Blunt had helped build the shed. The same shed under which Samantha Harold's body was found. And what's more, he hadn't mentioned it when he took down the shed or put up the coop. Not once in all the time he was working there, all the times they'd talked about Samantha. In fact, he had implied that Doug Harrison, buried in the corner of the cemetery, had built it very much on his own.

It was too weird. Johnny would have immediately mentioned that he helped build the shed unless there was a reason that he didn't want anyone to know.

And as far as Julia could think, there was only one good reason that anyone would have to deny knowledge of that shed – and that was if they knew about the body under it. The only reason Johnny could have had for not mentioning it was that he knew the body was there. And if he knew the body was there, he knew how it had got there. Either he'd put it there himself, or Doug Harrison had and Johnny was protecting him for some reason.

But then why had he let her pull down the shed? Julia thought back to that day. Johnny hadn't known anything about pulling down the shed, she recalled, until it was already done. It had all been young Brendan, working so hard to impress his grandfather. But instead he must have given his grandfather the fright of his life.

She thought about gruff Johnny in his blue knitted hat. Johnny bossing his grandson about in a fatherly way. Taking out his hearing aids to still the world. Putting them in to hear Julia, once it was established she was not a complete idiot. She tried to imagine him killing and burying a young woman. Or covering up for someone who had. It was inconceivable. It made no sense. Except it was the only thing that made any sense.

If Johnny had buried Samantha here, why would he even agree to come back to the scene of the crime to dismantle his hiding place?

Again, she made herself replay the conversation on the first day they met, back at the cafe. There had been no mention of the shed, only the coop. She may even have mentioned putting it under the plum tree. And she hadn't told him she lived at the Steadmans' place until after he'd agreed to do the job. Perhaps Johnny had then agreed to do it so that he could make sure she didn't find the body. Only she and Brendan had taken things into their own hands.

She tried to think back to Johnny's reaction when he'd realised that the shed had come down, but nothing came to her.

She reached for her phone. She needed to tell Hayley.

37

Hayley answered her phone, thank goodness. Julia told her about the Steadmans' revelations about Johnny's involvement in building the shed, and her own theories about his role in Samantha's death.

'Johnny Blunt? The shouty old guy with the woolly hat and the nice polite grandson?' Hayley said, incredulous.

'Yes, Johnny Blunt. Or Johnny Butler, actually. Blunt is a nickname.'

'You think he killed Samantha?'

'It is hard to imagine, I know, and to be honest I will be devastated if it is so, but how else would you explain it? He had the opportunity to hide the body. And he didn't mention the fact that he'd built the shed.'

'Does sound suspicious. I'll look into his record, see if anything pops up. We've already checked out Doug Harrison – nothing more than a parking ticket on that one. And then I reckon it's time to bring Mr Blunt in for questioning, see what he says.'

'I think so, and...'

Whatever Julia might have thought was drowned out by

Jake's excited barking. Julia looked out of the sitting room window and saw Johnny Blunt coming up the path towards her, a hammer in his hand.

'Dammit! He's here,' she said to Hayley.

'Johnny?'

'Yes.'

'Were you expecting him?'

'No.'

'But why do you think he's there?'

'I don't know. Maybe some last-minute fixes. He's got a big hammer.'

'Knock, knock. Julia, are you there?' came Johnny's voice.

'I'll talk to him. Gotta go.'

Julia put down the phone and called out, 'Coming.'

She went through to find Johnny on the doorstep. She saw, over his shoulder, that Brendan and Jake were engaged in a delighted reunion, rolling and wrestling on the lawn.

'Oh, there you are,' he boomed. 'Just came to fetch a few tools we left yesterday. You all right, then?'

'Yes.' Julia paused. It was awkward speaking to someone that you liked very much but that you now thought might be a murderer. She thought that her life as a social worker had prepared her for every imaginable awkward situation – but as it turned out, it hadn't. What she had learnt, however, was if you have just learnt an awkward piece of information, it often worked best to just pretend that you knew nothing, and act like you would have before. Often then, an opportunity would present itself to talk about the problem. Many a difficult custody conversation had been managed in this way. So that is what she did. 'Have you seen the chickens in their new home?' she asked.

'No, not yet.'

'Come and have a look.'

They walked round to the back of the house, where Johnny surveyed the happy hens with pride, rocking back and forth on the balls of his feet, his hands clasped behind him. 'Looks right nice with them in it.'

'It really does. I'm delighted. You did a super job, Johnny.'

'Ah well, not much to it,' he muttered ungraciously, but on his face there was a faint blush and a momentary smile.

'Come on now, that's not true. You're a true craftsman.' Julia took a deep breath before she said the next part. 'And to think that you built the original shed too.'

Johnny turned his head towards her, doing an absolutely terrible job of hiding his surprise.

'The Steadmans were here,' she said, keeping her voice calm and light. 'They came for a visit and they happened to mention it.'

'Long time ago, it was.'

'It was indeed. It's just... I'm rather curious about why you didn't mention it.'

He tapped his right temple and rolled his eyes. 'At my age...'

Julia raised an eyebrow and gave him a sharp look that stopped that sentence in its tracks. No way was Johnny going to play the old man card, he was as sharp as a tack. He had the good grace to look a little sheepish.

'I think it's time to come clean about whatever happened, Johnny. I don't know Doug Harrison, but I do know you, and I'm sure there must be a reasonable explanation for all this. Why don't you get it off your chest and then you and I will have a good chat about what to do next.'

Johnny hunched down into himself and pulled his cap down even lower over his forehead, as if he wished to disappear right into it. He said nothing. She had almost given up hope of an explanation, when he said, 'It was an accident. A terrible accident.'

'Samantha's death?'

'Yes.'

She waited, calm and still, admiring the roses as if she had all day.

'I... I...'

'It's okay, Johnny, just tell me what happened. I'm sure you didn't mean to kill her.'

He straightened up and looked at her in astonishment. 'Oh, I didn't kill her. Good Lord, no. I only buried her. Her body.'

Julia felt somehow relieved – she hoped he was telling the truth, that Johnny Blunt wasn't a killer, merely his boss's able assistant.

'What was Doug Harrison's relationship with her?'

'Doug? I don't think he knew her.'

'Why would anyone kill someone they don't know?'

'Gloria didn't know her.'

Julia had no idea what he was talking about. She kept her expression neutral and nodded encouragingly, and hoped he would continue. 'It was a Sunday evening. Gloria and me, we went to bed early, it being Monday the next day. I sleep like a log, but from the day Gary was born, Gloria always slept with one ear open, as she liked to say. Mothers, you know.'

His bright blue eyes misted at the memory. From the corner of her eye Julia saw Brendan, standing by the hedge behind Johnny. Listening, his arms wrapped tight around his body. Her gaze met his, but she quickly turned back to Johnny. She knew that if she alerted Johnny to his grandson's presence, he would break off the story.

'First I heard of it all was a loud noise. I woke up. No Gloria in the bed. Then I heard her cry out. I was out of there so fast, I tell you. Saw a light on in the kitchen. There was a girl sitting on the kitchen floor, holding her head. Gloria had the freezer open. Getting ice cubes into a clean dish towel. In a panic, she was, saying, "You'll be all right. You'll be all right, dear."

'The girl was moaning and mumbling. I couldn't make out half of what she was saying, but she kept saying, "Sorry, so sorry.

I wanted the tin. Just to borrow the tin." And Gloria crying and saying "sorry, sorry" too. The crying, the girl's moaning. I'll never...'

Johnny paused to take some deep, rattling breaths. His hands shook. The two of them stood still, looking at the oblivious chickens going about their business. The late afternoon air was thickly fragrant and buzzing with bees.

Johnny continued.

'And then... And then, just as I walked in, she had, I don't know, like a fit. Something. Her eyes rolled in her head and she slid to the floor. Gloria, my Gloria, going mad, screaming at me to call an ambulance, shaking the girl to wake her up.'

Johnny shook his head at the memory of it. Jake came trotting over and flopped down on Johnny's feet. No sign of Brendan. The poor boy had probably run off in shock after hearing his grandfather's gruesome tale.

'And the girl – Samantha – she died. Right there, in our kitchen. Must have been bleeding inside, you know. Like, in the brain.'

'Oh, Johnny,' said Julia, softly. 'What a horror.'

Johnny sighed, suddenly looking a hundred years old, and continued, 'It was all a terrible accident. So what had happened was, Gloria heard a noise, and thought the cat was shut in the kitchen and went to check. She didn't turn on the light, just opened the door and saw someone. A figure, in the dark. Picked up the old cast iron frying pan from the stove top, and hit the intruder. Just instinct, you know.'

Julia nodded, and waited.

'She saw it was a girl, soon as she put the light on. Samantha. The girl was dazed, but she told Gloria she'd had a fight with her mum. Samantha had been having it off with someone unsuitable and married, and Maeve found out. Maeve was appalled and said over her dead body, Samantha told Gloria. Maeve had said she'd confront him, tell the wife. Maeve was spitting mad, as Samantha told it, poor thing. Samantha needed to get out of town, and didn't have the train fare. All of us in those days, we kept an old tea tin on the top of the fridge. Any spare cash went in there – a fiver here, a tenner there. She'd seen it through the window and thought to come and borrow the tea tin money. Thirty pounds, I think it was. Planned to give it back, so she said.'

The running away money, Julia thought to herself. The money Samantha couldn't get from Kevin. The girl died for thirty pounds. She died for a train fare. Her throat caught at the sheer awful unnecessary pain of it.

'It was an accident,' Johnny said again, this time in a pleading tone, as if begging Julia to believe him. 'Gloria wouldn't hurt a fly. I swear, she was the most gentle... She didn't mean to kill her. She tried to help her, the ice and all. She was broken, she was. I just wanted to protect her, to protect my family.'

'So you buried Samantha.'

'I did. Good Lord, I don't know what I was thinking. But I didn't know what to do. We were both so frightened. Gary was such a disturbed young man back then. Expelled from school. He'd just got off the drugs, and there'd been a suicide attempt. His mum was the one keeping him together, like. Helping him start again. If they'd taken Gloria away, I don't know what we'd have done without her. We were only just making ends meet between the two of us. She was in an office, a receptionist, half-day. I had a job in the joinery, and was helping Doug out on the weekends for extra cash. I couldn't have anyone taking my Gloria away, when she hadn't really done anything wrong. And then I thought of the shed we were building.'

He gestured to where the shed had been. Julia nodded.

'It was my fault. I did a terrible thing. I panicked and I hid the girl's body. Not a day goes by I don't think about that night,

I can tell you. The body, how it felt, her face. It haunts me in my dreams.' Johnny shuddered.

'And what about Maeve?'

'I wanted to tell her, I felt so guilty, her waiting for the lass to phone. A hundred times I thought to knock on her door. But then a hundred times I thought of my Gary with both his parents in jail. Gloria for murder or some such, me an accessory. Him going off the rails again. And then Gloria died, just a few years later – never the same after the accident, was she? And Gary was so much better and Brendan was born by then. And there was Gloria's memory to think of. I didn't want her to be remembered in the village as a murderer. I couldn't tell Maeve.'

'I meant Maeve's death. What happened?'

'Now that I don't know. It makes no sense, does it?'

The time for subtlety was over. 'You didn't kill her?'

'Kill Maeve?' he asked. 'Oh now, Julia, do you think I'm some sort of murderer? Good heavens no!'

Julia heard a noise and turned to see Brendan, back by the hedge, Jake happily sniffing his legs. It was his gasp of horror that she'd heard, and his strangled 'No!' She had no idea how long he'd been back, but when he saw that he'd been seen, he ran to Johnny.

'Grandpa,' he said, hugging the old man. 'I overheard...'

'Oh, lad,' said Johnny sadly. 'I'm so sorry. I only ever wanted to be a good man. A good father and grandpa. But I wasn't. I did a terrible thing.'

'It was a mistake. It's not your fault. I phoned Dad, we can sort it out.'

Johnny shook his head, and gave his grandson a smile. 'You're a good lad, Brendan. It's a weight off my mind, to be honest, telling you. I'll tell the police too, tell them everything I know about Samantha.'

He turned to Julia. 'But I don't know nothing about Maeve Harold. Why would I kill Maeve?'

'To stop her from going to the police. Once it came out that the body was a young woman, her first thought would be that it might be Samantha's. And then the game would be up for you. Killing her would protect you and protect Gloria's memory. Once Samantha was identified, everything would come out.'

'I've not had a day without guilt on account of causing that poor woman's suffering. I would do nothing more to harm her. Besides, I was at the Buttered Scone the day Maeve died. I was finishing up my breakfast when the news came in that the police were down by the lake. I had nothing to do with it. And if you were going to accuse me of Patrick Callum's murder, now that you're in the murder accusing way, well I don't know nothing about that either. Go on. Call the coppers, I'll tell them the same.'

Julia found herself inclined to believe Johnny. He'd come clean about Samantha. The man had suffered so much guilt and trauma, he wanted it all over. But who else could have killed Maeve? And for what motive?

It came to her in a flash. The same motive.

But a different killer.

38

'There'll be no calling the coppers.'

It was not at all time for the post, but there was Gary, the postman, striding across the lawn pointing his finger at Julia. Julia looked around for Jake, who would normally have been greeting a new, unexpected and loud visitor. But he must have gone into the kitchen for a nap in his basket.

'What do you think you are doing?' Gary spat. 'He's an old man. He's done no harm. Leave him be. He didn't do the killing.'

'I need to sit down,' his father said, staggering to the low wall around the compost heap, and slumping down on it.

Gary turned to Julia. 'It was all a mistake. He was trying to help Ma.'

'You knew?' asked Brendan, looking at Gary in surprise. 'You knew about Grandpa and the body?'

'No. Yes. I mean. Not then. Only now, since. Since she, Samantha – or her body, rather – turned up. He told me. He was scared.' He turned to Johnny and said, 'You should never have told me. Look what's happened now! This is all your fault.'

Gary seemed furious, his body shaking. Julia could see that

he was in extreme stress. This was more than being upset about a crime that happened twenty years ago. It seemed her theory must be right.

She remembered Nicky, irritated that the postie had been late that morning, the same morning that Maeve died. Even Hayley had complained about the post running late that week. And Patrick, seeing the postman on the way to the lake that morning. The people in Patrick's street had only seen the milkman and the postman on the morning that Patrick was killed. And Gary was the postman; cloaked in his strange coat of invisibility. Nobody ever questions seeing the postman. But Gary had been at or near the scene of two murders.

Julia knew that she could not let on that she suspected Gary of two murders. He was too unpredictable. She needed to calm the frightened, unstable man, and try and find a way to call Hayley.

Johnny spoke dully. 'Let it be, lad. I know you mean well, but it's time for the police. I'll tell them everything I know. It will be a relief.'

'No!' shouted Gary. 'No police. We can sort this out ourselves.'

'Gary, I think we're beyond that point,' said Julia, in the calm, soothing yet firm voice she had so often used for deadbeat dads and teenage runaways. 'I'm afraid it's time for your father to tell what he knows and let the law take its course.'

'He can't go to jail... I mean he doesn't deserve... He was trying to do what was best, he shouldn't be punished.'

'Your father didn't kill anyone. He is truly remorseful, and his age will likely earn him some leniency. I think if he and your mother had told the truth back then, no charges would have been pressed. So I hope that the time that has passed hasn't made it all worse. But I do know the court puts a lot of value on remorse.'

'You're right, you're right,' Gary said, nodding. 'Yes.

Remorse.'

There was a chance that this dangerous situation could be defused, just as long as Gary thought no one was onto him.

Julia took out her phone to call Hayley. 'I'm going to phone the police now if that's all right with you, Johnny?'

He nodded.

Julia cautiously lifted the phone to her ear, not looking at Gary as she did so. He mustn't realise what she knew.

But Gary smashed the phone from her hand. 'No! No police. What about me?'

He was pacing around manically.

'Dad!' Brendan stepped forward, pale and shaking. 'Stop it, Dad!'

'What d'you mean, what about you?' said Johnny, his forehead creased with worry. Julia could see that he was one step away from realising the same thing that Julia now knew.

Gary looked at Julia's phone, lying on the ground, its cracked screen staring up at them like an apology. 'It's all right, son,' Gary said to Brendan. 'Sorry. I shouldn't have done that, Mrs Bird.'

Julia rubbed her smarting wrist and said, 'Gary, whatever you did...'

'I tried to make things right, that's what I did. I can still sort it out. If you'll just shut up and let me think.' He held his head in his hands as he paced, and muttered to himself, as if in an internal argument.

Julia spoke softly. 'You tried to help your father, Gary. You tried to protect him, and to protect the memory of your mother.'

'I did,' said Gary, looking at her with gratitude. Finally, someone understood. He continued more calmly, earnestly. 'Everything I did was for him, and for Mum.'

'But, Dad, what did you do?' Brendan said, clearly not following the steps. Julia gave him a warning look, hoping he would take the hint to stop his cross-questioning. He was too agitated to notice or care about Julia's look. 'What did you do for your mum? And Grandad?'

'I didn't want to kill anyone, I tried to talk to her. Just to make sure, you know, that she didn't think... So I went early, to find her before my rounds. But it went wrong. She got upset and angry. It all happened in a blur, and I was late for work. You know how I hate to be late.' He said this last bit to Johnny, who nodded sadly.

'You're a good postman, Gary. Everyone says. Like clockwork,' Julia said.

'I am, I am. Never late. Makes me stressed, being late. I need a routine, even the shrink said. I just wanted to sort it out. For Dad. But she made me late.'

'Maeve.'

He nodded. 'I tried to calm her, but she wouldn't... She was shouting.'

'Dad! *You* killed her? You killed Mrs Harold?' asked Brendan, appalled.

'Oh, Gary,' Johnny said, tears rolling down his face.

'And tell me about Patrick Callum,' asked Julia, quietly.

He was calm again, speaking in a robotic monotone. It was as if he was giving dictation.

'I saw Mr Callum there, when I was coming back from the lake. And then yesterday, when I was on my rounds, Mr Callum came out to greet me. He was my headteacher, at the school like, so I stopped. So he comes out and he asks me to be a witness, to tell the police that we'd spoken at the lake. That he'd turned around after, because he couldn't find Maeve. Seems the police didn't believe that he hadn't seen her. Thought he'd killed her, didn't they? But I couldn't do that, could I? I couldn't say to the police that I'd been at the lake.'

'No. Because that would put you at the scene of the...' Julia paused. 'Of the accident.'

'He got angry, kept asking why I wouldn't help him, what

was my problem, all that. All tied up in knots I was, and he was pushing and pushing. Big important man in town, thinks he can get what he wants. And I'm trying to think of a reason, you know, racking my brains. And the next thing... I just wanted him to be quiet, so I could think, and the garden cutters...'

Johnny started to cry, pathetic sobs. Brendan had his arm around his grandpa's shoulder, his eyes fixed on his father as he veered between calm and anger, reason and madness.

'This is all your fault,' Gary said to Julia, furious now, his face contorted and his hands clenched. 'If it wasn't for you, it would all be all right.'

He took three big strides and was up in her face, his hands on Julia's shoulders.

'It's okay, Gary,' she said calmly, trying to keep her voice from trembling. 'Let's not make things harder here. We can work this out.' But Julia wasn't sure that Gary was even hearing her. His rage had taken over.

Before Julia could think further, and before Gary could hurt her, Brendan came flying at them, shoving his father aside for Julia to step out of his grasp and away. Gary stumbled. Brendan came right back at his father, trying to pin his arms, to force him to the ground. Gary flung the boy away, shouting at Julia, 'It's your fault. I was doing my best. Mum, poor Mum.'

He lunged at her, missed, and came at her again. This time, Julia fell down, but Brendan was back on his feet and trying to stop his father. Jake came running out of the kitchen door. He barked loudly, and then ran towards Gary, a low growl coming from his throat, his teeth bared, his soft face transformed.

As the furious dog crouched, ready to launch himself at Gary, Gary picked up a spade and turned on Julia. Julia could see the madness in his eyes. She knew that he was about to kill again.

'Drop it,' came the voice of DI Hayley Gibson.

She was holding a taser.

39

All heads turned to Julia as she entered the library. The book club members had been prompt, and Julia was a little late.

Tabitha greeted her with a warm hug. They had spoken on the phone since the events of the previous day, but hadn't seen each other. 'Julia! So happy to see you, I wasn't sure if you would make it.'

Sean, already seated on a small sofa, caught her eye and moved a pile of books from the cushion next to his. He'd saved a seat for her. She gave him a small smile, and noticed Diane noticing, a smile on her lips too.

'Wouldn't miss it. Sorry I'm a bit late,' she said, sinking into the sofa. 'The day ran away from me rather.'

There was a flurry of, 'Oh not at all!' and 'Well, who can blame you!' and then an expectant silence. She realised that of course – this being Berrywick – everybody already knew about yesterday's drama, and they were all dying to know the juicy details from an eyewitness.

Jane was the first to crack, couching her inquisitiveness in concern. 'Poor you. You must be quite shaken after yesterday,' she said, her brow furrowed, her hand on her necklace. 'We heard... How terrifying for you.'

'Thank you, I'm really fine. There was just a bit of paperwork to take care of. A statement and so on. It's just been rather tiring.'

Pippa was the first to come out with a straight question, 'So who killed Samantha? Was it Johnny?'

Julia was surprised by her directness. 'Well, I can't say I...'

'I heard it was Gary,' said Jane, rather indignantly. 'Wasn't he arrested? My friend, Hattie, who lives in the Callums' road said she saw Gary being taken off in the van.'

'But that was for Patrick, or so they say,' said Pippa. 'It was Johnny who killed Samantha.'

'People say he was having an affair with her,' Diane piped up, twirling her hair around her finger, so it seemed to writhe like a shining orange snake. It was a nervous motion that Julia recognised from working with her at the charity shop. 'Isn't that true, Julia?'

'Johnny?' said Pippa in amazement. 'An affair?'

There erupted a general cacophony of questions and dubious claims.

'Yes. Dark horse.'

'No, not Gary, Patrick.'

'No, Johnny, that's why he killed Patrick.'

Tabitha stepped into the fray. 'Now, please. Let's not badger Julia. She has had a very stressful time, what with the body under her shed...'

'And then finding two more!' said Pippa. She must have heard the thrill in her own voice, because she added, tutting rather unconvincingly, 'A tragedy.'

'Now let's get on with the books,' said Tabitha firmly. 'And then tea.'

There was a general rumble of mild discontent, but no outward mutiny.

Julia felt wary about all these questions – a hangover from her social work days, when most of the things that she'd known were confidential. On the other hand, she had no official capacity, she wasn't an officer of the court, not a policeman, so she had signed no confidentiality agreement. And besides, it seemed that the story of what had gone down – or a series of incomplete, incorrect, and completely ludicrous stories – was all over town. She felt some duty to set the record straight, at least as regards Gary.

'Gary didn't kill Samantha,' she said. Everyone stared expectantly at her. Tabitha Too, with a cat's need to be the centre of attention, made a beeline for Julia and jumped up on her lap so that people might admire her golden stripes, while Julia answered their questions.

She stroked Too and continued, 'Gary didn't kill Samantha. It seems he killed Maeve, though, and Patrick. He has been sent for a psychiatric evaluation. He has a history, apparently.'

'That he has, my Hannah was at school with him. The poor boy was odd even then. Although I did think being the postie helped keep him on the rails,' said Jane, nodding sagely. Everyone was a psychologist these days.

The book club members started with follow-up questions, and Diane cut in: 'Shall we have tea, then? While we chat? I brought my chocolate fudge cake.'

'And I made sandwiches,' said Pippa.

'Ooh,' said Sean. 'Good idea. Tea before the books?'

They all looked at Tabitha who agreed, if rather reluctantly. 'All right then. Quick tea break, then books. We're talking about our favourite murder mysteries this week, remember?'

The members didn't wait for a second invitation. Who needed murder mysteries when you had a real life murder drama in your very own village, and a central figure and witness here in the library, prepared to spill the beans? There was a rustle of papers and handbags, and a scraping of furniture, as everyone started to move towards the tea table.

Julia dislodged Too from her lap. Sean moved the stash of books from his lap, and stood up from the sofa. He offered Julia his hand, and then hesitated, as if fearful of being too forward, just as she reached out hers. She smiled, and there was an awkward moment of extending and retracting hands, and almost touching. In the end, she stood without taking his arm.

The book clubbers were now gathering around the table with the steaming urn, the cups and saucers, the teabags, milk and sugar. And the fine-looking eats. Julia helped herself to two little triangle sandwiches, one cucumber, one cheese and tomato.

She was waiting her turn for the cake knife when Diane spoke. 'So, who did kill Samantha?'

'Gloria Butler killed Samantha by accident, and Johnny buried her to protect Gloria,' Julia answered, to a hum of disbelief and astonishment from the book club members.

'But why was Maeve killed?' Pippa asked, quickly adding, 'Poor woman!' as if people might think she wasn't sympathetic. Julia decided that there was no point in telling half the story.

'Remember Maeve was killed *before* the body had been identified as Samantha. Gary was worried that Maeve would come forward and suggest it might be Samantha buried under the shed, which would open up a whole investigation. From what he said, he intended to talk to her casually and sound her out, see if it had crossed her mind, but somehow things got out of hand. I don't think he meant to kill her,' said Julia.

'Well, that's as may be,' said Jane, crossly. 'But what about Patrick Callum? You don't murder someone with an axe by accident.'

Diane slid a large slice of chocolate fudge cake onto Julia's plate. 'Go on, have a slice,' she said. 'You need it after all you've been through.'

'It wasn't an axe, it was a pair of garden shears,' said Julia, plunging the knife into the moist, dark sponge. 'Patrick had seen Gary at the lake that day. Gary was worried he would tell the police. Whether he had planned the murder or whether it was an impulse thing, he just lost the plot.'

'Speaking of losing the plot, the chap in the greengrocer's was saying that Tessa Callum has gone off to a mental health clinic or some such. For a rest cure,' Pippa said, turning to Dr Sean O'Connor for confirmation. Him being a doctor. 'I must say, the drugs, the medications, you know, that would have something to do with it, don't you think?'

Sean stared her down, without saying a word, and then walked to the table for a supplementary sliver of cake.

Pippa looked shamefaced and backed off. 'Well wherever she is, she deserves a break. Being married to that man. His affairs and then, you know... the garden shears.'

Julia hadn't mentioned Samantha and Patrick's relationship, out of respect for the dead girl. The whole village didn't need to know. She was interested to hear that Patrick's philandering ways were common knowledge. She wondered which other newly ex-students had caught his eye.

'But how did you work it all out?' asked Tabitha. 'It does seem very involved, I must say.'

'A series of small clues – Gary was late for work on the day Maeve died. And then with Patrick, well, there weren't many people around at that time he was killed, but people kept saying that they had "only" seen the postman. And Patrick had mentioned seeing the postman at the lake. It all kept coming back to the postman.'

There was a good deal of nodding, and appreciative noises at that.

Julia continued, 'It's really very sad. If they'd only called the police when the accident happened, and explained everything,

I doubt that Gloria would have gone to jail. Maeve and Patrick would still be alive today.'

There was a lot of tutting and head shaking at the thought of it all.

'And poor Maeve would have known her daughter was dead,' said Tabitha, sadly. She had such a soft heart. 'That poor woman, thinking her daughter had cut ties, hoping for Samantha to come round, and telling us those stories about her just to keep up appearances.'

'I wonder what will happen to Johnny now,' said Sean. 'He's not a bad fellow, Johnny Blunt.'

'I shouldn't imagine there's a lot of appetite for prosecuting an almost seventy-year-old man on a twenty-year-old charge of accessory after the fact,' said Julia. 'But that's for the police and the courts to decide.' Julia sounded matter-of-fact, but she also couldn't bear the thought of Johnny in jail.

'Julia, I know I speak on behalf of everyone when I say how grateful we are to you for your part in solving these awful crimes, and filling us in on all the details. But I'm happy to say that our murders will all be of the fictional variety, in future. And so, back to the books.'

40

Julia sat at the small table she had put in the back garden, under the plum tree. Jake was at her feet, and they were both watching the chickens – Julia with a glass of wine, and Jake with a bone. Watching chickens, Julia had discovered, was an immensely peaceful occupation. It allowed her mind to wander pleasantly to the future, but somehow stopped her from getting stressed.

Peter and Christopher were coming for a weekend soon, and Jess had emailed and said she might manage a visit in winter. Strange child, she missed the cold. So those were things to look forward to, although Julia wasn't sure she'd ever entirely get her head around visits from her ex-husband and his soon-to-be husband.

Closer to home, Julia was making friends, starting to fit in. She had book club, and her work at the charity shop, and a village full of acquaintances who were slowly becoming friends.

'Julia?'

Julia looked up, her chicken reverie broken by the sound of Sean's voice.

'I just let myself in – knew I'd find you out back.'

Julia smiled. 'Help yourself,' she said, indicating the bottle of chardonnay and a wine glass that she'd put out in readiness for a visit from Tabitha. Although Sean's visit wasn't entirely unexpected – since the business with Gary, Sean tended to stop by of an evening. 'On my way home,' he always said, although they both knew that it was actually somewhat out of his way, in so far as anything in the village could be out of one's way.

'You've made it lovely and peaceful out here,' said Sean.

'Not like a murder scene at all,' laughed Julia.

'In fairness, the murder never happened here.' Sean poured himself a glass of wine, and sat down, scratching Jake behind his soft ears. 'I think that makes it better, don't you?'

Julia was not a squeamish woman, but she did agree with Sean. It was nicer knowing that Samantha had not met her end in Julia's garden.

'Yoohoo, anybody home?' Tabitha's head emerged around the corner of the cottage. She stopped for a moment, eyebrows raised. 'Not interrupting, am I?' she asked, a tease in her voice.

'Never,' said Julia. 'Won't you just grab a glass from inside?'

Country living had changed her, thought Julia. In London, she would never have expected anyone to just drop in. And if they had, she'd never have sent a guest to find their own wine glass. But everything was more relaxed here in the village, including Julia herself.

'I've got such an exciting event planned for the library,' said Tabitha, as she came out.

'Tell us all about it,' said Sean, and Julia liked the way he sounded genuinely interested in what Tabitha had to say. But Julia herself let the soft chatter of her friends wash over her, as she bathed in a sense of well-being.

A glass of wine, good friends, and the happiest dog in Berrywick. This was the life.

A LETTER FROM KATIE

Dear reader,

Katie Gayle is, in fact, two of us – Kate and Gail – and we want to say a huge thank you for choosing to read *An English Garden Murder*, the first Julia Bird cozy mystery. We have adored creating Berrywick, Julia and her trusted dog companion, Jake. We hope that you loved them as much as we do. Follow us on Twitter for regular pictures of the real-life Jake!

If you enjoyed the book, and want to keep up to date with all of Katie Gayle's latest releases, just sign up at the following link. Your email address will never be shared and you can unsubscribe at any time.

www.bookouture.com/katie-gayle

We hope you enjoyed reading about Julia's first adventure, and if you did we would be very grateful if you could write a review and post it on Amazon and Goodreads, so that other people can discover Julia too.

You might also enjoy our Epiphany Bloom series – the first three books are available for download now.

You can find us in a few places and we'd love to hear from you: Katie Gayle is on Twitter as @KatieGayleBooks and on Facebook as Katie Gayle Writer. You can also follow Kate at @katesidley and Gail at @gailschimmel.

Thanks,

Katie Gayle

 facebook.com/KatieGayleWriter

twitter.com/KatieGayleBooks